THE VILLAGE OF HAPPY EVER AFTERS

ALISON SHERLOCK

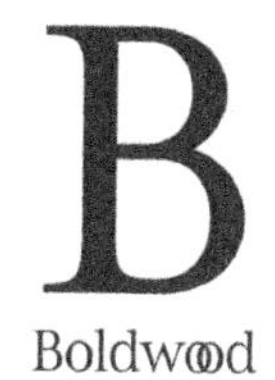

First published in Great Britain in 2022 by Boldwood Books Ltd.

Cover Design by Alice Moore Design

Cover photography: Shutterstock

A CIP catalogue record for this book is available from the British Library.

Paperback ISBN 978-1-80048-007-0

Large Print ISBN 978-1-80048-008-7

Hardback ISBN 978-1-80415-960-6

Ebook ISBN 978-1-80048-009-4

Kindle ISBN 978-1-80048-010-0

Audio CD ISBN 978-1-80048-002-5

MP3 CD ISBN 978-1-80048-003-2

Digital audio download ISBN 978-1-80048-004-9

Boldwood Books Ltd
23 Bowerdean Street
London SW6 3TN
www.boldwoodbooks.com

1

'When I said I was happy to help out with the Easter egg hunt, this wasn't quite what I had in mind,' said Molly Hopkins, her voice sounding muffled even to her own ears.

She had only been wearing the fancy-dress costume for an hour but already felt as if she was suffocating.

She took a careful look around, but other than her three best friends close by, there was no one else in sight on Riverside Lane that spring morning. So, with a grateful sigh, she removed the furry rabbit head from her Easter bunny outfit and breathed in the sweet fresh air of April.

'Just think of it like a really fluffy onesie,' said Amber Green, who was crouched down next to the veranda of her own shop, Cranbridge Stores, placing a handful of brightly coloured, foil-wrapped chocolate eggs beside the bottom step.

'Except it's one hundred per cent itchy polyester and I'm dying inside it,' Molly told her, wiping a lock of long blonde hair from her sweaty brow.

Easter was late that year and it was unseasonably warm even on a Sunday morning in April.

'You should have gone with the Playboy bunny outfit I suggested instead,' said Belle Carter, with a wink before she scattered a handful of shiny wrapped chocolates across the riverbank.

Molly rolled her eyes. 'Yes, I'm sure that wouldn't upset the parents *at all* when the Easter egg hunt starts later,' she replied, fluffing out the furry body of the costume to waft some cooler air inside.

Belle waggled her eyebrows in a suggestive manner. 'Certainly not the dads anyway,' she said, before unwrapping and popping a chocolate into her mouth.

'The eggs are supposed to be for the children,' said Lucy Conway in a pointed tone, as she placed a few more by the nearby bench.

'I'm doing the kids a favour by preventing all those future visits from the Tooth Fairy,' said Belle, with a grin.

Despite all of her friends being in an exuberant mood, Molly most definitely wasn't. She felt hot and uncomfortable and, surprisingly for someone whose outlook was normally so positive, a little fed up as well. 'I still don't see why I'm dressed up and nobody else is,' she said, looking down at her costume.

'Unfortunately, there can only be one Easter bunny,' replied Lucy, giving her a sympathetic smile.

Or only one person daft enough to agree to wear it, thought Molly. As usual, she had found herself volunteering for the role, expecting everyone else to follow suit, but they hadn't for various reasons and so she had ended up in the costume. Why couldn't she ever say no to anyone? Why did it feel as if she let everyone walk all over her most of the time?

'Well, I think that's all the chocolate eggs distributed,' declared Amber, looking around.

'Those that Belle hasn't eaten in any case,' added Lucy, giving her friend a nudge with her elbow.

'Don't blame me if you can't get into your bridesmaid dress,' said Amber, shaking her head.

Amber had asked all of her three best friends to be her bridesmaids for her wedding to Josh Kennedy at the end of the summer and they had excitedly agreed.

Belle grinned. 'That's the joy of being the seamstress for your big day,' she said. 'I can let out my own dress waistline in secret and you'll be none the wiser.'

Molly still couldn't believe that Amber and Josh's wedding day was only four months away. Time seemed to have rushed past since the big proposal the previous autumn. In fact, time seemed to be speeding up for all of her friends' lives. It was only her own life that felt as if it were at a crawl.

But at least it was Easter, which she loved. All that yummy chocolate to eat with no guilt, plus the delicious roast she had planned to cook for the family later. She couldn't wait for them all to be together around the kitchen table once more, and hopefully it would cheer her mum up as well. She had been particularly low since losing her job and Molly was worried about her.

At least having her two younger brothers, Adam and Ben, home from university for the Easter holidays would bring a bit of life to the place. Although knowing the twins and their penchant for mess and noise, that was something of an understatement.

So her family would be back together at last. Summer was just around the corner. She had a good job as digital manager for the community hub and her best friends were here in her home village. With Amber and Josh's wedding to look forward to as well, Molly didn't know what was up with her at the moment. She really had no reason to complain. Especially because there was no better place to live than Cranbridge, she thought, as she looked around. She had never even considered living anywhere else in her twenty-nine years. Why would she when Cranbridge looked as beautiful as it always did that morning?

It was a small village in the middle of the English countryside, with honey-coloured brick cottages lining the riverbanks and the surrounding green rolling hills peeping through from between each house. Instead of a main street, there was a wide shallow river running down the middle of the village, with three ancient pedestrian stone bridges connecting either side over the clear, bubbling water.

Molly turned to look down Riverside Lane, the only retail thoroughfare of the whole village. Cranbridge Stores was the shop on the corner. Amber had already decorated the wooden veranda which ran along the length of the shopfront with pastel-coloured bunting to match the beautifully decorated shop windows filled with Easter baskets and elaborately decorated eggs. The corner shop had been transformed by Amber and her fiancé, Josh, over the past year and was now the main destination for local people looking for food and any other necessities from local producers.

On the opposite side of the river was the newly renovated Black Swan Inn which Belle ran with her boyfriend, Pete Kennedy, Josh's brother. The makeover of the village inn had been remarkable and was now a hugely popular venue for delicious food and drinks. Belle had lived in the village almost as long as Molly, but she too seemed to have found her happy ending now that she and Pete were in love.

Lucy had come to stay in the village a year ago and she was busy in both her work and love life as she ran the community hub alongside her boyfriend, Tom. It was a thriving meeting place for villagers looking for advice or just company. There was also a number of small clubs held there, such as the Mothers and Toddlers group and various art clubs, and the hub was home to the local newspaper, *The Cranbridge News*. Lucy had taken inspiration and advice from Amber and now the hub was prettily decorated as well to match the shop next door. It was no wonder that both places were bustling with people heading in and out most of the week. A sense of community spirit had returned to the village once more.

Molly enjoyed her role there as digital manager, which included gathering all the information about the local community activities and then updating the village website, as well as posting on social media. Tom, her boss, had given her lots of training and her marketing skills had grown after only a year in the role. And yet, despite enjoying being so involved in the community, it wasn't her dream job. She knew, deep down, that she would love to bake cakes all day, every day. It was the only time that she ever felt fully confident in herself and her abilities. The longer she spent baking, the more relaxed she became.

At home, there were two large double-chocolate cakes ready for the Easter celebrations with the family. She was especially pleased with the intricately decorated eggs she had made for the top of each one. The trouble was that, although she hoped that she was a talented baker, she couldn't really make a career out of it. Besides, she wasn't professionally trained, only self-taught. And despite her family and friends reassuring her that she had a real talent, Molly was wracked by self-doubt about how good she really was.

So she was stuck in the rut. Much like the last two shops on the lane, she thought, looking at them. They were the only vacant shops in the village and particularly run-down as they had been empty for so long.

After the two empty shops, there was a good-sized garden which had a low wall at the front. But it was basically just an overgrown tangle of nettles and weeds having not been touched for many years. On the other side of the land, alongside a small tributary of the river, there was the old watermill. It had never worked in Molly's lifetime. It felt as if the success at the beginning of Riverside Lane had yet to spread its wings further along the street.

Molly watched the pink and red tulips on the riverbank bob their heads in a soft breeze. Normally she enjoyed the changing of the seasons, the excitement as life and nature moved on to the next chapter. But she had a growing restlessness inside her and she couldn't deny that something was missing from her life.

'Do you think the chocolate eggs will be OK in this sun for an hour or so?' asked Lucy, frowning.

'I don't think the children will care if the chocolate has melted by the time they find it,' said Belle, laughing. 'Besides, I'd be more worried about Keith eating it all and needing an emergency vet's appointment.'

Lucy glanced over her shoulder, where her dog, Keith, was watching them all with a sorrowful look on his shaggy grey face. He was tied up next to the doorway of the community hub, just in case his usual hoover-type habits included Easter eggs. With a heavy self-pitying sigh, he put his head on his front paws and closed his eyes.

'He'll never forgive me for tying him up,' said Lucy, shaking her head. 'Even though it's for his own good. I've told him that chocolate is poisonous to dogs, but I'm not sure he believed me.'

'He'll forgive you just as soon as dinner time rolls around again,' said Amber.

Molly watched her friends chatting and thought how grateful she was to have them in her life. The four of them had a close bond of friendship which Molly truly cherished. Her best friends were all happy in both work and love and Molly was truly happy for them all. And yet, she was still single and watched on as everyone else's dreams came true whilst hers faded away a little more with each passing year.

'Crikey, it looks like the church service is over already,' said Belle, glancing down the river to the other end of the village, where the congregation were spilling out of the tiny church of St Barnabus.

Lucy gave Molly a nudge. 'You'd better get back into costume before you give them nightmares about a headless rabbit,' she told her with a grin.

Molly selflessly slid on the heavy costume head and found herself grateful that the Easter bunny's smiling expression was sewn on.

She spent the next couple of hours hopping around and entertaining all the children as they squealed with delight upon finding another chocolate hidden along the lane.

Finally, with baskets and tummies full of chocolate, the children began to head home and Molly's job was done.

'Do you want to come back to the shop for a cold drink?' asked Amber.

'Thanks, but I think I'll head home for a shower,' said Molly, her voice still muffled from the rabbit's head.

With a wave to her friends, she headed around the corner to the back of the row of shops. It was a slightly longer way home than going alongside the river but she was hoping that she would be able to take her costume off along the way and get some much-needed fresh air to her overheated face and body.

Finding herself alone in the back lane, she suddenly felt very sorry for herself. She had been acting selflessly ever since her twin brothers had been born and where had it got her? Nowhere, it felt. She loved her friends and her family and yet she couldn't deny that she felt incomplete. She just had no idea what it was that was missing from her life.

In a sudden spurt of frustration, she whipped off the furry bunny head and flung it far away from her.

Just in time for a van to come around the corner and run the costume head over.

2

Logan Armstrong felt a rush of cold fear wash over him as he quickly brought the van to a halt. What on earth had he just run over? A wild animal? Someone's beloved pet?

Feeling sick, he clambered out of the cab of the van and forced himself to look at the front of the vehicle.

The mass at his feet was large, white and fluffy. Or at least it had been, before he had flattened it with his front tyre. But it didn't look like any member of the animal species, he thought, feeling somewhat confused.

He felt someone come to stand next to him and he looked around in a daze.

A pretty woman was staring down at the squashed white mess in front of them. Still horrified, he wondered whether it was her pet that he had just accidentally run over.

'Well, there goes my deposit on the costume,' she said with a wry smile, looking back up at him.

It was only then that Logan registered that she was wearing some kind of fluffy white fancy-dress outfit. And that it was missing the head of the costume.

He blew out a sigh of relief before saying, 'I'm sorry. I couldn't stop the van in time.'

She gave a shrug, which caused the fluffy white fur on her shoulders to rise and fall. Her head looked tiny against the huge white costume, especially with her long blonde hair swept back into a messy ponytail.

'It was my fault,' she told him. 'I'm the one who should apologise. After all, I threw the thing out into the road! Luckily I've finished my Easter bunny duties for the day.'

Her costume was beginning to make sense to him.

'Thank goodness,' said Logan. 'The last thing I need are any more headlines.'

She looked at him for a moment, her blue eyes frowning at him as if trying to figure out what he was talking about.

He was somewhat amazed. Was this woman the only person in the country who didn't recognise him? Who hadn't seen the endless media headlines about the breakdown of his marriage and his photograph plastered across every front page? Surely the gossip had spread everywhere, even sleepy Cranbridge?

'You're Stanley's grandson,' she said eventually.

He nodded. Everyone in Cranbridge knew his grandad, of course. Stanley had been the local school headmaster until only ten years ago.

'We were introduced just before Christmas in the Black Swan Inn,' she carried on.

'Hi. Yes, I'm Logan,' he said. Had they been introduced? He couldn't remember, although he would have thought he should be able to recall a pretty face such as hers. He had visited the village just before Christmas to spend time with his grandad, but he hadn't been back to Cranbridge since his life had imploded all those months ago.

'I'm Molly, but you can always call me the late Easter bunny,' she said, as she went over to peel the flattened costume head off the tarmac. 'Well, I'd better get going.'

'I can pay for any damages,' he said quickly.

'Please don't worry,' she replied. 'Well, I'll probably see you around the village.'

For all her laid-back attitude towards the accident, she looked quite a sad sight. The flattened head hung loosely in her hand as she shuffled away in that ridiculous costume, the fluffy tail wobbling as she went.

Logan ran a hand through his dark hair. Not exactly the fresh new start he had been hoping for. But at least he was finally in Cranbridge for a good length of time. He had all his possessions with him piled up in the back of the hired van. His marriage was over. The feeling of relief was matched only by the bitterness that still remained.

At least his reputation as the second most famous man in the tabloids over the past three months was unlikely to produce any more headlines here. Cranbridge wasn't a magnet for tabloid journalists and paparazzi. He would leave all that to his ex-wife and her notorious lover.

It really had been the scandal to top all scandals. The most famous man in the tabloids was Peter deVille, a presenter on one of the most popular baking shows on television. His womanising reputation had been intensified in recent months after being caught out passionately kissing one of his married co-presenters in the doorway of a London club. She just happened to be Logan's wife, Felicity.

Logan had never liked to think of himself as famous, but there was no denying that he and Felicity had built up a name for themselves over the past few years. His bespoke furniture-making business had always given them a steady income whilst his wife had been intent on becoming a household name as a TV presenter. But the ten-minute cooking slot on morning TV that she had miraculously managed to land hadn't been enough for his publicity-hungry wife. Soon she had graduated to *Yes, Chef!* which was the number one show for food lovers on evening television. And she had ended up working alongside Peter deVille. After two years of flirting with him on the television screen, their desire had spilled over all too easily into real life.

The press, to be fair, had mostly left him alone since the ghastly photos had graced the front pages. After all, Logan was just the cuckolded husband. But even so, it still hurt his pride to be so publicly humiliated like that. Instead of a private discussion that the marriage was over – something they both knew had happened a long time ago – it had been blasted all over the front pages of every newspaper in the country.

To his shame, only he knew the absolute worst secret of all. He had actually caught Felicity and her lover wrapped in each other's arms at home. It turned out that the passionate kiss that had been splashed all over the front pages had led straight to their marital bed. No wonder Logan hadn't slept properly ever since, despite moving to the spare bedroom.

At least Felicity had had the good grace to leave the marital home and move in with her lover. But Logan had found remaining in their house in central London gave him no peace either. There were too many reminders of their unhappy marriage and he had endured sleepless nights ever since, with the ghosts of his past marriage haunting him.

It didn't help that his London social circle had diminished into non-existence as well. One of their so-called friends had sold her story, along with various photos of Logan and Felicity at various parties, to the newspapers. A few more friends had chosen to side with his ex-wife and her lover, unsurprisingly for their own TV career advancement. Now he didn't trust anyone. Deep down he was lonelier because of it, but at least that meant that nobody else was going to let him down any time soon.

With the divorce going through the courts, their London home had sold quicker than Logan had anticipated. So he had taken a short-term rental on a place in Cranbridge near his beloved grandad. Finally, he felt back in control and ready for a fresh start in the next chapter of his life, whatever that turned out to be.

He opened up the back of the large van that he had hired. As well as his own boxed-up possessions, it was chock-full of half-finished furniture too. He was a cabinet maker and working quietly on each piece was the only thing that had kept him sane these past few months.

He hadn't been anywhere near the shop, of course, just in case the paparazzi decided to return. The fancy location on the legendary King's Road in Chelsea had all been his wife's idea anyway. Logan had always been happy just working out of the large workshop that he hired in the early days of his business. But, as usual, Felicity had wanted everything to be grander, more refined, more upmarket. Even him, he had realised, in hindsight. And what was a simple cabinet maker compared to the star of television? Nothing, apparently.

His wife had always strived to be something more and had quickly transformed from the woman that he had first known to the fame-hungry TV personality that she had become, almost within a few weeks of being married two short years ago.

'Good morning, my boy,' said a familiar voice behind him.

'Morning, Grandad,' said Logan, spinning around to see the elderly gentleman walking towards him. Stanley Armstrong was a little slower getting around these days, compared to the football-playing enthusiast of his youth. Hardly surprising now he was in his early seventies. But his mind was just as sharp as it had ever been despite the steel-grey hair.

Logan stepped forward to give his grandad a gentle hug. Despite talking on the phone every few days, it felt as if it had been a long time since Logan had last seen him at Christmas.

'Can't say it's been the best arrival,' said Logan when he stepped back. 'I've just run over the Easter bunny. Or rather her costume head. No one got hurt though.'

'Dear me,' said Stanley, his grey eyebrows furrowing in concern. 'You don't mean Molly Hopkins, do you?'

'Blonde hair, cheerful manner?' replied Logan. He didn't add the word pretty, even though he automatically thought it.

Stanley nodded. 'That's her,' he said, smiling. 'Lovely girl. Such a sweet nature.'

'I apologised,' said Logan quickly. 'Hopefully she won't hold it against me.'

Stanley shook his head. 'I shouldn't worry. I've never known Molly to have a bad word against anyone,' he commented. 'And I've known her all of her life.'

Logan smiled back at his grandad. As usual, he knew everyone in Cranbridge. Of course, it wasn't hard in such a small place, but Stanley's role as headmaster of the local primary school meant that everyone who had lived in the village had been in one of his grandad's classes at some point in their childhood.

In contrast, Logan had been brought up in the suburbs of a large city where everyone kept to themselves. To his surprise, he had always enjoyed his brief visits to the countryside growing up, and was looking forward to an extended stay in Cranbridge over the summer.

Logan relished the warmth of the sunshine on his skin as he stood in the narrow lane. He looked up at the blue sky stretching out beyond the row of shops and roofs. No skyscrapers here to block the view. Just an endless sky and the peace of the countryside, filled only with birdsong and the rustling of the fresh green leaves in the nearby trees.

'I've missed being here,' he found himself admitting. 'And I've missed you too Grandad. I'm sorry I haven't been back to see you so far this year. As you know, things have been somewhat difficult.'

It was a vast understatement, but was he still trying to protect his grandad, who was a little more frail these years, especially since he lost his beloved grandmother five years previously.

'The main thing is that you're here, my boy,' said Stanley, clamping a soft arm on his shoulder. 'Come on. Let's have a good look at where you're going to be living.'

'Temporarily,' said Logan quickly. He didn't want to get his grandad's hopes up that his stay in Cranbridge was anything more than just a short-term stop on the way to somewhere else. Which was why he had only leased the apartment and shop for six months. But the village, for all its familiarity, would hopefully be a safe haven for the summer. As well as giving him plenty of time to enjoy his grandad's company.

A conversation a few weeks previously about trying to find somewhere to reflect and mend his broken heart had resulted in his grandad sending him details of an empty shop in Riverside Lane. It hadn't been used for years, according to Stanley. But studying the floor plan online, Logan had realised it had enough space to work on the furniture downstairs and it came with the added bonus of an apartment to sleep in upstairs. And with the owner willing to rent it to him for a tidy price, Logan had leased the place without even viewing it in person.

'Let's see what home is going to look like for the summer, shall we?' said Logan, heading towards the back door.

He brought out the keys that he had just picked up from the landlord.

It was a fresh start, thought Logan, putting the key in the lock.

And there were worse places to ride out a media storm than Cranbridge in the summertime. Where his future lay beyond that he had no idea. But the way he felt at that moment, it would be alone as it would take someone very special indeed to make him give up his heart to love again.

3

'Hello,' called out Molly as she stepped into the hallway of the tiny cottage that she had called home all of her life. The aroma of the warm cinnamon from the hot cross buns that she had baked the day before still hung in the air.

It was a modest but warm and comfortable place that was normally kept clean and tidy. However, on that Sunday morning, Molly found the hallway almost impassable, with towering piles of bags in her way.

Her brothers had been home for at least a couple of days from university and had finally found time to unpack their cars, it appeared. Although their bags had only made it as far as the hallway.

She shuffled sideways into the front room, where she found one of her twin brothers playing FIFA on the large-screen TV.

'Hey, sis,' said Ben, glancing up from his console briefly. 'I like the onesie. Not sure it's going to stop you from being single though.'

'It's an Easter bunny costume,' she said, with a sigh, glancing down at the flattened head in her hand.

'Suits you,' replied Ben, with a grin, before turning back to concentrate on the game.

Adam came around the corner from the kitchen carrying two cans of Coke Zero and what appeared to be a couple of large wedges of the chocolate Easter cake that Molly had been saving for tea later that day. Thankfully she had baked two in anticipation of just such an event.

'Looking good, sis,' he said with a wide smile, placing the food on the coffee table in front of the sofa.

Adam was the more affectionate of the twins, but they both had the same blonde hair, tall athletic bodies and cheeky grins. Now twenty years of age, they towered over her. She had missed them both terribly when they had passed their A Levels and gone to different universities two years ago. They hadn't been home since Christmas and the house always felt emptier without them.

'What time's dinner?' asked Ben, who had now paused the game to take a bite of the chocolate cake.

'Just let me get this thing off,' she said. 'I'm so hot. And, by the way, it's nice to see you too this Easter morning, little brother.'

Ben grinned and leapt up to smother her with an enormous bear hug. 'My gorgeous big sister. The light of my life. How do I compare thee to a summer's day?'

'Gerroff me,' she said affectionately, as he ruffled her long blonde hair. But she couldn't help but smile at him. It was so good to have them both around once more.

'Now, when's my roast lamb?' asked Ben again.

Molly loved her brothers, but they were somewhat demanding. Nothing had changed from the time when they had first arrived in the world. As usual, she and her mum would spend the next few weeks rushing around after them until they left for university for their exams before the summer break began, leaving the house a whole lot tidier for a while but also quieter too.

'The roast will be whenever it's finished,' she told him before adding in a pointed tone, 'And that cake was supposed to be for pudding.'

'There was another one on the counter,' Adam told her with his mouth full. They knew their sister all too well to anticipate that she wouldn't have had a backup cake, just in case.

'Where's mum?' asked Molly, looking around.

'In the kitchen,' said Ben.

'Is she OK?' said Molly, lowering her voice to a whisper.

'Seems a little better,' Ben told her.

Molly nodded. 'Good.'

It was probably because the boys were home, she thought. But any kind of better day was a good thing at the moment where their mum was concerned. She had always suffered with periods of low moods throughout her life, becoming frequently tearful and almost overwhelmed with the world as a whole for a few weeks at a time. But on those occasions, she had always been cheered up by her children and her job at the local textile factory. There she mixed with plenty of people and it had brought her some much-needed human contact when her social life had been near on non-existent for as long as Molly could remember. She had always seemed content just to be with her family.

However, the factory had been closed down six weeks previously and their mum had been forced into taking early retirement. That had paid off the last of the mortgage on the tiny cottage and any lingering money worries, but it was the empty days that had brought on her mum's latest spell of unhappiness.

With the boys away at university, it had been left to Molly to cheer her up. Sometimes using her grandmother's recipes to make her mum's favourite cakes had worked. But she still wasn't sure that she had achieved too much success in that area.

It was lovely to have the boys home again, she thought with a soft smile as she headed back out into the hallway. Of course, these days they were fully grown men, but still, the house was too quiet without their shouting, music and laughter when they were away.

But her smile slipped somewhat when she saw two separate duvet covers stuffed with what could only be a whole term's worth of washing to be done.

She sighed. It was the curse of the older sister, she knew. Their wayward father had just about managed to stay around when he had only one daughter. But the thought of twin boys had made him run for the hills and he had never looked back or bothered to even contact any of his children. Molly didn't care. She hadn't known him and their mum was their rock. As far as she was concerned, they were better off without him. But she'd had to abandon her own childhood pretty early on to help her mum take care of her younger brothers. Family was family, after all.

It was a lot of mouths to feed, so her mum had sometimes worked three jobs in a week to keep a roof over their heads and food in the cupboards. But with their mum so busy, Molly had assumed a lot of the roles before and after school. She had taken care of the laundry, making sure the disorganised boys got to school on time, finished their homework and made dinner. It was being in the kitchen day after day where she had honed her baking skills, most of all. The boys always wanted cake and Molly had been happy to practise, to do something that she enjoyed, when she had so little time to herself.

'Hi, Mum,' said Molly as she headed into the kitchen.

Rachel Hopkins looked up at her daughter and smiled. She looked older than her fifty-eight years, with a few extra lines across her pretty face. Her blonde hair was heavily streaked with grey these days.

'The kettle's just boiled,' said her mum, as Simon, the cat, leapt up from underneath the table to settle down on her lap.

'Thanks,' said Molly. 'I need it. How was your morning?'

Her mum shrugged her shoulders. 'Not bad,' she replied.

'Is there any bread?' asked Molly, hopefully. 'I need something to keep me going until the roast is ready.'

Her mum shook her head. 'Sorry, love,' she said. 'I didn't get round to baking any. I'm a bit tired today.'

'That's OK,' said Molly, quickly. 'I'll grab a couple of biscuits for now.'

It was another sign that her mum was struggling, thought Molly. There had always been freshly baked bread in their home. The aroma of the warm bread from the oven was the overwhelming memory of her childhood.

As she took down the biscuit tin, she glanced at the washing-up that had yet to be done, as well as the messy garden beyond. Their mum had pretty much given up doing any kind of housework and gardening since losing her job.

At first, Molly had hoped that her mum was taking a long overdue break. But as the days turned into weeks, she was more and more worried about her. She had lost interest in both the house and the garden. Only Molly and the twins seemed to hold her interest these days.

Her mum carried on stroking the cat's soft fur. 'How was the Easter egg hunt?'

'A bit hot in that silly outfit,' said Molly, with a grimace as she poured out a cup of tea for them both. 'I shall need a shower after this to freshen up.'

'I'm sure the children appreciated it,' said her mum.

Molly watched as her mum looked out vacantly at the garden through the open back door.

After sitting down at the table, she reached out and took her mum's hand in hers. 'Are you OK, Mum?' she asked, after a short silence.

'Of course,' said her mum quickly.

'Do you think you should have a chat with the doctor or someone?' carried on Molly. 'I'm worried about you.'

'I'll be all right,' replied her mum, squeezing her hand. 'I'm just tired, that's all. Once I'm rested, I'll be OK.'

'If you're sure,' said Molly, still uncertain.

'How were the girls?' asked her mum, changing the subject.

'Fine,' said Molly, thinking back to how excited her friends were about everything going on in their lives. Before she could stop herself, she found herself blurting out, 'Do you ever get the feeling that you're being left behind?'

Her mum raised her eyebrows. 'In what way?' she asked.

Molly instantly regretted her words, not wanting to worry her mum any further. But she had spoken and the truth was out there now.

So she replied, 'I don't know, Mum. In every way, I guess. Life, love and work. After all, I'm only a digital manager at the hub. It wasn't my dream. I just sort of fell into the job.'

'Everybody does that from time to time,' her mum replied. 'Besides, I thought you liked working for Tom and the newspaper.'

'I do but...' Molly's voice trailed off.

'But what?'

'Is that it for me?' said Molly. 'I mean, is that all I'm going to achieve?'

Her mum smiled at her. 'You're only twenty-nine, love. You've got your whole life ahead of you.'

Yes, thought Molly. But when was it going to start?

4

Logan had only seen his rental home in some very dark photographs that his grandad had taken through the front window of the shop.

At the time, he had been too numb and broken-hearted to care what he was actually leasing and what kind of state it was in. It was only now that he had turned the lock in the back door and was leaning against the door to open it that he began to realise quite what he had taken on.

He eventually got the door open, which did so with a huge creak and judder.

'*Luxury* living and working space?' murmured Logan to his grandad, who gave a chuckle in reply. That was how the place had been marketed to him via the landlord, Barry, a local man with a somewhat dubious reputation, according to his grandad, although it hadn't put Logan off from renting a property from him, such had been his desperation in getting out of London.

Logan flicked the lights on and stared around what appeared to be the back kitchen and storeroom of the shop. The cobwebs held no fear for him, nor the amount of mess. It wasn't an auspicious start, but it was the only place in Cranbridge that had been available with space for Logan to work. He needed a large workshop and the empty downstairs shop, with storage, would be perfect, whatever kind of mess it was in.

Less interested in the living space, Logan insisted that they viewed the potential workshop first. It had been a hairdressing salon at some point, but that had shut down many years ago, like the bakery next door as well.

The beige sinks looked dusty and were filled with cobwebs and there were still the old hairstyle posters on the walls, as well as some rusty mirrors. But he didn't mind those. It wasn't about style anyway. It was just to be used as a workshop, nothing more.

He wouldn't be opening up a shop in Cranbridge, having decided to move the business online to give him more freedom. Back in London, the shop on King's Road was slowly being wound down. It could carry on for a few more months without him as it was so well run. He had told the staff that it would take a while so at least they had time to find a new job by the end of the summer.

Any unsold pieces would be sent down to him in Cranbridge, then at least he would have everything together. After that, he had no idea where he would end up. The divorce would leave him relatively well-off as the house in Fulham had gone up in value since they had bought it and he would receive half the profit once the mortgage was paid off. He was comfortable and would get by, but being busy had been helpful these past few months to keep his mind off everything. Besides, his work was both his passion and his escape.

If only he could turn back time to when he had never met Felicity. He had been happy in those early days of the business. He had started off in his garden shed making dining chairs and the word had spread from there.

He had always enjoyed working with wood ever since watching

his grandad make a bookshelf in his own shed when Logan had been a young boy. Stanley had nurtured his fledgling talent and encouraged him to follow his dreams all the way to college, where he had studied furniture making. Slowly his skills had turned to making all kinds of furniture and people seemed happy to pay for bespoke pieces.

It was only when he met his wife that she persuaded him to open up the shop on the very expensive King's Road. Thankfully, his business had exploded into life and he could barely keep up with demand, which at least covered the extortionate rent.

The orders had continued to come in despite the scandal. He wondered if it was because people felt sorry for him. Perhaps they wanted a piece of furniture in their house to say, oh, yes, that's a Logan piece. You know his wife left him for Peter deVille, don't you? But he was hoping it was because he was a good furniture maker.

Anyway he was tired. Tired of busy, smog-filled London. Tired of the occasional demanding customer as well.

He looked out of the dusty front window across the lane to the river and beyond. There were a few people about on the bright and sunny day. It was Easter Sunday, of course. A time for family.

It would have been nice to have had his parents to lean on, but they were humble, modest people. His mum was warm and often rang him from Spain, where they had moved to as soon as he had finished school. His father was colder in nature and had instilled in his only child a sense of being self-sufficient.

'Nobody will ever help you without wanting something in return,' he had told his son one day before they had left. 'Remember that.'

Logan had tried to be more open-minded than that but he had found himself thinking back to his father's words many a time and he couldn't deny that he had begun to live by that advice over the past few years.

Looking out of the shopfront, Logan thought that the view of the river would be something to enjoy over the coming months. The river looked cold but clear as it ran alongside the fresh green of the riverbanks, dotted with faded daffodils and bright pink and red tulips.

To the left was the old watermill. It had never worked in his lifetime. And yet, his grandad seemed to have a fondness for the old place and had mentioned it many times over the years. On the other side of the river was the Black Swan Inn. It too had gained in popularity tenfold since being renovated over the previous winter. Logan had been in there with his grandad on opening night, which had been somewhat of a disaster, but his grandad had told him what a good job Belle and Pete had done over the winter with the inn and how much better it now served the community.

'I've got a table booked for us both later,' said Stanley, coming to stand next to him and looking across to the inn. 'The food's smashing these days now they've got a new chef and it'll be good to introduce you to a few local people properly.'

Logan frowned. He wasn't in the mood for introductions.

His grandad caught the look on his grandson's face. 'I'm sure everyone will want to see you again,' Stanley told him.

But Logan shook his head. 'I'm happy to see you, of course, but I have a backlog of orders to get through this summer. And, to be honest, I'm happy with my own company for the time being.'

'Everyone should make time for other people,' said Stanley softly.

'Not me.' Logan sighed. 'Look, I appreciate you wanting to help, but I'll be moving after the summer, so it's probably for the best that I keep myself to myself at the moment.'

'I see,' said his grandad in a sad tone.

Logan turned around, wanting to change the subject. 'What about upstairs?' he asked.

He let his grandfather go up the stairs to the apartment first. It was a slower ascent and Logan was once again reminded what a good idea it had been for his grandad to move into a bungalow nearby.

The little cottage that his grandparents had lived in for so long had been quickly sold over a year ago. He knew that his grandad had been upset at having to leave a place with such happy memories, but it made sense now that it was just him. He seemed to have coped as well as could have been expected with widowhood.

They both missed his grandmother, of course. She had had a warm and welcoming nature, much like her husband. Logan missed her soft laughter and sage advice.

'Here we are,' said Stanley, with a grateful sigh as they reached the apartment at the top of the stairs.

Logan looked around, careful not to show his dismay too much. It was clean, he supposed. But the paint was peeling and it wasn't a great space.

On the plus side, his soon-to-be ex-wife wasn't anywhere near the place and he could maybe find some peace there. In addition, there was a back door into the workshop and thus he could come and go to work without needing to bump into anyone. That worked perfectly for him.

He had begun to be something of a hermit in London, with no social life. He was still embarrassed by the humiliating way in which his marriage had fallen apart so publicly. Thankfully, the early rush of well-meaning nosy parkers had soon receded and he had been grateful for the peace of the past few weeks. He was the forgotten man and he was enjoying that feeling.

And yet, he missed social contact. He missed chatting about football and being with people of his own age.

But he would be fine by himself for the time being. He had never asked for help in London. For the most part, he didn't like to surrender control. Even more so now, having been so burnt by his marriage. He didn't want to seem incompetent or, worse, needy. And he certainly didn't need any more headlines. Besides, as his father had reminded him on quite a few occasions, the only person he could trust was himself. So he had kept himself to himself and that was the way it would continue. Despite being ever so slightly lonely.

'It's OK,' he said, with a firm nod.

Stanley looked at him in surprise. 'Are you sure? It's in a bit of a state, don't you think?'

Logan shook his head. 'As long as there's room for my bed somewhere, it'll be fine. Anyway, the contract's been signed. It'll do for now.'

It would see him through summer, at least. After that, he wasn't sure where his path in life lay. But, for now, Cranbridge would be a safe haven for him to keep his head down. He wasn't there to make friends. He would enjoy the time with his grandad and then be on his way again once more. He just wasn't quite sure where he would go next.

5

Monday morning in the community hub was always a busy start to the week for Molly. First, there was the weekend news to post about on social media for *The Cranbridge Times* newspaper, although she wasn't quite so keen on the photographs of her wearing the Easter bunny costume. She tried not to grimace whenever she saw it as she scrolled through her timeline.

Then there was the community hub itself, which had thrived as a meeting place for villagers looking for advice or just company ever since Lucy had established it the previous summer. The Mothers and Toddlers group was in full swing, filled with many of the families that had attended the Easter egg hunt only the day before. Luckily, none of the children recognised Molly as the Easter bunny.

Lucy was sitting on the nearby sofa with many notes spread across the coffee table, trying to organise some kind of volunteer group for a problem that had become more prominent over the past few months. So far, it was only Lucy, her boyfriend, Tom, who was the editor of the newspaper, Molly and Grandma Tilly, Josh and Pete's formidable grandmother, and a tour-de-force on the lane.

'So we're agreed that Riverside Lane is doing well,' said Lucy. 'Business is better than ever and there are far more people out and about than ever before. The trouble is that our own success, and Cranbridge Stores next door seems to only highlight how awful the rest of Riverside Lane appears these days. There's been a few complaints online, haven't there, Molly?'

Molly nodded. 'Just people saying how messy the two empty shops look and that the piece of land between the shops and the watermill is so overgrown that the weeds are spilling over onto the lane itself.'

'Humph,' said Grandma Tilly, looking cross. 'That Barry Melville owns both shops and the land too. They look awful. Such a state. I've tried giving him a piece of my mind, but the man has such thick skin I'm not sure any of it sank in.'

She paused to look up at her lifelong friends, Frank and Stanley, as they came in through the open front door.

'You're late this morning,' said Lucy to her uncle Frank, as she gave him a kiss.

'We nearly didn't make it at all,' Frank told her, sitting down on the armchair with a grateful sigh. 'We almost got run over by young Ben Hopkins on his electric scooter thing.'

Molly was horrified. 'I'm so sorry,' she said. 'Are you both OK?'

'We're fine, my dear,' said Stanley, with a wave of his hand. 'Just took us by surprise, that was all. But at least your brothers are not at school any longer so the science lab won't be in danger of being blown up this term.'

Molly frowned. 'I'll have a word with Ben to say that he can't use it around the village,' she said.

'I hope not,' replied Frank, with a smile. 'I was hoping he might give me a lesson on it.'

'Absolutely not, Uncle,' spluttered Lucy, aghast.

'Spoilsport,' said Frank, giving his niece a wink. 'So what's on today's agenda? Now that Stanley's sorted out his grandson in the shop next door, we're at a loose end.'

'Next door?' asked Grandma Tilly, turning to look at Stanley, who had sat down next to her. 'He's taken over the old hairdressers?'

Stanley nodded. 'I didn't want to say anything before now until all the paperwork was signed, but my grandson, Logan, has rented the shop and apartment.'

Molly found herself blushing. She was still feeling somewhat mortified by the way she had met Logan. She hadn't realised he would be working next door to the hub as well.

'I didn't know he was a hairdresser,' said Grandma Tilly, giving her grey curls a pat. 'I wonder if he'd give me a purple rinse. I fancy a change.'

'He's just renting the old hairdressers as a workshop. He actually makes bespoke furniture,' Stanley told her with raised eyebrows. 'But perhaps he could make you a new mirror to admire any kind of new hair colour.'

'We must pop in and say hello to him,' said Lucy, looking across to Tom.

Tom, however, was looking thoughtful. 'He might not want any fuss at the moment, given the circumstances of his hasty retreat to Cranbridge from London.'

Lucy frowned. 'Oh. Yes. I see what you're getting at.'

Molly hadn't considered that Logan himself might be more embarrassed than her when they had met, given the way his marriage had fallen apart so famously. She actually felt quite sorry for him given the wretched time he had endured, according to his grandad.

'A little fuss might do him some good actually,' said Stanley.

'Well, if you think so,' said Tom, sounding hopeful. 'I can always invite him over to the Black Swan for a pint once he's settled in.'

'That's a good idea,' Lucy told him. 'Then you can have a boys' night out and us girls can have a catch-up.'

Molly nodded. It had been a couple of weeks since they had last had more than a passing conversation as their lives had become so busy.

'So I was telling the others about my idea for tidying up the rest of the lane,' said Lucy, looking at her uncle. 'Just to give the two shops a bit of a spruce up. You know, maybe some pots and a lick of paint.'

'Except now that Logan is living and working next door, that only leaves one shop to tidy up the front of and that walled garden at the end of the lane,' added Tom.

'You'll have to run it past Barry,' said Frank, with a frown. 'After all, it's his land and shopfront.'

Barry had owned the last two shops on Riverside Lane for years, both of which were quite neglected which he had often declared didn't really matter as he lived in Aldwych town and didn't have to see them every day.

'Having seen the state of the shop and apartment that my grandson has just leased,' said Stanley, 'I don't think Barry will be at all concerned. Logan spent yesterday cleaning up just to make it habitable.'

Grandma Tilly tutted. 'He always was a shocking landlord,' she said.

'Well, I'm sure Barry will be happy to lend us a hand clearing it up,' suggested Lucy.

Grandma Tilly chuckled. 'No, he won't, love. He'll be happy for us to do it for him though.'

'But it would be for the benefit of everyone,' said Lucy, frowning. 'I mean, I think it will take a bit of hard work to clear the land, but it would give everyone some cheer to see it look a bit tidier. And seeing as how there's only one shop empty now, it's less work than we'd originally thought.'

'I can talk to Barry but I'm not sure how much good it will do,' said Tom, still sounding unsure. 'How about Molly puts something out on social media for volunteers to help us?'

'I can do that,' said Molly, nodding.

'Folks are pretty busy these days, so don't expect too much help,' said Grandma Tilly. 'I can lend a hand though. When shall we start?'

'This weekend?' suggested Lucy. 'But it's quite a mess and I don't want anyone to strain themselves too much.'

Molly knew that her friend was trying to be kind and prevent the pensioners from having to work too hard. Hopefully they would have many volunteers to help out.

'You're going to need some serious help to clear some of those weeds,' said Frank, giving his niece a pointed look. 'Thankfully, us old folk know our dahlias from our dandelions.'

'I'm not sure how many dahlias there'll be in a wasteland like that,' remarked Stanley.

'What's a dahlia?' asked Lucy.

'My point exactly,' said Frank, smiling.

'Well, it's going to take a fair bit of work whatever we find in there,' said Lucy. 'Hopefully we'll have many hands to make light work of the mess.' She looked across at Molly. 'You haven't got anything on this weekend, have you? I'll ask Amber and Belle as well.'

Molly hesitated to reply. After all, with the twins home, life was going to be busy enough. She had also yet to tell anyone how worried she was about her mum, so she was shouldering the burden of keeping the house clean and tidy as well for them all.

'We'll all chip in when we get a spare hour,' said Tom enthusiastically.

'And Keith will always help with the digging,' added Lucy, glancing down at the dog who was currently sleeping on her feet.

'Excellent,' said Tom. 'Shall we say nine o'clock on Saturday morning?'

Molly looked up from her notes to find him smiling at her.

As usual, she found herself nodding automatically. 'Of course,' she replied, her heart sinking. Once more she been roped into something she hadn't planned to be a part of. Whilst she liked to help her friends and the village, she had planned to do some experimental baking that weekend with a new recipe for salted caramel brownies that she was keen to try out.

As always, baking relieved her stress. Feeling anxious about her mum's mental health was causing Molly a few sleepless nights. But baking calmed her, reduced her worries into the background whilst she followed the recipe. And, of course, seeing everyone enjoy the results made her feel better as well.

But now she was going to have to help clear out the overgrown garden instead. Why couldn't she ever say no and risk upsetting people? Hadn't she learnt from her past?

Only the previous summer, her awful ex-boyfriend, Gary, and best friend from school, Bridget, had made her question every shred of confidence in herself. Even when they had left her life, the old doubts had lingered and she was just as unsure of her abilities as she had ever been. She wondered if she would ever find herself a backbone or at least the ability to say no to anyone.

Probably not, she decided, making a note in her calendar to help clear the overgrown garden at the weekend.

6

Logan had been reluctant to head out that evening. But he could never say no to his grandad, so when Stanley had invited him for a pint of beer in the pub garden later that week, he had no choice but to go along.

His back was aching a bit, having moved all the furniture in by himself into the shop over the past couple of days. Not for the first time, he wondered about his decision not to make any friends in Cranbridge. He certainly could have done with the help.

At least it was a pleasant enough evening, he thought. And Cranbridge was always lovely on a sunny evening. With Easter being so late that year, May had nearly arrived and there was a touch of warmth in the air already, the promise of a long, hot summer hopefully.

The last time he had been in the Black Swan Inn, it had been a somewhat disastrous restaurant opening on a dark, cold winter's night. Back then, his marriage was on the cusp of falling apart. He just had no idea how publicly or spectacularly that would happen.

Almost four months on, he was enjoying himself far more. He and his grandad were seated in the beer garden, which was mainly laid to lawn with a white picket fence running along one side. On the other side of the fence, he could see the river through the gaps, the evening sun dappled on the crystal-clear water. Along with the inside of the pub, the garden appeared to have had some type of makeover and was filled with many beautiful hanging baskets and pots of overflowing colourful flowers. Where there had previously been just well-worn wooden picnic benches and wobbly tables, there were now comfortable chairs with coloured cushions and matching umbrellas on the new tables.

The garden was almost full and the sound of lively conversation and laughter filled the warm evening air.

'This is very pleasant indeed,' said Stanley, sipping his pint.

Logan couldn't help but nod in agreement with him, despite feeling weary. He was still not sleeping very well even after working all hours to clean the filthy apartment and shop. His mind was still restless and agitated and he found himself going over and over his failed marriage, trying to work out where it all went wrong.

'Have you heard from your parents lately?' asked Stanley.

'Mum rang the other day,' replied Logan. 'They're both well. Dad, well, you know. Dad was never one for chatting anyway.'

Stanley was quiet for a moment before saying, 'My son was never much for communication.'

That was an understatement, thought Logan. His dad was about as absent emotionally as a person could get. So different from his warm-hearted grandparents.

'Thank you, Belle,' said Stanley to a dark-haired waitress as she placed a couple of plates of spring pie and mash between them. 'This looks marvellous.'

'Our chef's new special,' said Belle, with a wide smile. 'It's really good.'

She gave Logan a warm smile before touching Stanley on the shoulder and heading off.

'Pete and Belle have done really well here,' said Stanley, reaching out for his knife and fork. 'I know it was a bit of a disaster last time you were here, but it's all changed for the better now.'

Logan couldn't help but agree, especially when he tried some of the pie. It was delicious, as were the root mash and vegetables.

'It's always good to have a great local pub on your doorstep,' said Logan.

'Everyone appears to be doing well around here these days,' noted Stanley. 'The pub, the village shop, the newspaper, even the community hub is busier than ever. It feels as if life has come back to Cranbridge at last.'

Logan did think that there were more people around than there had been before.

'What I'm saying is that it might be a good place for you to put down some roots,' said Stanley softly. 'Yet another successful business in the area would be good for the village. And maybe for you too.'

'Well, the website is still taking on commissions so business is good.' Logan fixed a look at his grandfather. 'But this is just a temporary set-up until I'm back on my feet,' he said. 'I'll probably end up in London again.'

'Is that what you want?'

The question startled Logan. 'Yes. At least, I think so.' He had yet to work out where his life would lead him next and he had to admit to himself that the extra space in the workshop was nice. As well as being away from busy, pollution-filled central London.

Stanley nodded thoughtfully. 'I just thought that perhaps you'd had enough of city life.'

'For now.' Logan gave his grandad a smile. 'Anyway, there are definitely worse places to be whilst the gossip and heat dies away.'

'Yes, there are,' said Stanley, raising a pint at him before taking a sip.

Logan looked across at Riverside Lane. His grandfather was right; the two businesses at the beginning of the lane were doing really well. His temporary workshop was somewhat more tatty-looking, as was the empty shop next to it. The old signs were faded and the paint on the windowsills was cracked and flaking.

He moved his view past the tangle of the abandoned garden, or whatever it was, to the watermill beyond. 'Whatever happened with your fundraising plans for the mill?' he asked.

It had been a long-time dream of his grandfather's to see the watermill working once more. It had provided flour to the local community until the 1940s when it had fallen into disrepair during the war. Stanley had organised various fundraising events over the years, which had brought the mill somewhat forward with regards to repair, but it had been quite quiet recently.

Stanley sighed. 'We were almost there, but then one of our main fundraisers passed away and the donations have dwindled down to nothing.'

'That's a shame,' said Logan.

'It's the sound of the water that I miss the most,' said Stanley, staring across the river to the mill. 'I'd love to hear that water rushing over the wheel once more. It was the sound of my childhood, you see. I used to fish next to the mill with your great-grandfather.'

Logan watched his grandad's face grow sad and wished he could take the pain away from all the loss that he had endured. 'Perhaps we can do a little fishing this summer,' he suggested.

Stanley looked more cheerful. 'That would be nice.'

As Logan carried on eating his delicious pie, he realised how much he had missed his grandfather's company these past few months and hoped that they would both benefit from his stay in Cranbridge over the summer.

7

Molly glanced over to where Logan was sitting with his grandfather before trying to concentrate on the conversation at her own table once more.

She was still so embarrassed about the way that they had met earlier in the week. She had lost the deposit when she had returned the flattened bunny costume to the fancy-dress shop, not that it had been a great surprise. He would obviously think her a total fool. Hopefully she wouldn't run into him too often, despite the news that he had actually leased one of the run-down shops to work and live in.

She tuned back into the girly chat and, as had been the case for the past few weeks, all talk turned to Amber's wedding once more.

'Mum's driving me insane,' muttered Amber, not for the first time.

Molly gave her a sympathetic smile. Amber's mum had turned into a mother of the bridezilla almost as soon as the engagement had been announced. Now, as the day began to draw nearer, it was getting worse and worse.

'I still can't believe that she persuaded you to book that fancy hotel in Aldwych town,' said Lucy.

Amber rolled her eyes. 'Apparently the idea that we would only have a small reception in the village hall here in Cranbridge is just not the done thing,' she replied. 'Even though it's our wedding!'

'I thought Josh liked the idea of a simple wedding day,' said Lucy.

'He does and so do I,' Amber told them with a heavy sigh. 'Suddenly, it's all about what fancy canapés should be served and how many flower arrangements we can cram into one large room. And don't get me started on her outfit and all the drama that's involved.'

Belle picked up her drink. 'Like you said, it's *your* wedding,' she said, before taking a sip of her gin. 'And you should have the day of your dreams.'

'I know,' said Amber, looking downcast. 'But I'm her only daughter so she just wants it to be perfect.'

Belle shook her head. 'I tell you, if Pete ever drags me down the aisle, we're going to elope to some desert island, just the two of us. I couldn't bear the fuss.'

She glanced at her boyfriend and landlord of the pub garden they were sitting in and gave him a soft smile. Pete gave her a wink as he walked past.

'Well, at least our shared future mother-in-law hasn't gone the same way,' said Amber.

Josh and Pete's mother, Cathy, was thankfully far more relaxed about the wedding than Amber's mum.

'Mum did have one good idea though,' said Amber, somewhat to everyone's surprise. 'She thought I should ask you to make the cake.'

There was a short silence as Molly looked around the table.

'I'm pretty certain that Amber was talking to you,' Lucy told her, laughing. Her lack of culinary skills were legendary in their awfulness.

'Me?' spluttered Molly, beginning to shake her head. 'Are you mad?'

'You make cakes all the time and they're delicious,' said Belle.

'This isn't just a cake for coffee morning or for a charity fete,' said Molly, still aghast. 'This is for Amber's wedding day! One of the biggest days of her life, like you just said!'

Belle shrugged her shoulders. 'Yes. And?'

'And it'll be in all the photographs and will need to be perfect,' Molly told her, beginning to feel pretty stressed.

Amber reached over to squeeze Molly's hand. 'When have any of your cakes been anything but perfect?'

But Molly was too busy panicking to be reassured.

'Maybe I could give it to you as a gift and then you won't have to pay me,' she said, thinking out loud. But that didn't ease her worries as the wedding cake would still be central to the celebrations.

'Of course we're going to pay you,' said Amber.

Molly began to feel even worse. She loved baking but felt uncomfortable asking for money for something that was really just a hobby. It brought out all her doubts and uncertainties.

'Look, we'd both really love you to make our cake for our big day,' said Amber, giving her hand a squeeze. 'It would make it personal and special for me and Josh. You know, your best friend and the guy you've known for years and think of as a brother.'

'That's blackmail,' said Molly, with a sigh.

She should say no, she thought, to ease the anxiety, but, as usual, she just remained quiet and panicked within.

She looked across the garden towards the river, deep in thought. Of course, it would be nice to plan and design a cake like that. Which recipe to use though? She had seen a rose and pistachio sponge which might be good to try out. Or there was always the classic vanilla cake. Perhaps even a chocolate layer?

Her mind drifted through all the different scenarios as the conversation carried on about the wedding and the bridesmaids' dresses which Belle was making.

'So we've got plenty of the pale mauve material that you wanted,' said Belle. 'It's so pretty. It's got a slight sheen and almost shimmers in the sunlight. It'll look super in the photographs.'

Molly was rifling through her mental catalogue of decorations that she could use for the wedding cake. Simple and elegant? Or fancy and original? She couldn't decide.

'When do we get to try them on?' asked Lucy.

'Next week, if I get a wiggle on,' said Belle. 'As you know, they're all slightly different in shape but mostly the same in style. Mine's a halter neck as I'm so flat-chested. You've got more curves than me, so I've gone for a figure-hugger for you. And Molly's design is a miniskirt with plenty of cleavage on show.'

Molly, who had been in a bit of a dream about cake decorations, finally blinked back to life. 'Er, what was that about cleavage?' she asked, shocked.

Belle grinned. 'Just wanted to test that you were listening. But, hey, maybe short and sexy is the way to go for your dress.'

Molly blushed furiously. 'It's a wedding,' she said, in a pointed tone. 'And Amber's day. All attention should be on her.'

'Oh no,' said Amber, who had always been shy. 'I'm more than happy for someone else to take away some of the attention.'

'Not like that,' muttered Molly.

'Why?' asked Lucy, shaking her head. 'Because it might attract someone single and handsome?'

'I don't think there's anyone on the guest list like that,' said Molly. 'Unless you include your uncle Frank or Stanley.'

'Don't forget Stanley's grandson,' said Lucy, her eyes gleaming as she nodded indiscreetly across the garden.

Molly refused to look over at Logan. 'He's OK to talk to, but no, I don't think so,' she said in a prim tone of voice.

'When did you two meet?' asked Amber, raising her eyebrows in surprise.

'I bumped into him the other day,' said Molly, her cheeks beginning to grow red. 'Literally. Just after the Easter egg hunt when I was heading home.'

After a short silence, Belle shook her head at Molly before saying, 'Right. So what are we going to do about the hen night?'

Grateful for the subject being changed, Molly tried to join in, but was still concerned about the wedding cake. Baking for family and friends was one thing. A wedding cake was in a different league altogether and she just wasn't sure she was up to the task. She would have a word with Amber when it was just them and explain that she just wasn't good enough. The last thing she wanted to do was ruin her close friend's wedding with a lopsided cake.

Maybe one day she would have enough confidence, but for now, she was still happy to keep practising.

Except a small part of her knew that she wasn't really happy these days. And she wasn't sure how that was ever likely to change.

8

At the end of the first week in May, the weather had turned unseasonably warm and so Logan had thrown open the front and back doors of the shop to get some fresh air through whilst he worked.

It didn't do any harm to get the place aired anyway, having been empty for so long. It had taken a few days of clearing and cleaning before he was happy to place his precious handmade furniture inside the workshop area downstairs. Upstairs, in the apartment, had also required a good clean, but it was habitable at least. He wasn't too fussed beyond that. It wasn't as if he would be entertaining anyone up there.

His phone continued to buzz with messages and calls and he continued to ignore them all, finally switching it onto silent. Some of the messages were orders which could be emailed or ordered through his website. The others were from his ex-wife, no doubt demanding something else from him. She'd had his heart and half the house in the break-up already, what else was left to give?

He looked around him, thinking that she'd love to get her hands on the lucrative profits which he had built up for himself. But she would never get hold of his furniture business. His solicitors had seen to that, thank goodness. It was the one thing that he had left. The one shred of legacy to his name.

He looked down critically at the sideboard that he had just begun to make. The walnut wood was especially beautiful. He ran his hands over the slightly rough surface. When it was finished, the wood would be waxed and buffed and would run smooth. But he liked it best like this, a little bit ragged, not quite perfect. But still the knots and veins of the wood shone through. The beauty of wood continued to surprise him, even having worked with it for all of this time.

He had just bent down to check his measurements for the drawers when a grey blur rushed in through the front door.

Logan stared down at the shaggy grey dog which had crashed to a halt in front of him, looking somewhat confused as it stared up at him, a long tongue panting heavily.

'Hello,' said Logan, somewhat bemused.

'Keith!' said a man, appearing at the doorway. 'Come here, you idiot.'

Keith wagged his tail at what appeared to be his master but stayed sitting in front of Logan.

The man looked at Logan and rolled his eyes. 'Sorry,' he said, stepping over the threshold to collect his dog. 'He's not blessed with the biggest of brains and I think he just mistook your place for ours next door.'

Logan looked at the man. 'You work in the community hub,' he said, putting two and two together.

The man nodded and held out his hand. 'Work, run, fund it, you name it,' he replied with a grin. 'Tom Addison. And this hairy mutt is Keith.'

'Logan Armstrong,' Logan told him as they shook hands.

Tom looked around the shop, smiling at the cracked, dilapidated sinks along one wall, a remnant of when it had been a hairdressers. 'Nice to see the place finally being used after all this time,' he said. 'It's been empty since I've been here and that's a couple of years now. Gosh, that's a beautiful sideboard.' Tom had spotted a corner cabinet of sheesham wood.

'Thanks,' said Logan, as always feeling proud of his work. 'I've only just finished that particular piece.'

'Nice to have a skill like that,' replied Tom, with a sheepish grin. 'My only skills are words, although luckily my girlfriend, Lucy, seems happy with my shortcomings.'

'Words?' asked Logan, a little confused. 'Are you one of the teachers who runs the writing courses in the hub?'

Tom laughed, shaking his head. 'No, I leave that to the professionals like your grandad! I'm the editor of the other side of the business. *The Cranbridge Times* newspaper.'

Logan instantly lost his smile and found himself scowling at the newcomer. 'I see,' he said, shortly. 'Well, good to meet you, but I must get on with my work.'

As usual, any mention of the press these days caused him to shut down.

'Hey,' said Tom, looking concerned. 'There's no judgement here, especially from me. I used to be married to Andrea Johnson, as it happens. So I know what the attention can be like.'

Logan looked at Tom thoughtfully. Andrea Johnson was a semi-famous newsreader who had a string of ex-boyfriends and apparently an ex-husband or two to her name. The latest one being a media mogul. It had been quite the scandal in his social circle at the time before he too had suffered a similar fate in his own marriage.

'Anyway, *The Cranbridge Times* is a local newspaper,' carried on Tom, who didn't seem particularly upset at the mention of his ex-wife. 'All of our news is about local people and what matters to the community. We don't slander anyone. Except the big corporations who try to do us over, of course.'

'Of course,' murmured Logan, nodding thoughtfully.

'Look, come and have a pint with me sometime,' said Tom, before smiling. 'Or not. No pressure, honestly. But there's a nice, small group of us here and you'll be amongst friends.'

'Thanks,' said Logan. 'That would be good.' Inside though, he wasn't so sure. The embarrassment with his marriage break-up was still too raw.

'By the way, don't be alarmed if a beautiful dark-haired woman suddenly starts painting the windowsills at the front of the shop,' Tom told him. 'My girlfriend, Lucy, runs the community hub next door and is desperate to clean up the rest of the lane. Have you heard about the plans for the clear-up of the land just past the next shop?'

Logan nodded. 'My grandad told me all about it.'

'It's a real mess,' said Tom, with a grimace. 'Would be a good opportunity for you to meet a few of the locals if you lend a hand.'

'I'd be happy to but I'm a bit behind with some of the orders thanks to the time it took to get this place habitable,' replied Logan.

Tom nodded. 'I understand. Your landlord has a lot to answer for, if anyone can actually ever get him to pick up his phone, of course. You know,' said Tom, as he took Keith by the collar to steer him out of the front door, 'my wretched past turned out to be the best thing to happen to me. I moved here, met Lucy and the rest is my very own happy ever after. Hopefully you'll be the same.'

Logan hesitated. 'I'm only here for the summer unfortunately. And I'm happy to stay single forever, to be honest.'

Tom laughed. 'Yeah, I remember that feeling. Anyway, I'm only next door if you need anything. See you.'

'See you.'

As Tom disappeared from the doorway with Keith following on, Logan heard him say, 'Good morning, Stanley.'

His grandfather appeared by the front door almost immediately.

'Morning, Grandad,' said Logan.

'Good morning,' said Stanley, heading inside. 'Nice to see you finally meeting with a few people.'

'His dog ran inside by mistake.'

Stanley smiled. 'Dear Keith,' he said. 'Always reminds me of one of my old school pupils, Rickie Davison. Permanently confused but happy to be so. Tom's a nice fellow. And you need to start trusting people again.'

Logan raised a sardonic eyebrow. 'Recent history would prove otherwise.'

Stanley shook his head. 'I've known these folks for quite a few years now. They're good people.'

'And I was married for two years and look what happened. Turned out I didn't know her at all.' Logan bent down to take the measurements for the drawers once more. 'It's better this way.'

'Alone?' murmured Stanley with a sigh, as he moved to the back of the shop to make them both a coffee.

Stanley's words hung in the air after he had gone to fill up the kettle. Logan knew his grandfather was worried about him and perhaps he was right to be. He was often right about so many things. So Logan began to wonder whether he had perhaps got this all wrong after all.

9

Molly glanced out of the front window and realised that there was a heavy drizzle outside that Saturday morning. So much for the hoped-for heatwave that the weather experts were forecasting for the summer.

She went to grab her raincoat from the hallway before glancing into the kitchen.

'I'm off now to help clear that patch of land, Mum,' she said.

'Have fun,' said her mum before glancing down at the cat on her lap.

'Not sure how much fun it'll be in this weather,' Molly told her. 'The boys are going to have a wet match today.' Her brothers were out playing the first cricket match of the season whilst they were still home. Although they were due to head back to university that week. 'What are you up to this morning?'

'Not sure, love,' replied her mum.

'I'll certainly be working up an appetite given the state of that land we've got to clear,' said Molly in an overly bright voice. 'A slice or two of your delicious bread would be nice.'

The silence stretched out before her mum spoke. 'I'm not sure we've got any yeast left.'

'Cranbridge Stores will have some,' said Molly.

'I'll see.'

Molly gave her mum a kiss on the cheek before heading out into the drizzle. It appeared to match her mum's low mood, which didn't seem to be improving at all. The skies were overcast and more rain was forecast for the coming weeks.

Molly walked along the narrow pavement before it widened as it became Riverside Lane. At the other end were the shops, bustling with people, but alongside the watermill it was quiet. The watermill had been abandoned a long time ago. She couldn't remember it ever working and nor could her mum. The wooden wheel was rotten and covered in weeds and moss. There had been some work done on it about ten years ago, but it had long since been abandoned.

Much like the garden next to it, she thought. It had a low brick wall along the front. Beyond that, it was a large space filled with tall weeds, nettles and the occasional bramble bush. At the back of the garden, it looked as if there were a couple of apple trees, old and gnarly with age, but their pink and white blossom was pretty enough, even on a cloudy day.

A higher wall ran alongside the narrow stream of water that fed the watermill when it had worked. On the opposite side was the brick side wall of the last of the shops along Riverside Lane. A particularly rotten-looking back door was just about visible through the tangle of plants.

Molly pushed open the rickety gate in the middle of the low wall at the front and it nearly collapsed with the effort of being moved after so long.

'Good morning,' she said to Stanley, who was nearby, dressed in what appeared to be old gardening clothes.

Alongside him, Frank nodded and said good morning to her. And then, at almost half their height, was Grandma Tilly. Josh and Pete's grandmother was a pocket rocket of good humour and gung-ho attitude.

'Morning, Molly,' said Grandma Tilly. 'Lovely day for it, don't you think?'

Molly grimaced. 'Isn't it awful? What happened to the sunshine?'

'Don't you worry,' said Grandma Tilly. 'It always comes out eventually.'

'But perhaps not today,' said Stanley wisely, looking up at the endless grey skies above.

'Well, shall we get started?' asked Frank.

'Is it just us four?' asked Grandma Tilly, frowning.

'I'm sure it's not,' said Molly, checking her texts. 'Oh! Belle and Amber both have to work. So do Josh and Pete.'

'And Lucy and Tom have come down with heavy colds overnight, so I've told them to stay dry inside their apartment,' added Frank. 'Despite my niece's protests to the contrary.'

'Shame,' said Grandma Tilly. 'Many hands making light work and all that.'

'I did put out a request on social media for volunteers but it doesn't seem as if anyone else is going to turn up,' said Molly. 'So where do we start? I don't know much about gardening. If anything, to be honest.'

'How about we start at the front and work our way towards the back,' said Stanley. 'At least the front part should be relatively easy.'

For once though, Stanley was wrong. The front of the garden turned out to be a tangle of bindweed and stinging nettles which had formed some kind of thick jungle mat across the whole area. To add to the difficulty, brambles were hidden amongst it and despite wearing her gloves, Molly was soon scratched from the thorns and splattered with earth as she pulled up the weeds.

The hard work occasionally ground to a halt on the discovery of a rusty old barbeque, a couple of broken terracotta pots and even some abandoned car tyres.

Too heavy to carry, Molly rolled the tyres to the side wall so that they could be taken away at some point.

After a couple of hours, they had managed to clear about a quarter of the garden down to ground level.

'I think we all need a tea break,' declared Grandma Tilly.

So whilst Stanley and Frank leant carefully against the dilapidated wall for a break, Grandma Tilly produced a flask of coffee to be shared. Molly had also brought something for them all and dug into the carrier bag to bring out a choice of her classic shortbread and white chocolate and cranberry flapjacks, both of which went down very well.

'This is marvellous,' said Frank, in between mouthfuls. 'So delicious.'

'I agree,' said Stanley. 'The cranberries are a lovely addition.'

Molly blushed and smiled at their praise. Flapjacks were easy compared to making something amazing like Amber and Josh's wedding cake. She was still fretting over what she could possibly make for them and how good the cake would actually be given their inevitable high expectations.

'They're so good. You should think about selling your cakes,' commented Grandma Tilly, licking her lips after polishing off both a flapjack and a piece of shortbread. 'They're very professional. Have you ever thought about putting them into Cranbridge Stores for sale?'

Molly shook her head. 'I'm not much of a businesswoman,' she told them.

'So learn,' scolded Grandma Tilly with a chuckle. 'You've got a real talent, girl. It'd be a shame not to capitalise on that.'

Molly blushed and concentrated on packing away her cake tin back into the bag. She knew that Grandma Tilly was being kind, as always. Nobody would ever pay money for her cakes, would they?

She tried to change the subject. 'So any ideas what will happen to the garden when we've cleared it?'

She really hoped all their hard work wouldn't go to waste and that it wouldn't grow into another mess in a couple of months.

Frank shook his head. 'I don't think anyone's got any clue what to do with it.'

'Seems a waste of a good space.' Grandma Tilly suddenly broke into a wide grin as she nudged Molly with her elbow. 'You know what? It's the perfect spot for a tea garden, don't you think?'

'A tea garden?' said Molly, somewhat amazed as she looked around the tangled mess.

'Just think, a nice cup of tea and lots of your lovely cakes served up,' carried on Grandma Tilly. 'Sounds good, eh? Being your own boss for a change.'

For a brief moment, Molly allowed herself to imagine what it would be like to run her very own tea garden. What would it be like to be in charge and responsible for all aspects of the business? She immediately found that she was scared out of her wits.

And yet, a small part of her yearned for change and responsibility. To be her own person and to make up her own mind. But what if she failed? What if the business crashed and burned?

'What have you got to lose?' added Grandma Tilly in a more gentle tone, interrupting her thoughts.

What little confidence I have left, thought Molly, before quickly changing the subject.

10

Logan locked up the front door of the shop and wandered along towards the end of Riverside Lane. The light drizzle earlier in the day had turned into more persistent rain and he zipped up his hoodie as he began to walk a little more quickly.

It certainly wasn't an ideal day to be gardening, he thought.

His grandad had told him about the plan to clear the plot of land at the end of the shops, but Logan had expected a little more progress to be made after one morning. As he reached the surrounding wall, he saw that about only a quarter of the overgrown weeds and brambles had been cleared. He felt guilty that he hadn't been able to help his grandfather as he had an order for a piece of furniture that needed completing on time.

He felt even more guilty when he discovered that the only person who had helped that wasn't under the age of seventy was Molly. She was looking somewhat bedraggled now from the rain, which was growing heavier by the minute. But, for whatever reason, she was still smiling. He had to admire her sunny attitude, he thought, even when splattered with grass and earth, with her blonde hair flattened on her head from the wet. She was standing by an old rickety gate, chatting with Stanley.

'Hey,' Logan said, checking over his grandfather briefly with his eyes. Stanley looked less bedraggled than Molly, but his cheeks were glowing. 'You look like you've been hard at work.'

'Thanks to young Molly here we've got quite a bit done,' replied Stanley, giving her a soft smile. 'Not sure how much progress we'd have made if it were just us three old 'uns.'

Logan smiled and nodded to his grandfather's friends, whom he had brought into the workshop the previous day for introductions.

'Speak for yourself,' said Grandma Tilly, with a grin. 'I'm still twenty-one at heart.'

'Mental age too,' muttered Frank.

'But my bones are a little older than my spirit these days, so I must away and put my feet up with a cup of tea,' she carried on. 'I'm not sure I'll be much use this afternoon.'

'I'll walk back with you,' said Frank. 'I'm a little weary myself. We can always continue our work at a later date.'

As they headed off, only his grandad and Molly remained. Logan watched as she shuffled shyly from wellington boot to wellington boot.

'Well, I'm going to fix myself a sandwich from home before I carry on,' she said. 'Are you sure you don't want the last flapjack?'

Stanley smiled and shook his head. 'Delicious as they were, I couldn't eat another morsel. But thank you.'

There was an awkward silence before Molly looked at Logan. 'It's yours for the taking, if you want,' she said. 'It's white chocolate and cranberry flavour.'

'And highly recommended,' added Stanley.

Feeling he had no choice if he didn't want to offend her, Logan took the proffered cake and paper napkin and said, 'Thanks.'

'You're welcome,' she replied. 'Right. I suggest you get some rest as well, Stanley. You've worked just as hard as the rest of us.'

'I'm just going to take a walk with my grandson but perhaps I'll put my feet up for a while afterwards,' he replied.

'You've earned it,' she told him, reaching out to give his arm a squeeze before saying goodbye.

She walked away, leaving Logan and his grandfather by themselves.

'Are you heading home?' asked Logan.

'I wanted to show you something first,' said Stanley, turning to walk to the other end of the lane.

Logan followed him, his stomach rumbling as he had missed lunch. So he absent-mindedly opened up the paper napkin as they walked and took a bite of the flapjack. It had to be better than nothing, he hoped. As it turned out, it was incredible. The sweetness of the syrup which bound together the oats was offset by the introduction of cranberries dotted amongst the bar.

Stanley glanced at his grandson's surprised face and smiled. 'I told you that she was a good baker.'

Logan nodded, eager to keep eating.

Stanley's forehead furrowed into a frown. 'It's just sad that she's the only one that doesn't see it.'

His grandad didn't say any more and Logan didn't press him even though he found himself curious to know more about Molly.

Expecting to follow his grandfather along the narrow pavement towards his bungalow at the edge of the lane, Logan was surprised to find Stanley had suddenly walked off to the left across a narrow bridge which he hadn't remembered was even there.

They crossed a stream and stood in front of the wooden door in the side of the watermill.

'Conservation of our local lands and buildings has become a big topic around here, ever since the threat of the quarry last summer,' said Stanley. 'Luckily we were successful with that, but I'd be heart-broken if anything were to happen to the watermill.'

Logan had heard all about the village's fight against the building of a large quarry on their doorstep. Thankfully they had won that particular battle.

Logan pointed at the padlock in the door. 'Looks like you won't be able to show me around today unless the council have given you a key.'

Stanley gave him a soft smile and pulled out a key from his pocket. 'That's not a problem. You see, I own it.'

As his grandfather turned to fiddle with the lock, Logan was astounded. 'You own the watermill? Since when?'

'The council offered it to me many years ago in order to get the restoration on track,' said Stanley. 'Otherwise it was in danger of disintegrating into the water. As you can see, the pointing and brickwork on the outside was all redone, as was the roof. Unfortunately that was when the work stopped.'

'Why?' asked Logan.

Stanley sighed softly. 'I lost your grandmother,' he said, after a short pause. 'And, in all honesty, I lost interest. It sort of took a back step. But when I had to give up the house last year and move into the bungalow, I began to be aware of the passing of time and I really would like to see it working once again.'

Stanley unlocked the padlock and pulled open the door before stepping inside.

Logan followed him inside and was instantly mesmerised. The mill was made of the same honey-coloured brick as the rest of the village. However, inside there was no middle floor and so it was a double-height room and he could see all the way up to the oak beams holding the roof in place. In the middle of the space were two vast round stones.

'They're called querns,' said Stanley as he watched his grandson walk across to run his hand over the stone. 'The upper one is the handstone, the bottom one the saddle stone.'

Logan looked at his grandad. 'I see the schoolteacher in you is still alive and well.'

Stanley smiled. 'Always,' he said. 'Just like my mother before me. But my father, you see, was a baker.'

Logan was surprised. 'I never knew that.'

'Oh yes,' said Stanley. 'Back when I was a child, my father would get all his flour from this mill. Freshly baked bread is still a marvel to me, transporting me back to my childhood.'

'How old is the mill?' asked Logan.

'Three hundred years,' said Stanley.

'And you've bought it?' Logan was still amazed.

'A rare rash decision of mine,' said Stanley. 'Not that I regret it at all. As you can see, the main repair work has been done, but the wheel outside has rotted away, sadly.'

'That's a shame,' said Logan.

'You know, it was always my lifelong dream to see the watermill saved. There's been so much heritage in the area lost already.'

Logan nodded.

'It would be a shame to lose yet another piece of my history,' carried on Stanley. 'My own heritage. When I've lost so much already, with your beloved grandmother passing.'

Logan gave his grandad some side-eye. 'You were doing quite well until you started to lay it on a bit too thick at the end there.'

Stanley broke into a wide smile. 'Noted, dear boy.'

'Taking advantage of my kind heart and even mentioning Granny,' said Logan, starting to laugh. 'That constitutes emotional blackmail.'

'I know,' replied Stanley, joining in the laughter. 'And I feel ashamed of myself.' He paused. 'But it worked, didn't it?'

Logan sighed. 'I'm not sure what a cabinet maker can do with a watermill, but yeah, for you, Grandad, I'll take a look.'

'Excellent,' said Stanley, beaming. 'I'd be most grateful, my boy.'

'Don't thank me yet,' Logan told him. 'I might not be able to do anything to help.'

'Just do your best,' said Stanley. 'That's all I've ever asked of you.'

Logan wandered outside and looked down at the rotten waterwheel, figuring that it would be way beyond his own skills to restore. He could see quite a few broken spokes, and the remaining ones looked pretty rotten.

'If only I knew someone who knew and understood wood,' murmured Stanley, coming to stand next to him. 'Then perhaps we could get the mill going after all.'

Logan spun around to where his grandad had quickly planted an innocent look on his face. 'So the flapjack, the invite to look around the mill, all of this. It was all emotional blackmail to get me to fix the wheel?'

Stanley was still trying to look innocent. 'The invite to look around was just that,' he said. 'The flapjack I can take no credit for.'

Logan couldn't help but smile for a moment. 'Look, Grandad, you realise that I make furniture,' he said. 'I'm not a proper carpenter as such. I'm not sure what I can really do to help.' The silence stretched out, so he found himself pressing on. 'But, if you want me to help out that badly, of course I'll take a look for you.'

'It's for the village, not me,' said Stanley.

'OK,' said Logan. 'But I'll be doing it for you, Grandad.'

Stanley clapped a hand on his grandson's shoulder and gave it a squeeze.

Logan tried to sound confident but he really wasn't sure that his skills were going to be up to fixing the watermill. But he had to try, for his grandfather's sake.

11

On her way home for lunch, Molly was thinking about the garden that they had only just begun to clear. But she wasn't thinking about the amount of work left to be done to tidy the rest of the land. She couldn't stop thinking about what Grandma Tilly had said about turning the place into a tea garden.

She found herself imagining a few tables and chairs dotted around. Perhaps with the grass left long here and there for the insects, of course. The clink of crockery. Maybe some pretty teapots and freshly cut flowers on the tables. The murmur of conversation. And, of course, many varieties of cake.

Her mind was still racing as she headed inside the cottage and into the kitchen.

Her mum was once more sitting at the kitchen table and looked up as her daughter came in.

'Hello,' she said.

Molly nodded. 'Hey, Mum. I just came home for a sandwich. Shall I make us both one?'

Her mum looked guilty. 'I haven't made any bread, I'm afraid.'

'Not to worry,' Molly told her quickly. She wasn't even sure her mum had moved from her position at the table since breakfast time. 'There's still some rolls from yesterday, I think.'

Over lunch, Molly chatted away about how much work there was to clear the whole plot of land.

'There's still so much to do,' she said, blowing out a sigh as she slid her plate into the dishwasher.

'Oh dear,' said her mum, frowning.

She seemed so disengaged from even making conversation that Molly was seriously concerned.

The silence stretched out once more until Molly had a thought. 'What about you giving me a hand this afternoon?' she asked.

'Oh, I don't know,' said her mum, shaking her head almost immediately.

'It's only been Stanley, Frank and Grandma Tilly to help me,' Molly told her. 'And, to be honest, you'd be doing me a huge favour. Because they're all really struggling with the heavy work clearing the weeds and have gone off needing a rest.'

Her mum was still hesitating, so Molly quickly spoke again.

'You used to enjoy your gardening,' she said. 'So at least you'd recognise what a weed is, whereas I haven't got a clue.'

'I'm not up to much physical work these days,' her mum replied, looking hesitant.

'Just for an hour,' said Molly quickly. 'That would make a big difference. For me, Mum. Please? There's nobody else around this afternoon to give me a hand. It's a lot of work for one person.'

In the end, her mum nodded her agreement and Molly felt somewhat relieved. Her mum hadn't left the house for a few days, so this at least would be something.

When they returned to the walled garden next to the mill, her mum looked a little concerned.

'There's still an awful lot of work to be done here,' she said, looking around.

'We'll just do what we can for now. Shall we carry on from that cleared patch over there?' said Molly, picking up the nearby shears and starting to slice through the next tangle of bramble branches.

The gardening had turned out to be far harder work than she had imagined, especially as the ground had not been dug or even touched for so many years. Weeds ran rampant and she had lost count of the amount of scratches she had from wayward branches and rose thorns.

And yet, it had been pleasant to be outside doing some physical work for a change. Most of her job was sat behind a desk in the community hub. And although it was nice to see so many different people on a daily basis, she still preferred to be active and moving around.

It was drizzling once more, but Molly had given up putting up the hood on her raincoat as it made her too sweaty with the gardening. But at least her wellington boots kept her feet dry.

She glanced over at her mum who was concentrating on digging up some kind of bramble bush at the roots.

They worked on for a while in comfortable silence until someone called out from the other side of the wall.

'Am I too late?' he asked, looking embarrassed.

It was Molly's old teacher from school, Mr Turner. A fair headed man in his late fifties with a friendly face, he had always been one of her favourite teachers.

'I had to go into Aldwych this morning,' he continued. 'But I saw your notice earlier in the week on the newspaper website and thought I could lend a hand.'

'You're not too late at all, Mr Turner,' said Molly, grateful for another pair of hands.

He smiled at Molly. 'I think you can call me Geoff now that I'm retired and you must have left school well over a decade ago.'

Molly smiled at him. 'When did you retire?' she asked.

'At the end of the summer term last year,' he told her. 'I have to confess, it's been a bit more difficult than I'd anticipated.'

'Oh really?' asked Molly, a little surprised. 'You miss the children?'

'I miss all the company, to be honest,' he replied. 'The teachers, the parents, even the kids. Being a bachelor, it can get a bit lonely rattling around the place on my own.'

Molly looked over at her mum, who was listening to the conversation but had remained quiet so far.

'Mum's just taken early retirement as well,' she told him, trying to draw her mum into the conversation a little. 'I think she misses her friends at the factory as well.'

Her mum blushed and looked away briefly.

'Hello, Rachel,' said Geoff. 'Nice to see you. Are you a gardener?'

'Not for a long time,' Molly's mum replied, finally speaking. 'What about you?'

'Not sure I've got particularly green fingers. Especially if you'd have seen my failed attempt with some salvias last year. I'm better off growing vegetables,' he added, laughing.

'Salvias I can handle. But vegetables were something I never got the hang of,' said her mum, her voice lifting a little as the passion filled her voice. 'My tomatoes were always a disaster.'

'If you like tomatoes then I always have a glut come the summer,' said Geoff. 'I'd be happy to pass some on to you.'

'Thank you,' she told him. 'That's very kind.'

They smiled at each other for a moment before getting down to clearing more of the area.

With Geoff helping, they were able to dig out the bigger bramble bushes from the roots to stop them growing again.

They had made steady progress but by early evening, they were all beginning to flag.

So they all said their goodbyes and headed home with a promise to return the following weekend.

'Mr Turner, er, Geoff, is nice, isn't he?' she said to her mum as they walked back.

Her mum nodded but didn't say anything.

Molly had never seen her mum go out on a date or have any kind of romantic interest in anyone. She had always assumed that her mum was too badly bruised from their dad leaving them all those years ago. But at least that afternoon she had managed to get her mum out of the house. That in itself felt like an achievement at the moment.

But what about her own achievements? Molly found herself wondering. A tea garden? Could it actually work?

She started to feel excited. It was an idea. She just needed to be brave enough to go for it. At once, her confidence failed her. But, as she reminded herself, what did she have to lose?

12

Monday evening brought another get-together for Molly and her friends. They sat on the comfortable sofas inside Lucy and Tom's apartment which was above the community hub.

'How was your weekend?' asked Amber, as she leaned forward to fill up their gin glasses.

'A bit tiring,' said Molly, laying out some home-made raspberry and white chocolate brownies on a plate in the middle of the coffee table. 'It was pretty back-breaking trying to clear that land when it hasn't been touched for so long.'

'I'm so sorry,' said Belle looking downcast. 'Pete had to meet with the bank so I ended up having to work.'

Lucy laughed, which turned into a coughing fit. 'I wish that had been my excuse,' she said. 'I was thick with cold and felt awful. Feel OK now though, once I get rid of this cough.'

'And I had to help out in the shop as we had an early delivery.' Amber gave Molly a sheepish smile. 'I just figured everyone else would be there.'

'No, it was just me, Frank, Stanley and Grandma Tilly,' said

Molly with a soft sigh. 'I managed to get Mum along to help out in the afternoon though.'

The silence stretched out as her friends exchanged a look of guilt until Belle finally spoke. 'OK, listen, we're all sorry for letting you down. Is there room on the naughty step for all three of us?'

But, for once, Belle's humour didn't lighten Molly's mood.

'It's just, well, it always seems to me that gets stuck with these things,' she said. 'Like the Easter bunny.'

'I'm so sorry, this was all my idea,' said Lucy, looking uncomfortable. 'But thank you for starting to tidy it up. We'll rally the troops for next weekend, I promise. And hopefully some good will come out of it.'

'Maybe even a tea garden,' murmured Molly to herself.

However, her friends heard her and stared at each other.

'A what?' they all chorused.

Molly gave a start. 'Oh, it was nothing,' she said quickly. 'It was a silly idea.'

And yet, she hadn't stopped thinking about it.

'What are you talking about?' asked Lucy, looking confused.

Molly sighed. 'Grandma Tilly and I were talking about what could be done with the space when it was cleared and she said that I should open up a tea garden. Isn't it the craziest idea you've ever heard?' She laughed and expected her friends to join in, but they were all too busy nodding their heads.

'She's right,' said Lucy, looking excited. 'With a bit of work, it would make a really pretty place to eat outside.'

'But we have the pub beer garden already,' Molly reminded them, frowning.

'So?' said Belle, with a shrug. 'More the merrier where the village is concerned. Besides, we only serve big meals at lunchtime. A tea room would be perfect for everyone else's needs.'

'But what about Amber's takeaway coffee from the shop?' said Molly, still thinking through the negatives.

'It's a shop,' said Amber, with a soft smile. 'The takeaway coffee counts for a tiny percentage of our profits. It wouldn't be a problem.'

'But how would it work?' asked Molly. 'Who would run it?'

'Well, you would, of course,' said Belle, rolling her eyes. 'Who else knows everything about cake?'

'I don't know that much about cake,' Molly told her quickly.

'Of course you do,' Amber replied. 'Why else would we ask you to make our wedding cake?'

'Look, about that,' began Molly, shaking her head. Surely now was the time to tell Amber that her doubts about being up to the task were very real.

But she was interrupted by Lucy springing up. 'I'm going to go and get Tom off his PlayStation,' she said, rushing towards the closed bedroom door. 'He knows all about starting up businesses.'

Whilst they waited, Molly's mind raced. She had expected her friends to laugh at the idea. The last thing she had expected, despite secretly hoping for, was for them to approve of the idea.

Lucy returned with Tom, who smiled and said hello to them all.

'I hear there's a delicious brownie in it for me if I can give you some business advice,' said Tom, sitting down on the end of the sofa.

Molly held out the plate of cakes for him. As she was feeling a little overwhelmed about the whole idea, she let Lucy tell Tom about the proposal for the tea garden as he nibbled on his brownie and nodded thoughtfully.

Alongside him, Keith the dog was eyeing up the delicious fare, so Amber immediately moved the plate to the much higher kitchen counter.

'Sorry, Keith,' she said, giving the dog's shaggy head a stroke. He sat and stared at the counter, his tongue lolling out in expectation.

Finally, Tom spoke. 'Well, first off, you're obviously going to need to check with Barry as owner of the plot of land. Although he doesn't seem to care what's done with the properties and land that he owns, given his less than interested attitude about us starting to clear the garden.'

'Except he'll want paying, I'm sure,' added Belle. 'That's all he's interested in.'

'Indeed,' said Tom, nodding. 'So, assuming that the rent he demands isn't too high and that the landlord is OK with this, my advice would be to give it a trial run to see if it's a proper business concern,' he told Molly. 'You can have a pop-up food business for twenty-eight days with minimal need for planning. Of course, you'll still need to meet certain hygiene standards and have public liability insurance in place. I can give you advice on that.'

'Twenty-eight days?' said Molly, frowning. 'You mean a full month? But what about my job?'

After all, Tom was her boss and she didn't want to upset him.

Tom gave her a wink. 'I don't care about that,' he said. 'Listen, you've got some annual leave saved up. Just use the rest of the time as a leave of absence. The community hub is our dream, not yours.'

Lucy nodded along with her boyfriend. 'He's right. It's time for you to think about yourself for a change.'

Molly sat quietly, still not quite believing everything they were telling her. Did they really mean it?

'The local authority will give you all the details that you need to comply with,' said Tom, before finishing his brownie and licking his lips. 'And with baking skills this good, I reckon you should go for it.'

'You really think so?' Molly bit her lip, still plagued with doubt. 'I don't know.'

'You love baking,' Belle reminded her. 'Imagine doing that for a living every day.'

'Go for it,' said Amber, softly.

'It's only for a month. What's the harm in that?' added Lucy.

Even Tom was nodding his approval.

Molly finally looked at Belle. 'Are you sure it won't be a problem for the inn?'

Belle looked at her friend for a moment before saying, 'Well, as you're going to be my main competition, I guess our friendship's over.'

Molly was horrified until she saw Belle's grin.

'Kidding!' said Belle quickly, reaching across and giving her a hug. 'Not everyone wants to go to the inn for a drink. Some want a nice cup of tea and a slice of your yummy cake. Me included, for the record.'

Molly was silent for a moment as she looked around at her friends once more. Could it work? Could she really run a tea garden for a month? There was so much work to be done on the garden itself, let alone setting it up. Would she even get permission to have a business there? What if Barry said no?

Her head was trying to impress upon her all the negatives, but her heart was singing at the thought of running her very own tea garden.

Molly glanced down at the plate which was now nearly empty as everyone had devoured her cakes, and finally, with a hesitant nod, she said, 'OK. Let's go for it.'

13

Logan had put off starting work on the watermill for a few days whilst he was busy with his own business, but in the end, the guilt over letting down his grandfather weighed too heavy on him.

So, on Tuesday evening, having completed a few more commissions for pieces of furniture, he stood in the dusty air of the mill and looked around him. There were some positive signs, he thought. His grandad had told him that the heavy round stones that ground the flour had been oiled and were ready to ground any grain into flour. And the complicated timber leverage system high above him in the double-height ceiling had already been fixed and should work.

The trouble was, the wheel itself was what was needed to get everything moving once more. And that was a huge problem.

He wandered back outside through the front door and looked at the giant waterwheel at the side of the building. From what he could see, the metal that held the wheel to the wall was incredibly rusty and that was nothing compared to the state of the wheel itself. It was covered with years of weeds and debris. The parts that were showing looked very rotten, in addition to the broken spokes. He suspected that he would have to replace nearly every spoke. And then who knew if it would even work?

First things first, he told himself. He would need an old pair of shorts to wade into the water and a large flashlight to study it up close.

So Logan went to his apartment to get changed before heading back to the watermill once more.

Riverside Lane seemed quiet that evening, but it was school term so there were no families about. No one at all, from what he could make out, especially there down the quieter end of the lane.

But as he went past the shop at the end of the row and on to the walled garden, he realised that someone was actually around. Molly was standing in the middle of the cleared patch of land, muttering to herself.

He was going to carry on and mind his own business when he realised that she was clutching her arms around her and frowning as she paced back and forth.

'How would it ever work?' she said to herself.

Logan found himself hesitating. She looked very anxious and he needed to make sure that she was OK. He didn't know why. Perhaps he was still feeling guilty over the whole Easter bunny roadkill accident.

'Hi,' he said, pushing past the rotted wooden gate and heading across the grass towards her.

Molly gave a start. 'Oh! Hi,' she said, her steps faltering as she finally stopped pacing.

'Some people say it's a sign of insanity talking to yourself,' he told her. 'But I also say that it's the best conversation you can have some days. Depending on the company, of course.'

She looked at him with a blank look. 'Sorry?'

He gave her a soft smile. 'I heard you muttering to yourself and just wanted to make sure that you're OK.'

She gave a shrug of her shoulders. 'I'm not sure how to answer that,' she said.

'What's going on?' he asked.

She blew out a long sigh. 'I'm trying to decide whether it's even worth me setting up a tea garden here.'

'Really?' Logan was surprised. She hardly seemed like the business entrepreneur type.

'See? Even you don't think I can do it.'

'That's not what I said,' he told her, shaking his head. 'So, tell me what you're worried about. What's the problem?'

'There are many problems,' she said, beginning to pace across the grass once more. 'How would it work? What are the customers going to sit on? How much do I charge for food and drink? Where do I store it all? And they're all valid questions but still not the biggest problem of all.'

'Which is?' he asked.

'I doubt whether Barry would even let me use the land in the first place,' she said, in a dull tone.

She really did seem very defeated already, he thought.

'I don't think you should wave the white flag until you've talked to him,' he said. 'And I think that a tea garden sounds like a good idea.'

'I bet you've never been into a tea garden in your life,' she told him in a wry tone.

He laughed. 'You might have a point! But, listen, so I don't know anything about tea gardens, but I know about business. I mean, the garden isn't exactly looking pretty yet, is it? But it's a great setting with the river on your doorstep. And having tasted your flapjack, I'm pretty certain the rest of your bakes are likely to be excellent too.'

She looked embarrassed at the compliment, her cheeks blushing an attractive rose pink in the soft evening sun.

'As for serving up the food...' he said, looking around the garden, trying to work out where that could even be done.

'I was thinking about investing in an old caravan or something,' she said. 'It's got to be weatherproof.'

'Not exactly aesthetically pleasing though, is it?' he replied. 'Besides, how are you even going to get it onto the land in the first place?'

'You're right,' she said, with a sigh. 'Let alone where on earth am I going to do all the baking. Maybe it's not worth it. After all, it's only supposed to be for twenty-eight days. A pop-up business, I think Tom called it.'

Logan looked across at the empty shop next to the garden. 'What about that empty place next to mine?' he said. 'That's not being used.'

She shook her head. 'Barry won't rent it to someone like me.'

'You won't know unless you ask,' he told her, thinking how eagerly his landlord had accepted his offer to rent his own place. 'And besides, it's not making anything for him sitting there empty.'

She looked at him for a moment before glancing back at the shop. 'I don't know,' she said. 'It's a bit big for what I had in mind.'

'So think big,' he told her. 'Dream big.'

Molly bit her lip, still looking unsure, and he didn't want to push what appeared to be a very fragile confidence.

'Ask Barry,' he said. 'If he says no, then that'll be it. But you never know. Stranger things have happened.'

'OK, well, thank you,' she said.

He smiled at her. 'I figured I owed you one for the Easter bunny disaster.'

She smiled back, her pretty face lighting up momentarily. 'I think that was a joint disaster, so maybe I can help you at some point.'

'Do you know how to fix up ancient watermills?' he joked.

'Oh! Are you fixing the watermill?' she asked, looking thrilled. 'That would be amazing. I don't think I've ever seen it work.'

'Well, don't get your hopes up yet,' he told her. 'It's not anywhere near fixed yet.'

He caught her smile and was pleased that she seemed a little happier.

As he walked back down the lane, Logan found himself pondering how her blue eyes lit up when she was happy and how much pleasure he had briefly had in watching them.

14

Molly was still dithering about the idea of the tea garden by the time the weekend rolled around again.

Thankfully, she didn't have much time to think, as nothing could happen in the garden until it was cleared. But perhaps it might not take as long as she had thought, she hoped when she arrived.

'This is a good turnout,' said Amber, looking around at the twenty or so people who had gathered there.

'It's certainly an improvement on last weekend,' said Molly. 'Maybe we'll get more done today after all.'

Her postings all over social media calling for more volunteers had certainly ensured that more people had turned up.

Unfortunately, her brothers had headed back to university to take their second-year exams and, as expected, her mum had decided not to come with her. Her brief good mood had faded once more over the past week with her sons' departure. However, Molly was pleased to see Geoff standing by the wall, and waved at him.

'Nice to see you here, Del,' said Stanley, looking surprised as someone else joined the throng.

'Someone said something about cake?' replied Dodgy Del, with a grin.

Del, who was the local coach driver, was always trying to be helpful around the village. It was just that his way of dreaming up dubious ideas to help the village and himself had earned him the nickname Dodgy Del a long time ago. His heart was generous, even if his methods were somewhat questionable.

'And I've brought my niece with me to give us a hand.'

He pushed Olivia forward, a young woman in her late teens. Molly didn't see her very often around the village, but she always seemed to have an air of sadness about her.

Michelle, Olivia's mum and Del's sister, had been trouble ever since school. A few years older than Molly, she had been in detention more often than in actual classes. And trouble had followed Michelle throughout her adult life as well. The previous year, Michelle had given birth to a younger brother for Olivia, although there was no sign of the father. Or Michelle either in the Mothers and Toddlers group. She had never struck Molly as the caring, parental type although thankfully Del was far more of an involved family member.

'Bit early for cake. Isn't it best to work up an appetite first, Del?' said Amber, in a pointed tone.

'Nah, I need a bit of energy,' he replied with a wink, before grabbing a piece of the seeded banana loaves that Molly had already sliced into generous wedges.

'Leave some for the rest of us,' grumbled Josh.

'So what are we up to first?' asked Del, his mouth full of cake.

To Molly's horror, everyone looked at her for the answer.

'You're the boss,' murmured Lucy, standing alongside her. 'Or hopefully you will be.'

Feeling the blushes appear, Molly began, 'Well, as you can see, we only managed to clear part of this space last week. All the weeds need pulling out by the roots and the brambles need cutting down. The idea is to clear the space back to hopefully just the grass and then see what we're left with.'

Everyone seemed agreeable to this and began to move out in all directions.

Molly looked at Lucy. 'You know, this is really your project,' she told her.

Lucy shook her head. 'If this is going to be your tea garden, you should be the one to take charge.'

Molly opened her mouth to reply but didn't get a chance as Dodgy Del barged up to them.

'You're turning this into a what?' he said, eyes agog.

'A tea garden,' Molly told him. 'Hopefully. Maybe. I've yet to get permission or anything like that.'

But Del wasn't listening. 'You mean cakes and all that? Terrific! My old mum would love that. And I'm guessing all of your menu will need tasting beforehand, yeah?' He looked at Molly hopefully.

'Join the back of the queue, Del,' shouted Tom from nearby.

'Lots of work to do before then,' said Stanley.

Molly nodded in agreement. It certainly needed a fair amount of work to turn it into any kind of garden that would be welcoming to visitors. But at least, with the 'many hands making light work' principle, the morning certainly produced some more dramatic results than they had managed the previous weekend.

By lunchtime, at least half of the plot had been cleared and by later in the afternoon, nearly all of the brambles and weeds had been pulled out and piled up in one corner ready to be carted away later. Even Keith the dog had helped dig up a few weeds before settling down with a nice stick to chew on.

Most of the garden was laid to lawn and now that the grass had been cut short it looked far more presentable, albeit not quite up to Wimbledon standards. By contrast, the area next to the far wall nearest to the watermill was looking far more barren. There was no green there, just soil which was beginning to be dug over by Tom and Josh. It looked tidier but a bit more like an allotment than she would have liked if there was any way it was to become a tea garden.

As well as her Mum, Molly couldn't help but notice another absentee.

'No sign of your grandson today?' Molly asked Stanley.

Stanley shook his head. 'I believe he has some commissions that need to be completed to meet some kind of deadline.'

Molly wasn't quite sure she believed him. Perhaps he just wanted to keep himself to himself. On the other hand, she was grateful for the crowd of people as it meant that most of the land was cleared by the end of the day.

They came across a few old benches which were wobbly but perhaps could be made more stable with a few extra nails so they kept them to one side.

'What's them tall things then?' asked Dodgy Del, peering down at the ground near the back of the garden. 'More weeds?'

Geoff wandered over to give his expert opinion and was almost too late as Del was already putting his garden fork into the ground to dig them up.

'Wait!' called out Geoff suddenly. His gasp of surprise was heard across the garden and so everyone went to see what they had discovered.

Molly followed everyone's gaze and saw that there were about twenty or so of a similar plant dotted around the back of the plot.

'I do believe that those plants are hops,' announced Geoff, looking delighted.

'Hops?' asked Molly, somewhat confused.

Dodgy Del rolled his eyes. 'You know,' he said, giving her a nudge with his elbow. 'What they make into beer!'

Molly looked back down at the green plants. 'Really? They become beer?'

Geoff nodded. 'Absolutely. With a bit of tender care over the summer, we may yet get a harvest from their flowers come the autumn. It's the flowers that produce the beer.'

'Our own beer!' said Del, his eyes now gleaming. 'How much do you reckon we'll be able to make?'

'I'm not sure,' Geoff told him. 'But if the plants are encouraged to grow high and flower profusely, then you might just have enough for your very own pint in any case.'

'Great. This one's mine, OK?' said Del, going to stand next to the largest plant.

Everyone else laughed. 'Del,' said Belle. 'You can't just nab a hop plant for yourself.'

'Why not?' asked Del, looking put out.

'What will Barry say?' asked Belle.

'We won't tell him,' replied Del quickly. 'He probably didn't even know they were back here as he's left the place run wild for so many years. Anyway, there's no way he's getting his hands on my pint.'

'Perhaps it might be a good way for us all to learn about hops growing,' suggested Geoff. 'We could allocate them out to those who'd like to learn.'

'How are we gonna know whose is whose?' asked Tom.

'This big one's mine,' said Del, quickly.

'Yes, we know that,' replied Molly.

Lucy, however, was tapping her chin in thought. 'It's an idea,' she said slowly, as if to herself.

'You're going to need to spell it out to us a bit more than that,' Belle told her. 'Unless you're also talking about beer. And we have plenty of that over at the inn.'

'Well, we've now got hops at the back of the garden and all this soil over the other side that needs planting or something made of it,' said Lucy, looking around. 'I wonder whether Molly could have the lawn area for her tea garden but perhaps this other part could become a community project for anyone who doesn't have a garden or just needs a bit of company to do a bit of gardening.'

There were a few murmurs of agreement in response.

'You know, I've heard about some wonderful projects where people have a garden for the whole community,' said Stanley, nodding thoughtfully to himself. 'Gardening can be hugely beneficial for those with different needs.'

Molly thought back to how much happier her mum had been the previous weekend, however briefly, and found herself nodding in agreement.

'Do you mean growing vegetables?' said Geoff, looking back once more at the newly dug soil.

'Flowers too,' replied Stanley.

'And hops,' added Del with a grin.

'So we could have one area for vegetables and flowers for people to grow.' Lucy tapped her chin in thought. 'Say, along that other side near the far wall. And this side with the lawn nearer the building could be for Molly's tea garden.'

'A tea garden?' said Stanley, sounding delighted. 'That sounds wonderful.'

'Excellent!' announced Lucy, beaming. 'It sounds like a plan, doesn't it?'

As everyone chatted away excitedly about the plans for the area, Molly joined in. The community garden did sound like a good idea, she had to admit.

But she wondered whether, like Del with his grow-your-own-beer idea, she had bitten off far more than she could chew with regard to the tea garden.

15

Once Molly began to delve a little deeper into the business aspect of running a tea garden for the summer, her already fragile confidence began to seriously waver. It turned out that setting up a pop-up business wasn't quite as easy as Tom had thought. She needed to register with the local authority as a business. The Environmental health officer would then need to sign off the inspection and the licence.

It was going to take some time to get everything authorised.

'It'll be June already by the time I finally open,' said Molly with a groan as she read the email from the council.

'But that's good,' said Amber nodding enthusiastically. 'That'll be the start of the summer season. Lots more people about. Potential for more customers.'

'I suppose it gives me time to retrain Lucy on social media for the month that I'm off,' said Molly, biting her lip in thought. 'As well as source the chairs and tables I need for people to sit on. Along with the crockery and sorting out the menu.'

As she began to list everything that needed to be done, she was almost grateful for at least the twenty-eight days' grace period because it all sounded a bit overwhelming.

Most pressing of all was finding somewhere to do all the baking. Her home kitchen was too small, and besides, somewhere would be needed to serve up tea and coffee as well as the food and cakes.

She thought back to Logan's suggestion of the empty shop at the end of Riverside Lane, right next to the garden. Many years ago, it had been a bakery, but it had been closed for almost a decade.

So when Molly arranged a viewing with the landlord, Barry, she wasn't surprised at the amount of dust in there. She was, however, amazed at the space in the kitchen. It was a really good size, as were the old industrial-sized ovens which still worked. With a proper clean-up, she could begin to see the possibilities. There was even a small toilet that the customers could use. If any customers came, of course.

There was the empty shop at the front of the building, but she just didn't have the time to clear all that dust and dirt. Besides, she was only interested in the tea garden so she could just leave the front door closed. Because, best of all, the kitchen had a side door which led directly into the garden.

'It's perfect,' she said, as she walked around the side of the shop to look at the front door again. Perfect was perhaps an overstatement for the state of the shop's interior, but the rest of the place would certainly work.

'Glad you like it,' said Barry, the landlord, with a sneer. He wasn't particularly friendly. 'So let's talk business. I'll give it to you for £1,200 a month.'

Molly was stunned. 'How much?' she stammered. It was way beyond her meagre budget. She had a small amount of savings, but this was way beyond what she had expected.

She was just blinking back the tears and watching her dream dissolve into dust when Logan suddenly appeared.

'Couldn't help overhearing,' he said, gesturing at the front door to his workshop which was also open. 'I gotta say, that's a bit steep considering the lady only wants to use a quarter of the space, as in just the kitchen. Not the shopfront as well.'

'I've got bills to pay,' said Barry with a grunt.

Logan turned to look at Molly. 'I wouldn't take it if I were you. There must be other places in the area.'

She thought he had given her a ghost of a wink, so nodded whilst she remained silent, wondering what to do. She knew that there weren't any other places in Cranbridge that would be remotely suitable nor included space for a tea garden.

The landlord frowned. 'Fine, I'll do it for £950 a month.'

But Logan shook his head. 'Let's be honest, it's only for one calendar month. With maybe a few more weeks thrown in as it's such a mess.' He ran his finger along the faded and cracked windowsill at the front of the shop and grimaced. 'Pretty awful how neglected the whole place is. Mine was the same, by the way. I've yet to file my complaint and talk to my solicitors. I mean, I was promised luxury accommodation and yet it was in as bad a state as this.'

Barry frowned at him. 'No one never said nothing to me about it.'

'If I could get you to answer your phone, I'd have told you plenty about it before now,' said Logan smoothly. 'Of course, I'd drop any lawsuit over flagrant misuse of advertising if you were to lend out this place to Molly free for the time that she needs it.'

'Free!' Barry's eyes goggled in shock.

Even Molly turned to look at Logan in stunned surprise.

'Listen,' said Logan, putting his hands in his pockets. His stance was casual but his tone of voice was forceful. 'The place was sitting here empty anyway. Molly's going to do you a favour by cleaning the kitchen up. Afterwards, you might just be able to sell or rent out the whole building. But nobody's going to touch the place like this. So, in a way, you owe her.'

Barry frowned as if struggling to keep up with Logan's logic. 'So let me get this straight,' he said slowly, scratching his beer belly. 'If I lend this place to the lady for a few weeks, I get nothing in return.'

'Oh, I wouldn't say nothing,' replied Logan quickly. 'I'm sure Molly would be willing to oblige you with some of her delicious cake every once in a while.'

'Cake?' Barry's eyebrows nearly reached his hairline.

Logan shrugged his shoulders. 'I don't think it's too much of an ask and would certainly help me forget all about that lawsuit,' he said.

The word lawsuit hung in the air as Molly stood and waited for Barry's reaction.

Finally, Barry nodded slowly. 'Well, I suppose so. For only a month, mind you.'

'After the few extra weeks I'll need to clean it up,' added Molly quickly.

'Excellent,' said Logan, smiling. 'Just think how great it would be for the village. And it's good to give a young entrepreneur a fighting chance, don't you think?'

Barry puffed out a sigh in reply.

'Oh and don't forget she'll need the garden thrown in for free as well,' said Logan.

'Now hold on a minute,' began Barry, but Logan was already holding up his hand.

'The garden is a mess and the villagers have already begun to tidy it up for you,' he said, gesturing at the space outside. 'To be honest, if she hadn't, I was going to get onto the council about it. Don't want rats or worse in the neighbourhood, do we? Those environmental officers come with some pretty hefty fines, from what

I've heard. And it's always the poor landlord that has to pay up, isn't it?'

Barry sighed heavily. 'This is going to ruin me,' he muttered.

Logan looked at him with a hard stare. 'It's an empty shop and what was a very messy garden,' he said. 'She's doing you a favour.'

'Fine. I'll get the paperwork sorted,' said Barry looking exceedingly grumpy before wandering away.

Molly was still stunned at the way Logan had so expertly handled the conversation.

'Thank you so much,' she said, turning to look at him. 'I'm not much of a business person, if at all, to be honest. That was amazing. So kind of you.'

'I just don't like to see anyone taken advantage of,' he told her.

She suddenly laughed. 'Then you're definitely talking to the wrong person,' she joked.

But he didn't laugh. 'You need to stand up for yourself a bit more,' he said.

She quickly looked away before staring at the shopfront once more. 'So maybe I'm going to open a tea garden next month after all,' she said, deliberately changing the subject.

'Well, seeing as my stomach's already rumbling with hunger, you might find me being your very first customer,' he told her.

'Oh!' she said, bringing out the large bag she was carrying on her shoulder. 'I've got something you can have.' She brought out a couple of blueberry muffins and handed one over to him. 'I meant to give them to Barry,' she carried on, as she watched Logan stare down at the cake. 'As a bribe.'

'He definitely didn't deserve them. Well, if you're sure,' he said, leaning against the wall and taking a first bite.

As he ate the muffin, Molly stared around, frowning.

'Mmm. This is delicious. But what's the matter?' asked Logan, between mouthfuls. 'Don't you want to open a tea garden?'

'Oh yes,' she told him. 'I just can't see it succeeding.'

There was a short silence whilst she felt him studying her as she looked down at the pavement.

'Well,' he finally said, 'I can only tell you that your cake is brilliant. But surely you already know that.'

She blushed and shrugged her shoulders, her usual response to any compliments. 'I've tasted worse.'

'And I've not tasted better,' he told her in a firm tone. 'Believe me, this is good. I don't normally even like muffins. You've got a real talent, you know.'

'It's just cake,' she said. 'Not like the way you can make a piece of furniture. I couldn't do that.'

'And I can't bake a cake to save my life,' he replied. 'People just have different strengths, that's all.'

She nodded, wanting to believe him. 'Thank you,' she told him. 'For everything.'

'Just being neighbourly,' he replied, with a smile that suddenly made his face far more friendly and handsome. 'On the other hand, I might be high from all the sugar that I've just consumed.'

She laughed. He was really nice, she thought, as he headed back into his own shop. There was a kindness there.

And she was smiling to herself as she went out into the garden to begin to plot out the next stage of opening up the business.

Her very own business, in fact. She could hardly believe it.

16

As Molly began to put her plans together for the tea garden, the idea for the community garden was also becoming a reality.

'I think it's a great idea,' said Geoff, nodding his approval as he looked around the area that Friday afternoon.

'So do I,' Molly told him.

Apparently Barry had finally issued a somewhat reluctant agreement to Lucy that they could use the space for a community garden. After all, he really had no response or comeback to the argument that the whole plot had not been maintained for many years. So what harm could it do?

'It might be a lot of work though,' said Molly. 'I'm not sure there's too many people with your knowledge of gardening.'

Geoff shrugged his shoulders. 'Happy to have something to fill the days, to be honest.'

'How are you both?' asked Stanley, heading through the rickety gate and into the garden. 'I heard that we have the full go-ahead for the community garden.'

'I'm only here to look at the kitchen,' Molly told him. 'I'm afraid I'm no gardener.'

Stanley nodded thoughtfully to himself. 'And your dear mother? Will she be joining us today?'

Molly was reluctant to speak in front of Geoff, who, picking up on her hesitancy, wandered over to inspect a climbing rose which had been discovered underneath all the weeds and was flopping away from the wall, needing tying in.

'Mum doesn't get out the house much at the moment,' said Molly, finally allowing herself to meet Stanley's eyes.

He gave a soft sigh of understanding. 'I see,' he said. 'I've known Rachel for a very long time. She'd do anything for her children. Especially if they needed help with, say, a community garden. Given the right leverage, of course.'

Molly looked at him for a moment before excusing herself to type out a quick text to her mum.

Have you got 5 minutes? I urgently need your help. x

Then Molly kept herself busy sizing up the area for the tea garden whilst she waited.

She was somewhat relieved not to receive a text back in reply but could see her mum had read the message. She was even more pleased when, ten minutes later, her mum appeared at the wall of the garden and headed towards her, looking concerned.

'What's up?' she asked, somewhat breathless. 'Is everything OK?'

'Everything's fine,' Molly told her with a smile, before lowering her voice. 'But I don't think the community garden idea is going to become a reality.'

'Why ever not?' asked her mum, looking surprised.

'It's just too much work for Geoff on his own, I reckon,' she whispered. 'You can't expect Stanley to help out much at his age. But who else has got the time to do anything about it?' Molly sighed heavily before wondering whether she was overdoing it. 'My other concern is that it doesn't exactly fit with the ethos of the tea garden. I mean, it's hardly pretty and countrified, is it?'

'It'll be fine by the time you open,' said her mum, following her daughter's gaze to the large patches of bare soil on the other side.

'I'm not so sure,' Molly told her. 'I mean, it's so bare. And whereas Geoff knows all about vegetables, a row of tomatoes and pumpkins wasn't quite the aesthetic I was going for.'

'I see.' Her mum nodded thoughtfully. 'Well, I suppose a few flowers here and there would help pretty the place up a bit.'

'I heartily agree,' said Stanley, who had been hovering nearby. 'The trouble is, my arthritis doesn't lend itself to much planting and potting up these days. I don't suppose you could give me a hand if you have a spare hour this afternoon?'

There was a short silence before her mum said, 'Of course, Stanley. It certainly needs a bit of colour around here.'

'I agree,' said Stanley. 'How about I donate some of the many seedlings that I've got all lined up in my greenhouse?'

'Are you sure?' asked Molly, worrying about how much all the plants would cost.

'They're all free, my dear,' Stanley told her, guessing her concern. 'I grew them all from the seeds that I saved last year. Of course, your mother was always a dab hand, or should I say green-fingered, where flowers were concerned.'

Her mum blushed. 'I haven't gardened properly in years,' she admitted. 'But I certainly used to save my own seeds.'

'Never too late to start again,' said Stanley. 'But if you could give me a hand with carrying them over from my garden, I'd be most grateful.'

Molly thought that Stanley gave her a ghost of a wink as he led her mum out of the garden and towards his bungalow.

By the time they returned, Molly had poured out a couple of

mugs of tea and took them outside. Thankfully, the good weather was continuing to last and was giving the grass and soil time to dry out.

'Here you go,' said Molly, walking over to where her mum and Geoff were standing, looking at the wheelbarrow full of small plants of varying colours and types. 'I figured you would need something if you're going to get that lot planted up this afternoon.'

Her mum took the mug of tea from her daughter. 'Thanks, love.'

Molly handed over the other mug to Geoff, who also thanked her.

'Well, this is all going to make it look much better,' Molly told them, looking down at all the plants. Although that would still leave quite a bit of soil left to be filled.

'It'll look even better when the flowers come out,' said her mum. 'I chose pinks, purples and pale yellows along here. I hope that's OK with you.'

'It'll look great, Mum,' replied Molly with a smile.

'I've got loads more at home to place along the other walls,' said Stanley, coming to join them.

'I just hope it's not too much work for you all,' Molly said.

Geoff shook his head. 'Actually, I'm enjoying myself getting out and about. In a way, it's a good excuse to do something.'

Her mum nodded in agreement. 'You need a rhythm to the day, don't you find?'

Geoff smiled at her. 'That's exactly right,' he told her. 'Although I'm not sure how much beauty my vegetables are going to bring to the place. But at least we'll be able to harvest them in about five or so weeks.'

'Is that all?' asked Molly, amazed.

'Oh yes,' said Geoff. 'I thought we should plant things that wouldn't take long to develop, such as baby carrots and lettuce.'

'And that'll be just in time for your grand opening,' added

her mum.

Molly felt a pang of fear and tried to suppress it at the thought of being solely responsible for the tea garden.

'At least I'll be able to make carrot cake,' she told them with a smile.

'What about some herbs?' said Geoff. 'They might come in handy for your baking, although I don't know anything about that.'

'Me neither,' said her mum. 'I'm not sure where she gets her talent with cakes from. I only know about bread.'

Her mum smiled before taking another sip of her tea.

She was certainly looking more cheerful than Molly had seen her for a while.

'To be honest, gardening keeps me busy,' said Geoff, before draining his mug of tea. 'And my mind active as well. It's all I've thought about this week and it's not given me a chance to mope about the place as I had been doing since I retired.'

Molly saw her mum give a little start as if realising something. 'Maybe there's something in that,' she said, with a smile.

'Maybe there is,' replied Geoff, smiling back at her.

'How about I put a few posts on social media to see if anyone else feels the same way?' suggested Molly.

'That's a great idea,' said Geoff, nodding enthusiastically. 'I might need a few more days to plan out where various plants should go. I'll make a note in my empty calendar if you'd like.'

'Me too,' replied her mum, to Molly's surprise. 'I can always come along each day, if it would help.'

They shared a smile and Molly thought that perhaps there was a connection there.

Whatever the future of the tea garden would be, Molly was hopeful that it had already had a positive effect on her mum's mental health. And that was worth more than any successful business, as far as she was concerned.

17

Molly found that she was crazily busy for the next few weeks despite only planning to open up the tea garden for one month.

After work at the community hub, which now included training up Lucy on the social media side of things, any free time in the evenings and weekends during May was taken up with everything to do with the tea garden.

She had found the paperwork pretty confusing, so was immensely grateful to Tom for helping her to fill it all out with infinite patience. Once the legal requirements had been completed, it still left the practical side of things. Such as what everyone was going to sit on.

'I hear you're looking for chairs,' said Dodgy Del, coming into the community hub one morning.

'For the tea garden?' replied Molly, a little warily. 'Possibly. And tables as well.'

'Can't do you any tables, but for chairs, I'm definitely your man,' Del told her, with a winning smile. 'I've got a mate who's just cleared a whole load out of a club that's shut down in London.'

'I'm not sure how suitable furniture from a fancy place in London is going to be in a tea garden,' said Molly, frowning.

'What about a picnic area?' asked Stanley. 'I've got some nice tartan rugs somewhere.'

'And who's going to help us old folks up from the ground?' asked Grandma Tilly, rolling her eyes. 'If we can even get down there in the first place, that is.'

'Point taken,' replied Stanley, smiling. 'I forget how old you are.'

'Oi!' said Grandma Tilly, but she was chuckling to herself.

'So, chairs are needed, from the sounds of it,' said Lucy, urging Del on.

'Yeah, they'll be smashing,' replied Del. 'The guy says that it's all solid wood. And there's even some animals on the chairs. Rabbits and whatnot.'

'OK, well, thanks,' said Molly, in a faint voice. Animal design? Was it possible that they were for children? Although they might be better than nothing at all. 'That would be really useful. It'll only be for a month anyway.'

'Rubbish,' said Del. 'It'll be a roaring success and then you'll be open forever.'

Molly's smile became somewhat rigid. Everyone seemed to think that the tea garden was going to be wonderful, but she was still plagued with doubts.

'Well, that's good news,' said Lucy, after Del had wandered off to the shop. 'You need furniture after all.'

'It is,' Molly told her, still unsure. 'If the seats are actually fully sized, that is. But I still haven't got any tables. I don't want to fork out for some when they'll only be used for a month.'

'What about some old crates?' said Lucy, frowning in thought.

'Crates?' repeated Molly.

'I saw some in the pub the other night,' Lucy told her. 'We could turn them over and cover them with a pretty piece of material. That would do, wouldn't it?'

Molly nodded. 'That's a good idea,' she said. 'But there's still so much else to decide on. Such as what kind of cutlery and crockery to use.'

'You can get some really cheap paper plates and stuff from the cash and carry,' said Lucy.

'Not very environmentally friendly though, are they?' murmured Stanley, who was sitting on the nearby sofa with Keith the dog alongside him.

'I always like drinking out of a cup and saucer,' said Grandma Tilly.

'It feels like a special occasion, doesn't it?' agreed Molly.

'Although I seem to be the only one these days,' said Grandma Tilly. 'I've got loads in my attic that are never used. Proper china from all kinds of different places.' She suddenly looked at Molly with a delighted expression. 'So they're yours.'

'Are you sure?' asked Molly. The last thing she had envisaged was serving up her tea and cakes on Grandma Tilly's old china. What if she broke a plate or cup that was expensive or worse, sentimental?

'I'd rather they were used, my dear,' Grandma Tilly told her.

'And we can always ask around if anyone's got any more,' added Lucy, looking pleased.

'Thank you so much,' said Molly. 'That will be wonderful. I'm not sure how much I can pay you for them.'

'I don't want money,' said Grandma Tilly. 'In fact, I was going to ask if I could help out.'

'In the tea garden?' asked Molly.

'I thought it would be rather fun,' replied Grandma Tilly, looking at Stanley. 'We both did, in fact.'

'You don't think that it would be too much for you both?' Molly told them, trying to hide her dismay. 'You know, on your feet serving for all that time. Not that there'll be that many customers, I'm sure.'

'We can start with a couple of hours and see how we get on,' said Grandma Tilly, looking pleased. 'If that's OK with the boss lady, of course.'

'Of course,' replied Molly, with a fixed smile on her face. 'It'll be great fun.'

'And I'm sure there'll be plenty of customers to keep us busy,' added Stanley, reaching out to give Keith the dog's head a stroke.

Molly was feeling thoroughly depressed. Everyone was being so kind and yet none of their suggestions were her own. As usual, she felt she couldn't say no to anyone and hurt their feelings.

But it felt as if everything was running away from her when she hadn't even had a chance to decide on her own ideas.

18

Molly was still fretting about the tea garden when the weekend finally came around. However, the biggest problem she was having was trying to work out what kind of food to serve.

What she needed was a research trip, so she invited her mum along for a Saturday afternoon visit to the nearest competition in the area.

They sat down at a table in the sunny courtyard of Willow Tree Hall and looked around. It was certainly quite a setting, with the beautiful huge stately home nearby. They had been to Willow Tree Hall a few times for its seasonal fairs, but it was the first time that they were visiting the courtyard tea room which had only been up and running since the previous year.

'Well, this is very classy,' murmured her mum, looking around. 'Thankfully, from what I know about the family they're very friendly. Old money, if you know what I mean.'

Molly nodded in response, but she was thinking how much happier her mum looked. She had begun to show up at the community garden most afternoons to start sowing the seedlings that Stanley had kindly donated. She had also mentioned in passing that she was sleeping well due to all the exertion. But it was more the improvement in her mental well-being that Molly was thankful for, as well as her mum's friendship with Geoff.

A friendly waitress came up to take their order.

Molly ordered a pot of tea for two and a slice of lemon and elderflower cake for herself, with her mum ordering a coffee and walnut bar.

'So to what do I owe this pleasure?' asked her mum. 'Not that I'm complaining, of course.'

'Call it research,' Molly told her, in a hushed tone. 'It's my nearest competition and I wanted to see how the professionals do it.'

'You'll be a professional too, once you start charging money for your cakes at last,' replied her mum.

Molly grimaced. 'I know. That's the scary bit.'

'Maybe the person who started this found it scary as well,' said her mum. 'Don't always assume that everyone has confidence.'

They sat and looked across the vast grounds for a moment. Molly felt grateful that she wasn't responsible for clearing that amount of land and only had her tiny garden to worry about.

'Do you?' asked Molly. 'Have confidence, I mean.'

Her mum leant back in her chair and thought for a moment. 'I've never really had a chance to consider it, to be honest. I've just had to make do. There was no question that I wasn't going to keep a roof over our heads and feed us all when you were all growing up, so I just had to get on with it.'

Her mum didn't say anything more as the pot of tea and cakes were placed in front of them.

The cake, as expected, was delicious. Molly had taken a discreet photo of the menu to get some idea of pricing but had to concede that the cake was worth every penny.

'Of course, they've got the whole fabulous stately home thing going on here as a backdrop,' she said, looking over at the gorgeous manor house once more.

'But you'll have a pretty garden and view of the river, which they haven't,' replied her mum, loyally. 'Plus the old watermill alongside as well.'

Molly nodded. 'I guess so. And, thanks mainly to you and Geoff, a few pretty flowers as well. Which reminds me, I've been so busy I haven't had time to post about the community garden yet online.'

To her surprise, her mum shook her head. 'Actually, I understand that Lucy has spread the word instead. The Mothers and Toddlers group are coming down this week to pay us a visit and get the little ones planting.'

'That's great,' said Molly, still feeling guilty that she hadn't played her part.

'You've been so busy, everyone understands,' her mum told her, guessing the reason for the look on her face.

Molly looked down at the rose-patterned cup and saucer with a matching plate. 'These are very classy, aren't they? Grandma Tilly has given me some crockery but there's only one or two of each pattern.'

'You can't expect the Earl of Cranley to have mismatched china,' her mum told her.

'No, but luckily I'm not the aristocracy,' said Molly with a smile. 'But it's more in keeping with the vintage vibe that I was going for. So I guess mismatched will have to do.'

And that was perhaps her main concern. That she was just making do and not wowing anyone, even herself.

'Are you missing your old job?' asked Molly, trying to concentrate on something else and not spoiling the afternoon with her worries about the tea garden.

'I miss the people, of course,' her mum replied. 'But I'm enjoying having the time to do a bit of gardening now. I'd forgotten how much I loved it. And I've got some lovely plants for you to use in the, er, well, you know.' She gave her daughter a wink, having checked that they weren't being overheard.

Molly laughed. 'You'd make a terrible spy, Mum.'

'I'd better stick to gardening then.'

They finished their cakes with a satisfied sigh.

'That was lovely,' said her mum, licking her lips. 'Not as nice as yours though.'

'You might just be a tiny bit biased about that,' said Molly, laughing.

They sat for a while in the sunshine, enjoying the warmth and the rare chance to rest and just be in the moment. She looked across the table and smiled to see her mum also revelling in the sunny afternoon and looking happy.

'Feels a bit like a holiday,' said her mum after a while. 'Or definitely a treat.'

'Well, why shouldn't we treat ourselves once in a while,' Molly told her. 'We've worked hard all year. We deserve this.'

Her mum looked amazed. 'Molly Hopkins,' she said, her eyes wide in surprise, 'I don't think I've ever heard you talk like that.'

Molly gave a defiant shrug. 'Well, maybe we'll have to get used to it. Not being taken advantage of all the time.'

'What's brought about this change in you?' asked her mum.

'Must be the cake,' said Molly, with a wink.

The joke ended the inquest, but as they sat in the pretty courtyard finishing their pot of tea, she realised that she knew that it was Logan's words coming out of her mouth. And that maybe, he had been right all along.

She had to start standing up for herself and believing that she could achieve her dreams. Then perhaps they could become real after all.

19

Logan yawned and decided that the next bit of checking he would do inside the watermill would be the last for that evening. He had already done a full day's work, finishing a complicated cabinet with many drawers for a client, when he had decided to quickly check on a few things inside the mill. That had been three hours ago.

It was now gone nine o'clock and the light was beginning to fade inside the mill.

He had forgotten to bring his torch with him, so figured that perhaps it was nature's way of telling him to go home and rest.

He went to the main door and looked up at the vivid red sky. He had forgotten quite how much he enjoyed the vast amount of sky in the countryside. With no tall buildings and skyscrapers to interfere with the view, he could just enjoy the endless raspberry-pink streaked sky.

'It's beautiful, isn't it?'

He looked over to see Molly closing up the garden gate before glancing up at the sky.

He nodded. 'Definitely,' he replied. 'You heading out somewhere tonight?'

She glanced down at her clothes and grimaced. He followed her gaze and saw that her shorts and T-shirt were heavily marked with grease and grime.

'Hardly! I'm filthy,' she said, with a short laugh at herself. 'That kitchen was a great idea of yours to use, but it's completely disgusting. Thankfully I scrubbed and cleaned every surface just in time for the health inspector to come along this afternoon and give me a pass.'

'Congratulations,' said Logan. 'I bet you've still got further than me.'

Molly looked at him. 'How so?'

'I'm having trouble with one of the mechanisms,' he told her.

She tried to peer past him, obviously interested.

'You want to see inside?' he asked.

'Sorry,' she said, almost immediately. 'I'm sure you haven't got time for that, have you?'

'No problem,' he said, turning around and heading back inside. 'Come on in.'

She followed him into the main area of the mill and he watched as she stared around with wide eyes. 'Wow,' she muttered. 'This is amazing.'

He was surprised she could see anything in the darkening light inside but found himself pleased that she approved.

'What does that do?' she asked, pointing up high at the timber ceiling.

'That's where the grain is stored,' he told her. 'In those wooden bins.'

She nodded. 'Then what happens to it?'

'The grain flows down those wooden tubes where, eventually, it gets fed down here.'

She stared up at the complicated spaghetti of wood tubes above them before finally looking at the large wooden vat in front of them.

'It's called the shoe, apparently,' he told her. 'Then, finally, it gets pushed between those two huge stones and milled into flour.'

She walked over to run her hand over the huge round pair of stones that would crush the grain.

Logan carried on. 'The millstones are actually French burr, which apparently is the finest stone for producing flour. They're called querns.'

'Where did they come from?' she asked.

Logan shook his head. 'Grandad didn't know. France is a long way away, especially all those hundreds of years ago when this place was built.'

'It's wonderful,' she said, looking around once more. 'Really magical.'

'It needs major repair, especially the waterwheel itself,' he said, with a sigh. 'And I can't get the mechanism to work because this metal pipe has corroded with rust. It's just so heavy.'

Molly looked to where he was pointing. A huge metal pipe connected the wheel to the querns. 'Will you be able to fix it?' she asked.

'I've got to,' he told her. 'For Grandad's sake. I'm in too deep now.'

'I know the feeling,' she muttered. 'Can't someone help you with all this? Can't Tom or Josh or Pete help you with the heavier parts?'

He avoided her gaze for a moment. The truth was that he hadn't ever made it over to the pub to meet them properly, only in passing in the shop and on the lane so far with a quick greeting.

'They're all really nice guys,' he heard her say.

He thought that they probably were, but instead he said, 'I'll be fine.'

For some reason, he didn't want her to think of him as someone who needed help. He needed to show her that standing on his own two feet was fine and that he was better for it.

So he went over to look down at the large rusted metal pipe and went to pull it out ready for replacing. But as he moved it, a large chunk that had completely rusted away fell off onto the ground, bouncing off the top of his foot inside the soft trainer he was wearing.

Logan immediately felt a rush of immense pain.

'Oh, God, are you OK?' asked Molly, rushing over to where he had sunk against the quern stones in agony. 'Logan? What is it?'

He felt the throbbing in his foot and said, 'I think I've just broken something.'

So much for appearing as if he could cope by himself, he thought, before wincing in pain once more.

20

Molly helped Logan very carefully remove his trainer and sports sock before they both stared at the foot which had already begun to look faintly bruised and swollen.

'That's not a good sign,' she murmured. 'It normally indicates a break.'

'Since when did you complete your medical degree?' he asked, trying and failing to smile. She could see how much pain he was attempting to hide.

'Since having two younger brothers who both play sports,' she told him, leaning back on her heels. 'The good thing for you is that I know the quickest way to the nearest Accident and Emergency department.'

He looked up at her with stern eyes. 'I'm not going to hospital,' he told her, his argument somewhat countered by what appeared to be another grimace of pain.

'Logan,' she said, shaking her head. 'You need to get it X-rayed.'

'No, I'll be fine,' he told her, slowly drawing up to his full height with only a small grunt of discomfort. 'I'll rest it overnight and then—'

'And then it will still be broken,' she reminded him. 'Come on, can you walk?'

'I told you that I'm not going to hospital,' he said, sounding nervous.

'Tough,' she told him. 'I'm not taking no for an answer. My car's just outside in the back lane.'

He sighed and after struggling to lock up the mill, he then began to hop out into the darkening night outside. Eventually, though, once he had banged his injured foot against the wall, a fence and a lamp post, he took her advice and leant against her for support.

'This is totally unnecessary,' he said, as she opened up the passenger door for him.

'Be quiet or I'll tell your grandad that you're injured,' she said in a stern voice.

'You wouldn't dare,' he replied, but quickly got into the car after that warning.

As it happened, he was right. She would never dream of worrying Stanley with the news that his grandson had hurt himself, but she decided to keep that information to herself.

What a night, she thought, as she slid into the car and switched on the engine. She was filthy from cleaning the kitchen and had been desperate for a long hot shower to get rid of the grease and dirt. But, for now, she needed to drive Logan to the hospital.

* * *

Logan's foot hurt so much that he could barely take in whichever route Molly was driving. He was absolutely mortified that she'd had to help him hobble to the car. Any sickness, such as colds and whatever, he had faced by himself. His ex-wife was certainly no nurse and had almost a phobia to germs. So he had become used to taking care of himself.

He knew he only had himself to blame. For some reason, he had ended up showing off the watermill to Molly, heaven only knows why, and whilst he'd been rambling on about the inner workings, he'd somehow managing to drop a great piece of metal piping on his foot.

To add to his embarrassment, once they reached the hospital, Molly found him a wheelchair and pushed him into the Accident and Emergency department in that, despite his protestations.

Having given the receptionist his details, they were told to wait in the seating area nearby.

'Would you like a drink?' asked Molly, as soon as they were settled. 'How about a cup of tea? Something to eat?'

But Logan shook his head. The pain was quite bad, and besides, he didn't want to eat anything in case the doctors recommended some sort of painkiller that needed an empty stomach. At least, that was what he was hoping for.

He just wished it could take away his embarrassment as well. He wondered about suggesting that she could leave now that he was at the hospital but figured that, given Molly's unexpected stubborn stance that evening, it was highly unlikely.

He hated being seen as needy and not able to take care of himself. Especially in front of Molly, he found himself thinking, although he had no idea why.

* * *

Molly stood in the queue for the coffee machine, also feeling wretched. Her stomach was rumbling and she grabbed a Mars bar from the vending machine as well to keep her going. She hadn't had dinner yet and it was likely to be a long time in A&E, given the amount of people already waiting in there. Not that she was going to leave Logan, of course. He was new to the area and although he could probably get a taxi back to Cranbridge, she would have hated to have been left by herself in A&E if she had been the patient.

She sent a quick text to her mum to let her know that she was going to be home late so that she wouldn't worry.

Logan was missing when she returned, so she ate her chocolate bar in quiet contemplation.

It wasn't long before he returned, this time on a couple of crutches.

'You've had your X-ray already?' asked Molly, in surprise. 'That was fast.'

He nodded. 'They say it shouldn't take too much longer to see someone and get the results.'

'You're lucky,' she said. 'When Adam broke his arm at rugby, we were here nearly the whole day. Sundays are the worst because of all the children's clubs in the morning. Although I wouldn't recommend Friday or Saturday nights either as that's when all the nightclubbers get injured. I had to drive all the way to a field once to rescue Ben when he gave himself food poisoning trying to barbeque a chicken when he was drunk.' She laughed to herself in memory.

'So you've always taken care of them,' said Logan, after a while.

'Between us, me and mum have just about kept them under control,' said Molly, smiling to herself. 'More or less.'

'Your dad isn't around?' he asked gently.

Molly shook her head, her smile fading. 'Didn't want to know us at all,' she said briskly. 'He left when the boys arrived. Although, according to Mum, he wasn't that hands-on even before the thought of twins frightened him away.'

The pain was still there. A dull ache even after so many years.

'So we brought up the boys between us,' she carried on. 'Especially as mum had to work so many jobs to keep a roof over our heads.'

'That's a lot of responsibility for you to take on, even as a child,' he said.

Molly shrugged her shoulders. 'It's family, isn't it? You do what you can. I was almost nine years old when the twins arrived, so I was old enough to help out. Mum and I have somehow got them to university and kept the two of them out of jail, so I figure we've done a pretty good job.'

She grinned at him, but he wasn't smiling back. Just watching her with thoughtful eyes.

'But what about your dreams? Didn't you want to go to university?' he asked.

She shook her head. 'I wasn't bright enough,' she told him, her smile fading once more. 'Anyway, that would have left Mum in the lurch and the boys were still only young. Plus, I would have been miserable away from my family, to be honest. And my friends too.'

'Well, that's where we differ,' he muttered.

'You're not one for companionship?' she asked.

'Maybe only Grandad,' he replied.

'He's going to be worried when he hears about your foot,' she told him.

'Maybe he doesn't need to find out?' he asked, looking at her hopefully.

But Molly laughed softly and shook her head. 'I think you're being overly hopeful about a dramatic recovery overnight.'

* * *

Molly's predication about his optimistic view of recovery turned out to be true.

Logan sighed as he thought back to the doctor's words as the hairline fracture in his foot was confirmed to him.

'It'll take anywhere between four to six weeks to heal hopefully. Rest, ice, compression and elevation,' he carried on. 'You're not going to want to put any kind of weight on it for a few days, so you can keep those crutches for now.'

Logan was horrified. He was going to be on crutches? What a nightmare. How was he going to work if he couldn't stand up for any length of time? But it appeared as if he could do nothing but grin and bear it.

Once he was loaded up with the crutch and some painkillers from the pharmacy, he and Molly headed back to Cranbridge in her VW Golf.

He felt even more embarrassed about his predicament now that he was on crutches but he was feeling a little grateful for her being there with him that evening.

As she parked the car at the back of Riverside Lane, Logan peered up at the back of his shop and apartment and wondered how he was going to go up the stairs.

'Perhaps you could stay with your grandad in the bungalow for a few days,' said Molly, guessing what he was thinking.

His mind was reeling as he tried to work out a strategy for staying in control of the situation he had got himself into.

'I'll be fine,' he said, opening the car door.

The thought of no stairs was indeed tempting, but he didn't want his grandad to worry. And besides, he would be better off by himself as usual.

'Do you need anything?' Molly asked, getting out of the car.

She was being very kind, but it just reminded him even more of his accident and he didn't want to be beholden to her. So he straightened his back to look as strong and as capable as he could possibly could before saying, 'I'll be fine. Thank you for driving me. I'm sorry to have mucked up your evening.'

'No problem,' she said.

But she was still looking worried and he could see that she was about to suggest something so he briskly said, 'Goodnight,' and hobbled over to the back door as quickly as he could.

He thought he heard her soft sigh in the evening air before she got back into her car, but he wasn't sure.

21

After her late night at the hospital with Logan, Molly was grateful that it was finally the weekend the following morning. Not that there was much chance of a lie-in unfortunately.

There was still so much to do. As well as all the work for the tea garden to open, she also needed to finalise the flavour and style of wedding cake that Amber and Josh wanted. She had never found the opportunity to tell them of her doubts and with time marching on quickly towards the wedding date at the end of August, it was now too late for them to ask anyone else. She just hoped her best was good enough for such an important event.

The community garden was coming along though, she saw at once as she opened up the gate. Small changes were beginning to make huge differences in the appearance. Geoff had built about half a dozen raised beds along the far wall, which were now filled with soil and tiny rows of what was promised to be various types of vegetables.

However, one bed had been allocated for the local children to use and was now filled haphazardly with burgeoning sunflowers, marigolds and brightly painted wooden flowers.

Along the front wall, her mum had planted up quite a few different flowers, which were just coming into bud and Molly could just about make out the soft pinks and yellows that they would turn into when the flowers bloomed.

But whereas the community garden was certainly making a difference outside, inside the shop, it was a different story altogether.

Thankfully, the kitchen was now spotless and up to health and safety standards. But despite not needing to use the area, Molly had decided to sweep and clean the shop to keep the dust and dirt at bay.

By mid-morning, it was looking a lot better and the final disinfectant was giving everything a cleaner aroma.

Molly opened up the front door to let in some much-needed fresh air. She peeked out and around the door frame and was pleased to see that the front door to Logan's workshop was open as well. She had wanted to check up on him that morning but didn't know his mobile number. So now she walked along the front of her shop before reaching the front door to his own place.

She hesitated for a moment, thinking about how he had been so adamant about not wanting help, before deciding to go inside.

'Good morning,' she said, seeing Logan almost immediately. He was sat behind a small cabinet with a chisel in his hand.

'Morning,' he said.

'How are you feeling today?' she asked.

'Rubbish,' he said, giving her a rueful grin.

'Are you in a lot of pain?' she said, heading over. He did look a little pale.

'When I'm standing for a long time, with all the blood rushing to the foot, it's pretty painful,' he told her. 'Hence this stool.'

'Well, that's a good idea,' she said. 'But do you have to keep working? After all, it's the weekend.'

'I've got orders that need completing,' he told her. 'But it's pretty slow progress. And I'm not sure what I can do in the watermill in this state.'

'Have you told Stanley?' she asked.

He nodded. 'Told me that it was perhaps some master plan of the universe to make me slow down,' he said, rolling his eyes.

'Maybe he's right,' she said.

'Don't you start,' he told her. But his eyes softened his snappish tone. 'Besides, I need to get that watermill up and running. I made a promise to Grandad.'

'He'll understand,' said Molly. She knew Stanley very well and he wasn't one to hold grudges. 'What's left to be done on the mill? It didn't look so bad to me.'

He laughed. 'That's because it was in the semi-darkness,' he told her, before his smile quickly faded. 'It's a mess, to be honest. That wheel alone was going to be tricky enough, but with this...' He gestured down to where his injured foot was encased in the sturdy-looking boot the hospital had given him, presumably to protect the broken bone from further knocks. 'How am I supposed to wade through the water now?'

Molly felt sorry for him. He really did seem very defeated. 'Look, can I do something to help?'

He shook his head. 'Thanks, but it's pretty heavy work. I mean, I'm not saying that you're not fit. You're definitely fit.' He looked almost embarrassed. 'What I meant was that your arms are very toned and all that. But it's going to take some serious muscle.'

'I know you're proud, but there's nothing wrong with asking for help,' she told him.

He sank further onto his stool. 'It's not that easy.'

'Yes, it really is,' she said. 'There are plenty of people that would be willing to help you. If not for you, then for your grandad. And everyone wants to see the mill up and running again.'

'I don't know anyone around here,' he told her.

She laughed. 'And whose fault is that? You've kept yourself to yourself. People understand why, with all that's happened in the newspapers. But nobody cares about that kind of thing. You know Lucy, my best friend who works next door in the community hub? Ask her about being the subject of gossip columns! She was on the front pages last year before she came here. Nobody cared. She's a good person with a good heart. That's all that matters around here. None of what happened to you was your fault.' She looked at him. 'But not asking for help? That's all on you.'

He ran a hand through his hair. 'Gee, thanks,' he said, before smiling at her. 'When did you get so wise?'

'I was always this wise,' she said, smiling back. 'That's why I'm such a great older sister!'

They continued to smile at each other for a while before her heart began to thump in her chest and Molly had to look away.

'Well, I've bothered you for long enough,' she said quickly. 'And that kitchen floor needs at least one more clean before I even contemplate baking anything in there.' She turned to leave before hesitating and drawing up the courage to turn back for a moment. 'Think about it,' she said softly. 'Most of the guys are in the Black Swan on a Sunday lunchtime. Just in case you were passing by.'

She quickly walked out before he could reply, but as she glanced through the window as she headed back to her own shop, she saw that he was smiling to himself.

22

Sunday lunchtime came and went, but Logan had decided against going into the pub. It was too embarrassing to ask almost complete strangers for help. He had considered what Molly had suggested but he didn't want to be a burden to anyone.

He just wasn't quite sure how he was going to get everything done by himself. But he was young and healthy-ish. Hopefully that would be enough, he'd told himself as he headed over to the mill.

But by mid-afternoon, his foot was throbbing in pain. He had managed to cut out most of the rotten pipework, but the effort of standing on his feet to do so had made his broken foot incredibly sore.

He looked down at his foot which was encased in the sturdy boot. Inside the boot, his foot was a spectacular rainbow of purple bruising, still swollen and painful. He sank against one of the millstones, feeling a bit light-headed. Perhaps he just needed a drink, he told himself, and took a sip from the bottle of water that he had brought with him.

But it was no use. If he didn't sit down soon and put his foot up, it wasn't going to get any better.

Frustrated and fed up, he knew he would have to give up working on the mill for the time being. Which meant yet another wasted day and a whole weekend had gone by without making any progress.

The sound of conversation and laughter came from outside. Probably some friends or family enjoying the spring sunshine. After all, it was Sunday afternoon.

But, to his surprise, the sound grew nearer and nearer. Then footsteps on the wooden bridge heralded the arrival of what sounded like a group of people. Finally, there was a knock on the door.

'Good afternoon,' said Tom, coming into the mill with his dog trotting in alongside him. 'Well, this is something else, isn't it?'

As he looked around in amazement at the gears and pulleys, he was joined by three other men, who were all nodding and smiling at him.

'Let me do the introductions,' said Tom. 'I don't believe you've met everyone properly yet apart from Keith the dog here. This is Josh, from the corner shop. His brother, Pete, who runs the Black Swan Inn, and Del here, who runs the local coach company.'

'And who runs up a high tab in my inn which he's yet to settle,' added Pete in a pointed tone.

'Nah, nah,' said Del, shaking his head. 'I haven't forgotten. It was just funds were a bit tight last month.'

'Aren't they always?' murmured Josh, before coming across to shake Logan's hand. 'Hi. Heard you were in a bit of a bad way at the moment.'

'It's just a broken foot,' replied Logan. 'Nothing too bad.'

'I broke a bone in my foot once,' Pete told him, frowning. 'Bloomin' painful, it was.'

'I remember that,' said Josh. 'Didn't your date push you over into a rose bush or something?'

'No,' replied Pete. 'It was definitely football.'

'Yeah right, bro,' said Josh, grinning.

'Anyway,' said Tom, coming to stand alongside them. 'We're not builders, but between us we've refurbished a shop, the hub and the inn.'

'With a bit of help from some talented workmen,' added Pete. 'But if we can help in any way, then we're here.'

Logan looked at them all for a moment. 'Molly sent you, didn't she?' he asked, guessing the truth.

There was a short silence as they all broke into a smile. 'It's very hard to say no to Molly,' said Tom. 'After all, I think it's the first time she's ever asked us for anything.'

'That's right,' agreed Josh, nodding. 'She's always the one who ends up doing everything instead.'

'I think fixing the watermill might be a bit out of her skill range though,' said Tom.

'I think it's out of mine as well,' remarked Logan, with a grim grunt of humour.

'What are you struggling with?' asked Pete.

Logan hesitated to confess all the problems but he actually found himself grateful as well that they were there so he could finally share the burden. 'The wheel is supposed to be connected by this metal pipe to the gears in here. That will then rotate the heavy millstones. But the metal corroded and landed on my little toe instead.' He pointed at the long metal pipe. 'I can weld reasonably well, but standing for any length of time is agony.'

'I've done a bit of welding in my time,' said Josh. 'I'm not particularly tidy, but the stuff holds together.'

'I'm not worried about it looking good,' said Logan. 'I just need it whole again so that it will turn with the wheel outside. Which is the other big problem.' He hobbled outside, with the group of men following him. 'It's completely snagged up with weeds that need clearing before I can remove the rotten spokes and get them replaced.'

'Right, time for your annual bath, Del,' said Pete, bending down to remove his trainers.

'Just don't frighten the fish with that lily-white skin,' added Josh.

'Gerroff,' said Del, pulling off his T-shirt. 'I'm beach-body ready, me, mate.'

Logan tried to protest to tell them not to worry and that they shouldn't be wasting their weekend doing this but they ignored him and carried on staring at Dodgy Del instead.

'I'm glad I've eaten already,' said Pete, with a grimace. 'You should have given us warning that you were going to bare that weedy torso of yours.'

Before Logan could stop them, Pete and Del had waded into the water and began to pull off the strands of weeds that were caught up in the spokes. Soon they were joined by Keith the dog who was also eager to help although perhaps more interested in splashing about and having fun. Meanwhile Tom and Josh worked on the metal piping by cutting off the rotten piece and welding a new one on instead. All the while, they chatted with Logan but kept the conversation light. They mainly talked about their families and girlfriends. Stanley's name came up a few times.

'He's like family to all of us,' said Tom, with a smile.

'So's Molly,' added Josh. 'Let's hope that tea garden idea of hers takes off. She deserves a bit of success.'

'That Barry,' muttered Pete, who was sitting on the riverbank drying off. 'He's even dodgier than you, Del.'

'Thank you very much,' said Del. 'Don't tar me with the same brush as that guy. He's a right rip-off merchant.'

There was a huge roar of dismay from everyone as Keith the dog finally clambered out of the river and proceeded to shake the water from his wet fur over them all.

Logan found that he already liked the guys. Their conversation flowed and nobody asked too many in-depth questions. He knew he was closed off but didn't know what to do about it.

Molly, on the other hand, was a completely open book. She couldn't lie if she tried. Except to help people. If anything, she needed protecting from herself.

He found himself wondering why he so badly wanted to volunteer for that job.

23

Molly hoped she hadn't overstepped the mark by asking her friends to help Logan. But if the man wasn't going to ask for help when he so obviously needed it, she didn't know what else she could have done.

Anyway, it was all done now. She had taken a peek out of the back door of the shop later in the afternoon and had spotted Dodgy Del and Pete waist deep in water, removing some of the debris and rotten timbers from the waterwheel.

With a satisfied sigh, she went back to working on the menu for the tea garden, which needed checking one final time before sending to the printers.

There was still so much to be done. Planning to open the Saturday of the following weekend, that left only five full days to organise getting Dodgy Del's chairs delivered, picking up the crockery from Grandma Tilly and having the menus printed. Then there was the marketing tweets and Facebook pages that needed organising. Tom had promised her a big splash in the local newspaper. It was all very exciting. And nerve-wracking as well.

But she still hadn't had time to source any teapots, let alone a coffee machine. She really didn't think serving instant coffee was going to make a very good impression.

Feeling the anxiety rising, she concentrated back on the list that would make up the menu. There was the obligatory chocolate cake, a classic Victoria sponge, an Earl Grey loaf that she was pleased with. Then she had added a fruit cake, some salted pecan and white chocolate brownies and various flavoured biscuits. Something for children would be needed as well, including some different flavoured juices. She then stared at her notes, wondering whether the options were good enough and even tasty enough for everyone to enjoy.

Deep in thought, she was sucking on the end of her pen when she heard someone open up the front door to the shop and come inside.

'Hello?' she called out.

'Hello to you too,' said Amber, as she walked into the kitchen carrying a large box.

Behind her, Belle and Lucy were carrying equally large boxes.

'Well, this is a nice surprise,' said Molly, smiling at her friends as they placed the large boxes on the kitchen counters.

'We've missed you,' said Amber, heading over to give her a hug. 'You've been so busy that we hardly ever see you these days.'

'There's just been so much to do,' Molly told them, with a sheepish grin. 'I'm sorry.'

'No need to apologise,' said Belle. 'We just decided that we'll come to you instead. What's this?' She peered at Molly's mock-up of the menu which was on the countertop.

'Just the menu that needs finalising before I send it off to the printers,' Molly told her.

Belle frowned. 'I can see a mistake already,' she said.

'Where?' asked Molly, aghast. She grabbed the piece of paper and ran her eyes up and down all the words. 'What is it? A spelling mistake?'

Belle shook her head and smiled. 'Right here where it says coffee,' she said. 'You haven't listed the different types. Cappuccino, latte and all that.'

Molly grimaced. 'I can't do all that with just a kettle.'

'Ah, then this should hopefully help,' said Amber, reaching into the large box she had carried in. 'Someone give me a hand here.'

Molly watched as Amber and Lucy slowly and carefully pulled out a large coffee machine from the box. 'But that's from your shop!' she said. 'What will you use?'

'Thanks to us doing so well, we've just upgraded to a newer model,' Amber told her. 'So it's all yours.'

'Oh!' Molly was stunned. 'That's amazing. Thank you so much.'

'My pleasure,' said Amber.

'That's not all,' added Belle, reaching into her own box. 'These are from the pub refit. I thought you could make them suitably country garden-ish.' She brought out a couple of small blackboards, which Molly instantly knew would look perfect in the tea garden. 'I've also got some spare highball glasses in here in case anyone wants a cold drink.'

'Oh, you are wonderful!' Molly told her.

'Wait! I've got something too,' said Lucy, grinning as she too rummaged inside the box next to her. 'Grandma Tilly and I had a great day out yesterday going into all the charity shops in Aldwych and buying up all their teapots. Hopefully these should set you up.' Lucy brought out a couple of teapots which had vintage flower designs on them.

'They're perfect,' said Molly, feeling overwhelmed with love and gratitude for her friends. 'I don't know what to say.'

'Then you'd better hold on for just one more minute,' said Belle, giving her a wink before pulling out another blackboard from her box. 'This was our idea, but we let Amber do her thing with it because she's the most arty out of all of us.'

The blackboard was larger than the other two and was already decorated and written up. There in large, bold letters were the words 'Molly's Tea Garden'. Along the edge were tiny little teapots, flowers and pieces of cake that Amber had drawn on.

It was beautiful, but Molly couldn't help but stare at the words: Molly's Tea Garden. It was her responsibility. All hers.

She caught a shaky breath. This was becoming all too real.

Her friends, seeing her expression, all stepped forward as one.

'You're going to be fine,' Belle told her.

But Molly was shaking her head, trying not to cry. 'I still think that I'm going to fail,' she whispered.

'We know,' said Amber, putting her arm around her. 'And we know why as well. Bridget and Gary did such a number on you last summer. They stripped you of almost all your confidence.'

'So you might not believe in you, but we do,' said Belle.

Lucy nodded. 'And we'll be with you every step of the way.'

Then her best friends brought her in for an enormous group hug and Molly could only think about how lucky she was to have friends like these.

24

Her friends left but only after Molly had promised to head over to the Black Swan Inn after she had closed up the kitchen. They made her swear that she would relax and join them all for a drink, obviously still worried about how anxious she was at the moment.

Molly looked at all the presents they had given her. They had been amazingly generous and the coffee machine, blackboards and teapots were all very welcome and would be great additions to the business.

So why did she feel sick? Her old fears and lack of confidence rose quickly to the surface these days. She only had days to go until the tea garden opened and was frightened that she had made a terrible mistake. She tried to think back to the positive messages her friends had told her. But the negative was always so much easier to believe than the positive, wasn't it?

She began to pace up and down in the kitchen, trying to catch her breath. What if she failed? What if she made a total and utter fool of herself by even attempting to run a tea garden?

'Hey.'

She gave a start and spun around to find Logan leaning against one of his crutches at the open back door.

'Are you OK?' he asked, looking at her with an amused expression.

'Why?' she asked. 'Why wouldn't I be OK?'

His soft smile didn't drop. 'Because you're marching back and forth muttering to yourself in a dark tone again,' he said.

She stopped pacing and sighed heavily, staring down at the floor. 'It's no good,' she murmured.

'What are you talking about?'

'This,' she said, looking up at him and waving her arm around at the kitchen. 'This business I'm trying to get off the ground.' Her shoulders sagged. 'It's going to be a failure.'

'Says who?' he asked.

But she didn't reply and began to pace again. 'What if I poison someone accidentally?' she muttered to herself. 'What if I burn the whole place down? What if someone sues me?'

She went to turn but couldn't as Logan had suddenly appeared in front of her and she crashed into his wide chest. He reached out with his one free hand to take her by the shoulder.

She was startled. Apart from when he had hurt his foot, she had never been this close to him. She could even see the flecks of green in his hazel eyes.

'Have you burnt down many places?' he asked, raising an eyebrow with an amused expression on his face.

She gave him a sheepish smile. 'Well, I set fire to the stove at home once,' she said. 'I was making choux pastry on the hob for profiteroles when Adam said that he'd been stung by a wasp. By the time I remembered, the kitchen was full of smoke. Thankfully it was only the saucepan that was ruined.'

'I see.' He smiled down at her. 'Well, luckily you don't need to fry your cakes. Listen, you need more faith in yourself.'

'Ha, easier said than done for someone as confident as you,' she told him.

He was astonished and dropped his hand. 'Me?' he said. 'The most humiliated person in the country? Whose own wife left him for a TV presenter and, let's be honest, someone who's an awful lot shorter than I am.'

'That's about your ex-wife, not you,' she told him.

'You don't think it reflects on our marriage in the slightest?' he asked. 'Or on me in particular? Because I do.'

She shook her head. 'I think it reflects on what a horrible person your ex-wife is,' she replied. 'I mean, to have an affair behind your back. To embarrass you like that. She's the one to blame, not you.'

He looked at her with bleak eyes. 'You really believe that?' he asked, his voice a little hoarse.

She nodded. 'I truly do. Look at how much you care for Stanley. How you sorted out Barry for me to get the rent scot-free.'

'That's because I trust and believe in you,' he said simply. 'And there's not many people I can say that about, believe me.'

She smiled. 'So I'm on an exclusive list? That's what you're telling me?'

He laughed, his face lighting up once more. 'Yeah, if that's how you want to put it.' But then his expression grew serious. 'You need to trust in yourself. Trust in your abilities. Because I do,' he told her. 'And if not, fake it until you make it.'

She looked up at him and tried to take comfort in his warm smile as he gazed down at her.

'How's the foot?' she said, changing the subject onto him once more. But looking into his eyes, she just felt dizzy for some reason.

'Pretty painful.' He looked at her with his piercing hazel eyes. 'I know what you did today.'

She suppressed her smile. 'You mean the fabulous menu I've just created for my future customers?' she said in an innocent tone.

'You know exactly what I'm talking about,' he told her. She figured that he was trying to look stern and yet there was a smile playing at the corners of his mouth. 'Sending the guys over to the watermill to give me a hand.'

'Oh. That.' She gave him a sheepish smile. 'Did it help?'

He deliberately looked away, frowning at the floor.

'So what are you complaining about?' she said.

'I don't need anyone fixing my life,' she heard him say.

'I'm not,' she told him. 'I wouldn't dream of doing that. Anyway, it was for Stanley, not you. I know how much the watermill means to him.'

He looked at her, smiling broadly now. 'Well played,' he said, nodding his approval. 'Pretty low, but you hit the right mark.'

'I thought it would,' she said, laughing. 'So what did the guys do?'

'Pretty much cleared the waterwheel ready for repair and helped fix the metal pipe that caused all this bother in the first place,' he told her. 'The one called Dodgy Del seemed to be a bit upset about his fancy shorts getting a bit slimy from all the pondweed.'

'Del doesn't have any fancy clothes,' she said, laughing. 'He's just worried about his hot date later. I dread to think what he'll show up wearing.'

Logan looked at her. 'You're going on a date?' he said, his voice sounding a little sharp. 'With Dodgy Del?'

'What? No!' Molly laughed. 'Can you imagine? No, we're meeting up at the pub because Belle's organised some live music this evening. It's good fun. You should come.'

'I would, but my foot is sore,' he told her. 'I haven't put it up all day so that'll be my exciting evening ahead.'

'Pity,' she said. 'Pete will probably play his guitar and he's really good. Certainly much better than my singing, anyway.'

'I'm sure both are a vast improvement on Dodgy Del's singing in any case,' he said, with a rueful smile. 'Well, I'd better leave you to it.'

But just as he began to spin around, his crutch caught on the door frame and he stumbled into Molly. She held out her arms to steady him and they somehow ended up extremely close to each other. So close that she could feel his breath on her face.

He looked down at her for a second before straightening up. 'Thank you,' he said. 'Sorry. I'm a liability with this thing.'

'It's fine,' she told him, trying to control her pulse which had begun to thump in her throat. 'I'm just grateful we both didn't end up on the floor.'

'Yeah,' he said, giving her a piercing look.

She found she couldn't look away and so was almost startled when he broke the eye contact and moved around, a little more slowly this time.

'Well, thanks for the meddling,' he said as he moved away. 'For Grandad's sake.'

'Any time,' she called out, but the doorway was already empty.

For a second, she leaned against the kitchen counter. She breathed in the fresh air coming in through the open doorway, but it didn't do anything to cool her hot cheeks.

Logan was a good-looking man. That was all. Wasn't it?

25

At midday on the first Saturday in June, Molly placed the sign which read Molly's Tea Garden against the wall next to the gate.

As she straightened up, she looked at the sky again, even though she had only checked five minutes previously. Despite the clouds being mostly grey, any rain had held off.

She felt a sigh of relief, especially as she had yet to source any kind of umbrellas or shelter from any rain. Hopefully the weather would hold and it would bring her good fortune for the opening of the tea garden.

Her phone beeped with a text from her brothers wishing her good luck with the grand opening and that they would be home later to hear how it went. She smiled to herself, knowing that her mum must have reminded them. In all the frantic build-up to the big day, she had forgotten that it was the start of the summer holidays for universities and that the twins would be home that evening.

As she walked back across the garden, she noticed that some of the flowers that had been planted around the edge had begun to bloom, providing dots of colour along the walls. Her mum was currently tying up some of the pink roses which were clambering up the walls. She glanced over at her daughter and gave her a tentative thumbs up, which Molly returned with a nervous smile.

Her mum and Geoff had been busy once more. Another of the raised beds had been planted up, this time with herbs, and Molly had found herself reaching out to brush her fingers over them as she often passed by before breathing in the sweet scent of the basil, mint and thyme.

She just hoped that the tea garden would be open long enough that perhaps she could use the herbs in her baking at some point.

Thankfully, Dodgy Del had come good on his promise of chairs at the very last minute, even though he was only just delivering them all now. Molly didn't have time to check them out properly, merely placing them in a circle around the upturned crates, which were to be used as tables. Belle had lent her various pieces of pretty vintage cloths, which certainly looked in keeping with the country cottage theme.

The chairs, however, were a bit of a mismatch as there was purple velvet on the seat pads and it didn't really suit the garden, but at least they were adult-sized and the customers had somewhere to sit and order their tea and cake. If they came, she thought, crossing her fingers.

Along the wall next to the kitchen door, she had placed a long trestle table that she had borrowed from the community hub. On top of a length of pretty flowered cloth, she had placed a large pile of laminated menus to be positioned on top of each crate before anyone arrived. There were also quite a few cakes, all covered in glass domes. She had baked a few different flavours, not really knowing quite how many she was catering for.

Inside the kitchen, the shelves and countertops she had cleaned were stacked with plates, teapots, cups and saucers. The coffee machine was plugged in, ready for the first hot drink order.

All that was needed was the first order. *Please let there even be a first order*, she thought. Any order. This had to work. She needed to prove to everyone that she could be a success. But mainly, deep inside, she needed to prove it to herself.

As Molly stood in the kitchen, she heard the front door of the shop open. She frowned, hoping the customers hadn't got confused and were coming into the empty shop instead.

'Good afternoon,' said Grandma Tilly, walking into the kitchen. 'I told you it wouldn't rain.'

'And I should have listened to you as per usual,' said Molly, with a smile.

'Like I told you, my bones are never wrong,' carried on Grandma Tilly. 'If my knees ache, I know that rain is coming. But yesterday and last night, I could have danced the fandango on them.'

'And did you?' asked Molly.

Grandma Tilly laughed. 'If I'd have had another glass of sherry, I may well have done!'

'Where were you last night?' asked Molly agog.

'Didn't I tell you?' said Grandma Tilly, settling down onto a nearby stool. 'The bingo ladies had a night out. And I've got that much gossip, you wouldn't believe it.'

As Grandma Tilly chatted away, Molly began to slice each large cake up. She wondered whether she was making the slices too big but then decided it was better to be too generous than too stingy in the early days of the business.

'Anyway, those that haven't been cautioned by the police are definitely coming to support you this morning.'

Molly looked over at Grandma Tilly with a start, wondering what kind of story she had just missed.

'In fact, I think I can hear Beryl now,' said Grandma Tilly, sliding off her stool and peering outside around the back door.

'They promised me that they'd come. Yes, our very first customers are here!'

Molly took a deep breath, grabbed a couple of menus and headed outside to where a small group of elderly ladies were sitting down at a table. This was it. The tea garden was open for business.

As she walked towards the table, Grandma Tilly kept pace alongside her.

'Isn't this exciting?' she whispered, with a grin.

Molly smiled back. 'Very,' she replied before arriving at the table. 'Good afternoon,' she said to her very first customers.

'These chairs are very comfortable,' said one of the women, wiggling in her seat. 'If a little of a strange choice for a garden.'

'They're only temporary,' Grandma Tilly briefly told them, before sitting down at the one of the empty seats and beginning to chat away with her friends.

So much for her extra help, thought Molly. But she didn't mind. These were actual customers! So she took their orders and was soon serving up pots of tea and plates of cake for them all.

As she headed back towards the kitchen, her mum crossed the garden and followed her inside.

'Well, looks like you're on your way,' she whispered, giving her daughter's arm a squeeze. 'I'm just going to head over and collect some more seedlings. Stanley's put me in touch with a local lady who's got lots of different varieties she's happy to donate.'

'OK, Mum,' said Molly.

'See you later,' replied her mum, giving her a kiss on the cheek. 'Good luck.'

'She won't need that,' said Lucy, as she, Amber and Belle walked through the shop and into the kitchen.

Her mum headed off after saying hi to the girls.

'We've made some spare time for an hour so what can we do to help?' asked Belle.

'I was going to ask Grandma Tilly to lay out the napkins on each little table, but I seem to have lost my helper,' said Molly.

They all glanced outside, where Grandma Tilly was sitting and chatting away with her friends.

'Right, give those to me,' said Belle, taking the napkins and heading outside.

'There's some more customers arriving,' said Amber, looking delighted. 'Shall I head over and serve them?'

Minute by minute, the tea garden gradually filled up. It was mainly local customers, but Molly was just thrilled that everyone had come along to support her. They all bought pots of tea, coffee and, yes, they bought her cakes as well.

By late afternoon, Molly was feeling relieved and happy. Albeit somewhat rushed off her feet as Amber and Belle had to go to work and Lucy had a hair appointment. Grandma Tilly was moving from one group of people to the next, settling down each time for a proper chat with her friends. She seemed to have completely forgotten that she was supposed to be helping with the orders.

Thankfully, Stanley and Frank had arrived to help as they had promised. They were less chatty than Grandma Tilly although their order technique left a lot to be desired.

'The lady with the big hair next to the wall says she's gluten-intolerant,' said Frank, making a face. 'Although I'd more inclined to say that she's manners-intolerant as there wasn't a please or thank you to be had from her.'

'Right,' said Molly, with a nod. She handed over the two slices of cake that she had just arranged on the plate. 'Here's the order for table three.'

'Which table was that again?' asked Frank, with a frown.

'The one alongside this wall,' Molly told him.

'Right,' said Frank, sounding a little unsure.

Molly's doubts were confirmed as she headed out to talk to the lady with the gluten intolerance.

'Excuse me, but this isn't the cake I ordered,' said a gentleman as she passed his table.

'Oh, I'm sorry,' replied Molly, taking the plate from his proffered hand. 'What was it that you ordered again?'

'Two slices of carrot cake and a Victoria sponge,' his companion told her. 'We seem to have three brownies and nothing else.'

'I'm so sorry,' repeated Molly. 'Let me get that for you.'

But as she went to move away, there was a large cry from nearby.

'This is an utter scandal,' said the woman, standing up. 'We shall leave immediately, Mavis.'

'Is everything all right?' asked Molly, heading towards the woman.

The woman made a face. 'Well, apart from receiving the wrong drink and food, I have no desire to be sitting in a place of sin!'

Molly stared at the woman, completely nonplussed. 'I beg your pardon?' she asked.

'This place! This furniture!' The woman waved her hand around in a wild manner. 'It's disgusting.'

Molly stared down at the purple velour chair and tried to work out what the woman was so upset about.

'Vice! Here in Cranbridge!' cried the woman.

'Vice?' Molly blinked at her uncomprehendingly.

'Don't pretend you don't know,' sneered the woman, spinning around the chair that she had been sitting on so that Molly could see the back. 'It's from a s-e-x shop.'

'It's what?' cried Molly, completely aghast.

She peered down at where the woman was pointing and then she saw. The animal that Dodgy Del had told her was on all the chairs was there, but unfortunately it was a Playboy bunny logo and not the far more appropriate Peter Rabbit that she had hoped for.

She had been so busy that she hadn't even spotted the decoration on all the chairs.

'I had no idea!' she said, absolutely horrified.

'A likely story,' said the woman. 'It's your tea garden, isn't it? Aren't you responsible for all of this?'

The woman swept away, taking her friend with her.

Molly stood and watched as a few more people began to stand up and leave as well.

'We received completely the wrong food and drinks,' said one man.

'You're lucky,' said another. 'We never received anything at all.'

To add insult to injury, the heavens opened at that precise moment and a heavy rain shower began. With no umbrellas or cover for people to shelter under, every customer made a swift exit out of the tea garden.

At that moment, Barry, the landlord, wandered through the crowd towards her.

'Not sure your temporary lease covers this many people,' he said, with a grimace. 'Nor all this extra furniture that's been placed everywhere. I think you and I had better have a chat about increasing your rent.'

Molly stood in shock, still holding the plates and feeling completely stunned.

She watched as the rain poured down, soaking the linen tablecloths and purple velvet, splattering into each cup and onto every plate. Her beautiful cakes were disintegrating in front of her eyes, as was her dream.

It was just as she had feared. Molly's Tea Garden was a total and utter failure.

26

Molly wasn't quite sure how she had got to the Black Swan Inn, but suddenly she appeared to be sitting at a table, surrounded by her friends, in something of a numb daze.

She vaguely remembered her friends suddenly appearing. They all rushed around in the pouring rain tidying away all the food and drink before locking up the kitchen. Then they had walked her over to the inn, where she was now sitting with a towel around her shoulders.

'It'll be fine,' Amber was saying, reaching out to give her hand a squeeze.

'Absolutely,' Lucy told her, nodding furiously.

'Couldn't get much bloomin' worse, could it?' said Belle. 'What?' she said, as the others rolled their eyes. 'Too soon? Look, so it went wrong, so what? It'll stop raining and then—'

'And then all I've got to worry about is the fact that my furniture came from The Playboy Club in London!' said Molly, with a small sob.

Lucy pushed a large glass of wine across the table towards her, but Molly shook her head. She didn't even want to get drunk.

She just wanted to hide away in her bed and never come out again.

Keith the dog seemed to sense her sadness and leant his head on her knee for support. Molly reached out to stroke his soft fur, grateful for some kind of distraction from what had just happened.

'I've had a word with Barry,' she heard Lucy murmur. 'I told him to come back another time about the rent.'

'I texted your mum,' said Amber. 'She said she can come over here, if you want to see her.'

Molly shook her head. Her mum was only just beginning to recover from her low mood and the last thing she wanted to do was set her back by being the teary, miserable mess that she really felt.

'OK,' said Amber, typing into her phone. 'I'll tell her that you're OK and will be home in a while.'

'Please eat something,' said Belle, pushing a plate of pizza towards her. 'It's your favourite.'

But Molly was still too numb. She shivered, her clothes soaking her through to make her skin cold.

'Del!' shouted Belle, making them all jump as she leapt up from the table. 'I want a word with you and it won't be a pleasant one, so brace yourself.'

Molly glanced up to see Belle charging over to where Del had just walked through the front door.

Belle continued to rant at Del, but Molly couldn't stand the humiliating looks from all the other customers any more so made an excuse to go to the ladies' toilet. But she kept on walking, out into the pub garden, where she found it was still raining. She didn't mind. She couldn't feel it. She wasn't sure she was ever going to feel anything ever again, and certainly not happiness.

She looked back at the door to the bar and decided that she couldn't face anyone at the moment, so she sent Amber a text that she was heading home to see her mum and to get changed into warm, dry clothes. Then she headed around the side of the inn, through the small gate and across the narrow pedestrian bridge over the river to Riverside Lane.

The rain was coming down quite heavily now, so there was nobody about. The shop and community hub were shut for the day so at least there was no one around to talk to.

So much for flaming June, she thought, as her trainers soaked up the water from the many puddles.

She carried on, deep in thought, until she reached the tea garden. She stopped briefly to look across at it. In the pouring rain, it looked pretty dismal, even with the Playboy bunnies smiling at her from the back of the chairs. She thought she could laugh with the ridiculousness of it all if her heart wasn't breaking.

She gave another shiver as the rain began to seep through her T-shirt to her bare skin. Perhaps a shower would make her feel better, she thought. Or perhaps she would just climb into bed and stay there forever.

But as she turned to carry on walking past the garden, she saw Logan watching her from the doorway of the watermill.

'Hey,' he said, walking slowly with the aid of the crutch to head across the small bridge to stand in her way on the path. 'How are you doing?'

He seemed oblivious to the rain pouring down over them both.

'You heard what happened?' she asked, guessing by the pitying look on his face.

He nodded.

She sighed. 'It's fine,' she said. Except her voice broke and she could finally feel the tears beginning to come.

'Molly,' began Logan, reaching out to take her arm.

'Please don't be nice to me,' she told him, brushing away the rain on her face. At least she hoped that they were masking her tears.

'Come inside,' he said. She could feel the warmth of his hand on her cold skin. 'You're freezing.'

She shook her head. 'I'll head home and take a shower,' she told him.

But as she went to walk away, she couldn't stop herself from staring back at the tea garden one more time.

She looked at it for a while longer before she felt Logan come to stand next to her.

'Don't suppose you want a slightly used Playboy Tea Garden?' she joked, attempting a smile, but feeling that it didn't quite hit the mark. 'Only one useless owner.'

'You're not useless,' he told her, in that quiet tone that he often used.

'I'm not so sure about that,' she said, her voice cracking. Now she could definitely feel the warm tears mingling with the cold rain on her cheeks. 'Who was I trying to kid? A great British summer without any rain?'

And she rushed away as she couldn't bear for him to see how humiliated she really was.

Once home, she shut the door behind her and leaned against it for a moment.

Her mum rushed out of the lounge and stood in front of her with her arms wide open. Molly gave a sob and rushed into them, despite knowing that she was going to make her mum wet as well.

'It'll be all right,' murmured her mum, as she held her close. 'You'll see. We've got through worse.'

Molly relished the warmth from her mum's embrace for a moment longer before pulling back.

'Sorry, Mum,' she said, with a sniff, wiping a long lock of wet hair away from her forehead. 'You don't need all my drama at the moment.'

'You're my daughter and we'll face everything together, just as we always have done,' said her mum, sounding stronger than she had for many weeks.

Molly realised that her mum was stepping up, just when she needed her. And that she didn't need to be the strong one, for once. For today, she could be true to herself. And then the tears really began, her wonderful dream of owning a tea garden in tatters.

27

Logan watched Molly trudge away in the rain and wondered for a moment if he should follow her. But he remembered how he had just wanted to be left alone when he was at his lowest and so let her walk away. Although it didn't stop him watching her until she was out of sight at the end of the lane.

He leant on his crutch and sighed. He knew exactly what had happened. He had spent the day at the watermill and had therefore seen and heard all the drama. He had caught up with his grandad at the end of the day and everyone seemed to be keen to tell Dodgy Del exactly what he had done wrong.

'He's kind enough and he means well,' Stanley had told Logan. 'But when Del does you a favour, you normally end up picking up the pieces for many days afterwards.'

The trouble was, from what Logan had overheard, it wasn't just the furniture. The lack of rain cover hadn't helped and then there was the fact that the only staff that Molly had employed were his grandad and friends, all of whom weren't exactly professional waiting staff.

He went back into the mill, but his mind was elsewhere and he couldn't concentrate on the mechanical workings any more. So he locked up and headed back over the bridge.

'Oh, hey,' said someone nearby. 'Have you seen our sister?'

Logan looked up to find two tall, young men staring across at him from the riverbank. They were almost identical to look at and, once he had registered the blonde hair, he surmised that these were the Hopkins twins, Molly's younger brothers.

'You've just missed her,' Logan told them. 'She's gone home to dry off.'

The heavy rain had slowed to a steady drizzle but it was still damp and cold outside.

They looked at each other. 'Maybe she's better off on her own with Mum,' said one of them.

'Hi. I'm Logan,' he said, holding out his hand.

One of the men introduced himself as Ben.

'And I'm Adam. So we've literally arrived back from university this afternoon,' said the other brother, looking concerned. 'From what Mum text us, the grand opening of the tea garden didn't exactly work out?'

Logan shook his head. 'I'm afraid not. Your sister's pretty upset,' he told them.

'Wish there was something we could do,' said Ben, frowning. 'But what do we know about tea gardens?'

Logan blew out a sigh. He had been thinking exactly the same thing. All he knew about was furniture. Which gave him an idea.

'You really want to help your sister?' he asked them.

Adam and Ben exchanged a quick look. 'Of course, we do,' said Adam.

'Then follow me,' said Logan, heading towards his shop. He winced a little as he walked but the pain in his foot had begun to recede a little day by day.

Once back inside the workshop and out of the damp weather, he turned around to look at them both.

'You're right,' he told them. 'I don't know anything about tea gardens or cakes either. But furniture is something I know all about. So how about you help me rip that ghastly purple velvet off every chair and sand down those awful Playboy logos so that they can at least be used without offending anyone.'

'We don't know anything about furniture either,' muttered Ben.

'I'll teach you,' Logan told them. 'You both must be bright to go to university. What are you studying?'

'He's doing the easier course,' said Adam, rolling his eyes at his brother.

'You're calling Business Studies easy?' said Ben. 'Anyway, I like the idea of bossing people around.'

'Bullying, more like,' muttered Adam.

'And what are you taking?' asked Logan, somewhat bemused at their ease and teasing of each other.

'Psychology,' said Adam, who appeared to be the quieter one of the two. 'Then anyone who has to work with him can come to me for therapy afterwards.'

They were supremely confident in themselves, thought Logan. Unlike their older sister. As if she had given them every shred of confidence she had and had none left over for herself.

'So how about we give your sister a bit of a hand?' he said.

They both nodded so he asked them to start bringing in all the chairs whilst he worked out where they could put everything.

It took some time to bring but eventually all the awful chairs from the tea garden were inside the workshop.

Logan instructed the boys to remove the sodden purple velvet padding. Although, once removed, the chairs perhaps looked even worse. What was going to take some time was removing the line of studs around the top and sides of each chair so that they were much tidier. Then they needed sanding down so that the wood appeared uniform in colour.

And this was all times twenty, thought Logan. But he was determined to get it done for Molly. And, he was pleased to find, so were her brothers.

The twins were hard workers once they actually settled down and stopped bickering and taking the mickey out of each other. So the three of them got down to work for the next few hours.

Later on in the evening, Ben asked what Logan had been doing in the watermill.

'I'm trying to get it up and running for my grandad,' said Logan. He didn't add that he wasn't succeeding at all in his efforts so far.

Ben shuddered. 'Not sure how many times your grandad put me in detention over the years.'

'Did it work?' asked Logan.

Adam broke into a wide smile. 'What do you think?'

'Do you really think this will help the tea garden?' asked Ben, looking at the chairs that they had already sanded down.

'I hope so,' replied Logan. He so desperately wanted Molly to succeed. 'If the chairs don't offend anyone, then surely the customers will stay next time.'

'If there is a next time,' said Ben, looking upset.

'There will be,' Logan told them in a determined voice. He wouldn't let Molly down, nor would he let her business fail.

'I'm not sure what else anyone can do for the time being until the fuss dies down,' said Adam.

'Unless Molly wears that Easter bunny costume again,' joked Ben, with a grin to himself.

'The only thing that she could wear to bring in the customers is to dress like a Playboy bunny not an Easter one,' said Adam, laughing.

Logan found himself briefly envisioning Molly's long legs in black stockings and had to drag his mind back from that enticement, shocked at how much it made his pulse race.

With a shake of his head, he concentrated back on the furniture, hoping it would help keep Molly's business afloat.

28

Late in the evening, Logan cooked a couple of pizzas, which they all eagerly devoured. And then the work on the furniture for the tea garden continued long into the night.

Logan found that he enjoyed Adam and Ben's company. So these were the infamous Hopkins twins, he thought, with a smile to himself. He could certainly understand why they had been such a handful at school for his grandad. And perhaps he could see why Molly was the quietest one. After all, who could even begin to get a word in edgeways with these two around?

When he asked about their university exams, Ben chatted away about his plans to be a millionaire by the time he was thirty. Adam was quieter and seemed more interested in Logan's work on the watermill.

'I almost took history before I chose psychology,' said Adam, frowning to himself. 'Not sure I should have followed my gut instinct, to be honest.'

'The course isn't going well?' asked Logan.

'Oh, it's fine,' replied Adam, quickly. 'Just maybe not for me. But it's a bit late now, I guess. I've still got another year to go in any case.'

'You can always give it up,' said Logan. 'No point wasting a year when you could be doing something that you enjoy instead.'

'You mean real work?' said Ben, who had been listening into the conversation from the other side of the room. 'Nine to five and all that? You must be joking, right, bro?'

Adam nodded, but Logan wasn't sure he quite believed him.

Eventually, the brothers' energy began to fade. Logan tried to persuade them to head home, but they said they only needed a power nap before continuing work, so Logan let them go upstairs to sleep for a time whilst he carried on.

However, Adam and Ben never woke up, so Logan worked through the night, finishing off the last chair just as the sun rose above the treeline.

He looked around with a self-satisfied smile. Despite his weariness and the ache in his foot from standing for so long, the chairs looked much better. They had ended up sanding away the dark gloss to reveal a golden oak underneath and were now more rustic and in keeping with being used outside. He stretched his back and sighed. It was worth it. Hopefully it was a big step forward in resurrecting the tea garden.

As if by magic, Molly appeared at the window soon afterwards, knocking gently on the door once she spotted him.

'Good morning,' he said, opening the front door and immediately checking her face, concerned about her. She looked as if she had cried herself to sleep.

'Oh, er, hi,' she replied with a small smile. 'I don't suppose you've seen my brothers, have you? They texted Mum last night to say that they were here. Was that right?'

He smiled. 'Don't worry. They're OK,' he assured her. 'Why don't you follow me.'

She followed him into the workshop and came to an abrupt halt. 'What's all this?' she asked, her eyes wide as she looked at all the chairs and then the pile of velvet on the floor. 'Are those my chairs? The Playboy bunny ones?'

'I figured that if you're going to reopen, then perhaps the bunny logo had better go,' he told her.

She turned one of the chairs around, where the back had been sanded down and the logo had completely disappeared.

'I don't believe it,' she said, genuinely amazed as she ran her hand along the top of the chair back. 'They look wonderful. So different. I would never have recognised them. Thank you so much. That's incredibly kind of you.'

He found himself uncomfortable at her grateful words, for some reason. 'It was no problem,' he said quickly.

'Are you kidding?' she said. 'You must have worked all night.'

'Well, I had help,' he told her, gesturing with his head for her to follow him upstairs.

As they headed into the apartment above the shop, Molly gave a gasp of soft laughter. In the lounge area, both of her brothers were sprawled out fast sleep on the sofa and armchair.

'They didn't really help you, did they?' she asked, sounding totally disbelieving.

'Actually they did,' said Logan, smiling at her.

She giggled once more in disbelief and it was that which made the brothers slowly begin to wake up.

'Wassup?' said Adam, struggling up to a sitting position. 'What's all the noise?'

'Oh, hey, sis,' said Ben, peering at her with sleepy eyes and yawning as he ran a hand through his messy hair.

'You really helped Logan with the furniture?' she asked, still sounding as if she didn't believe it.

'I've got the blisters to prove it,' said Ben, holding out his hand. 'The man was a real taskmaster.'

Molly turned to look at Logan with raised eyebrows.

'They each got a whole pizza to eat and crashed out around 1 a.m.,' he told her.

'Well, I can't believe it, but thank you all so much,' she said, her eyes shining.

'You're welcome, sis,' replied Ben. 'I'm starving though.'

'Aren't you always?' said Molly, laughing.

Ben jumped up. 'How about breakfast?' he asked.

'I'll grab some bread from the shop,' said Adam, quickly joining him. 'Bacon butties all round?'

As her brothers made their way downstairs, Molly turned to look at Logan. 'Well, thank you,' she told him, still looking stunned. 'For taking care of them and for the chairs as well.' She gave a little sigh. 'I'm not sure what good it'll do.'

'Don't give up,' said Logan, unable to stop himself from reaching out to take her hand. He was desperate to have cheerful Molly back, not this defeated sad soul in front of him. 'You can do this.'

She nodded as if trying to believe him. 'Maybe,' she said.

'Definitely,' he told her.

They stared at each other for a long time before she finally broke the gaze to look down at his hand holding hers.

As she looked back up at him, it seemed as if she were about to speak when they both heard Adam and Ben coming up the stairs.

Logan dropped her hand and the moment was lost as they all went into the kitchen to prepare breakfast.

29

The failure of the opening of the tea garden weighed heavy over Molly all day on Sunday. So she spent the day quietly with her family.

The twins didn't seem too weary after their late night working with Logan and they watched rubbish movies and taught her how to play some of their games. She was grateful for their support.

Her mum had also stepped up, as if her own daughter needing help had given her some much-needed impetus to address her own mental health. Thankfully the community garden appeared to have achieved wonders in that respect. She even baked some bread for them for lunch before cooking them all a delicious roast dinner later.

Her friends too had been calling and texting and Molly was thankful for their love and support as well.

But by Monday morning, she couldn't put it off any longer. She had to face the tea garden once more.

'Are you sure?' asked her mum, when Molly told her of her plans for that day.

Molly nodded. 'I've still got twenty-six days left on the licence that the council have given me for this pop-up business. So I'd better try to make a profit whilst I can. I'm just not sure where to start.'

'I find an old-fashioned to-do list often helps,' said her mum. 'I'll be in the back garden here if you need me.'

Rachel headed outside, where she had already begun to work on clearing the borders outside ready for some new plants. Her mum was still battling her low mood but was keeping the fight going so Molly knew that she needed to do the same as well.

Molly headed over to the tea garden, walking slowly as she went. At least it had stopped raining, she thought. For now, anyway. Any kind of rain covering or umbrellas had to be top of her list, she thought.

She brought out her phone and began to make notes on her to-do list.

Then there was the matter of the furniture. Thanks to Logan and her brothers' hard work, she had quite a few chairs that were no longer Playboy bunny decorated. But that still left the problem of a lack of tables. The upturned crates had sort of worked but were a bit small and low for people to use. She had no idea what she could use in their place.

Lastly, there was the matter of staff. This was a little more tricky as she desperately needed someone else to help out without offending Grandma Tilly, Frank or Stanley.

But she would cross that bridge when she came to it.

* * *

Later that afternoon, Molly hesitated before heading into the hub, where she knew Grandma Tilly, Frank and Stanley were having their weekly Monday stint helping out Tom on the newspaper.

Still hovering on the pavement outside, she spotted Olivia, Dodgy Del's niece, heading out of the shop with some milk.

'Hi,' she said, grateful to put off the tricky conversation in the hub for a few minutes longer.

'Oh, hi,' said Olivia.

There was something downtrodden about the young woman, thought Molly. As if she really needed a lucky break or something to get a step up in life.

From what Del had told her, his niece had been having trouble finding a job without any qualifications to her name as she had dropped out of college. Though not through any lack of ability apparently as Del had told her that she was quite bright.

'How's things?' Molly asked. 'Any luck with the job hunting?'

Olivia shook her head.

Then Molly had a brainwave. 'How are you at waitressing?'

Olivia stared at her, seemingly hesitant to speak.

'I need someone to help out at the tea garden,' carried on Molly, pointing up the lane to where it was situated. 'Just taking orders and then making up pots of tea. That kind of thing.'

'I thought it wasn't open any more,' said Olivia, frowning.

'Oh. Well,' said Molly quickly. 'We had a bit of a disaster, to be honest with you. But we'll be back up and running again by this Saturday. I'm not sure how many customers we'll get, but I'll pay you a flat rate. At the very least, we should be open for the rest of the month.'

The silence stretched out.

'I could really do with the help and at least it'll give you some wages for now.'

Olivia looked at her for a second, her face betraying her complete lack of trust, thought Molly.

But Molly was an open book as well and her own desperation shone through as Olivia suddenly nodded her head.

'OK,' she finally said.

'That's great!' replied Molly, a little overenthusiastically. 'I'm so pleased. Is 10 a.m. on Saturday morning OK with you? I'll be in the shop kitchen at the back of the garden.'

'All right,' said Olivia. 'I must go now.'

'See you Saturday!' called out Molly as Olivia rushed away.

Molly stood and nodded to herself. This was good. Or, at least, Olivia couldn't be worse than her current staff.

Talking of which, she couldn't put it off any longer. So she headed into the community hub, where she found Grandma Tilly, Frank and Stanley chatting on the sofa, their work on the newspaper obviously finished for another day.

Lucy looked up from her desk and smiled at Molly. 'Hey,' she said. 'How are you doing today?' she asked.

Molly smiled at her friend. 'OK,' she replied. 'Well, you know, better than Saturday.'

'I think that awful Mavis Turner was overreacting,' said Grandma Tilly, frowning. 'She made a big deal over nothing. I mean, what's a Playboy bunny between friends.'

'You'd have to be really good friends,' muttered Frank, waggling his eyebrows.

Stanley remained quiet but smiled at his friend.

'Anyway, I was thinking that perhaps you might have been a bit weary afterwards,' began Molly. 'You know, with all the rushing about.'

'I certainly slept well that night,' said Frank, nodding.

'Much like Keith over there,' said Stanley, pointing to where the dog was sprawled out in the warm rays of the sun shining through the open door.

'Yes, well,' rushed on Molly, 'I was thinking that perhaps it was all a bit much for you all.'

The silence stretched out uncomfortably and she rushed on to fill it.

'And I just saw Olivia, you know, Del's niece and she really needs a job, you see. So I was thinking that perhaps it might be better if she helped out for the time being.'

'You mean replace us with a younger model,' said Grandma Tilly, frowning.

'Molly would be hard-pushed to replace us with anyone older,' said Stanley in a pointed tone.

'And that family do struggle,' added Frank. 'Plus, it would be nice to have our weekends back, so we can watch the odd cricket match.'

Stanley nodded in agreement.

'I see.' Grandma Tilly pressed her lips together.

The elderly gentlemen seemed happy enough with the changes, but Grandma Tilly was looking positively put out.

'Of course, I'd love for you to carry on helping if it's not too much work for you,' said Molly, desperately.

Grandma Tilly immediately cheered up. 'I'd love to,' she said, breaking into a wide grin.

Frank rolled his eyes, but both he and Stanley remained quiet.

'Well, that would be great,' said Molly.

Hopefully Grandma Tilly and Olivia would work well together and that at least one problem had been resolved that morning. But she was worried that perhaps she had managed to create another one in its place instead.

30

Late on Monday afternoon, Logan threw down his screwdriver in frustration. For some reason, the piece he was working on just wasn't coming together. It was a tall cabinet with many drawers and was a complicated build. He would work it out in time but for now he needed a break.

He wandered over to the large front window and stared out across the river. It was at least drier that day and the clouds had begun to clear. He found that he was enjoying looking out at the view each day. Day by day, he was appreciating living in the country just a little bit more. It seemed to soothe his soul, watching the water and the trees nearby. Even the ducks waddling along the riverbank quietened his mind.

However, even they couldn't quiet his stomach, which grumbled at the lack of lunch that he had forgotten to eat, so he grabbed his front door keys and locked up.

He had started to leave the crutch behind most days as his foot began to heal although he was still walking a lot slower than he was used to, due to the ache inside as the bones mended.

But rather than heading to the Cranbridge Stores, he found his feet turned left and he headed towards the next shop along. He hadn't seen Molly since Sunday morning and was worried that perhaps she was still upset about the disaster on Saturday. However, the front door to her shop was locked and as he peered into the darkness beyond, he couldn't see any lights or signs of movement inside.

What he could hear, however, was the sound of a hammer somewhere close by.

Intrigued, he headed towards the garden, where he found Molly hammering a nail into what looked like a somewhat dilapidated long seat.

'Hey,' said Logan, pushing open the rotten gate to head into the garden. 'What are you up to?'

Molly straightened up and looked around to see who had spoken before breaking into her usual wide smile. 'Oh, hi. I'm making a table,' she told him in a proud tone. 'Or, rather, fixing up an old bench and hoping it will make do as a table.'

'I see,' said Logan, wandering over to look at it. There were a few nails sticking out and it wobbled alarmingly when he touched it.

'So, I've fixed it,' she told him, with a firm nod.

Logan smiled. 'I'm not sure that you have actually,' he told her. 'Is it even strong enough to hold a teapot?'

'It'll be fine,' said Molly. 'I'll show you.'

She leant gently on it, whereby it promptly collapsed underneath her. She dropped to the damp ground with a squeal of surprise.

Logan laughed and held out his hand to help her up.

'I don't understand,' she said, letting go of his hand to brush the grass off her jeans.

'It's rotten wood,' said Logan, lifting up the bench and turning it over to show her. 'See this bit here?' The wood crumbled in his fingers. 'No amount of nails is going to keep this from falling apart.'

Molly frowned. 'Do you think they're all like that?' she asked, gesturing at four benches nearby that he hadn't noticed until that moment.

Logan went over and studied each one carefully. He moved two away from the pile before Molly came to stand next to him. 'Those two will be fine,' he told her. 'The rest will only do for firewood when they're dry.'

'Oh no,' she murmured. 'I was banking on using them for tables. The crates were only supposed to be a temporary option.'

'Could you not buy some?' he said.

She sighed. 'I'd love to, only I'm a little short on funds, what with taking on a new staff member and needing to buy cover for when it rains as well. I was really hoping for some kind of weather-proof tables out here but also rustic, if you know what I mean? That was the vibe I was going for. If anyone ever returns to buy anything, that is.'

Molly was looking downcast suddenly. Almost defeated. Logan found himself desperately thinking of a way to cheer her up.

'I've got some offcuts in the workroom,' he found himself saying. 'I can knock up a few tables out of them, if you'd like.'

She looked amazed as she turned to him with wide eyes. 'That would be incredible, but I can't pay your kind of prices.'

'On the house,' he said, with a shrug. 'Call it a neighbour helping out another neighbour.'

Her eyes immediately filled up with tears. 'Oh, that's so sweet of you. Thank you so much.'

Logan suddenly felt awkward. He had been called many things over the years but sweet wasn't one of them. 'It's not a big deal,' he muttered.

'Of course it is,' she said immediately, her eyes still shiny with tears. 'You're giving me this huge present. I must give you something in return.' She looked around for her bag and brought out the familiar cake tin. ‘Here,’ she said, thrusting the whole thing into his hand. ‘Take it all.’

He lifted the lid and found an enormous layered white and dark chocolate cake inside. It looked utterly delicious.

‘If I eat all that I’ll go into a kind of diabetic coma,’ he told her with a grin.

She rolled her eyes. ‘How else can I thank you for being so generous?’ she said.

There was a moment when they locked eyes and Logan had an unexpected idea pop in his head that he wanted to kiss her. He quickly thrust the cake tin back into her hands and turned away, wincing as his foot protested with the sudden movement.

‘Just leave the tables to me,’ he told her. ‘Otherwise you’ll have a lawsuit on your hands if someone ends up with hot coffee in their lap. I’d better get going.’

‘Logan,’ called out Molly as he left.

But he was too busy retreating from the garden to carry on their conversation. It was fine, he told himself. It wasn’t as if he had anything else to do in the evenings. A few rustic outdoor tables would make a nice change from his normal pieces of furniture. But as he headed back into his workshop and stood staring at the wood pieces that he could use, he wasn’t thinking about designs for the outdoor tables at all. Nor even his rumbling stomach.

To his surprise, he was thinking about kissing Molly and wondering whether it would be as wonderful as he imagined.

31

That evening, Molly arrived home feeling a little defeated.

Despite Logan's kind offer of making her some tables for the tea garden, the other main item on the to-do list was still not completed.

'I just don't know what to do,' she said, as she sat down at the kitchen table with the twins.

Her mum placed a plate of pasta and salad in front of her.

'What's up?' said Adam, reaching out to grab a piece of garlic bread from a plate piled high in the middle of the table.

'I've been looking up the cost of large umbrellas,' she told him. 'You know, for the tea garden so that when it rains all my customers don't need to leave again. But they cost a fortune! Especially as I need so many.'

Adam nodded thoughtfully. 'Well, that sucks,' he said, before taking a bite of the bread.

'Couldn't you use the inside of the shop when it rains?' asked Ben.

Molly shook her head. 'It's only for the next few weeks,' she told him. 'And it's licensed as a tea garden only, not an indoor space, which means I'd have to obtain other licences. And I'm pretty sure Barry would want to charge me for the use as well. You know what he's like. Besides, the décor in there is pretty awful. All yellow and brown walls.'

'I remember when it used to be a decent bakery,' said their mum. 'Such a shame to have only the shop and hub as local businesses now.'

The twins remained quiet, but something must have sunk in as the following evening they bounded into the kitchen as excited as puppies.

'Hey, sis!' said Adam, grinning from ear to ear.

'What's going on?' asked Molly, looking from one excited twin to the other.

'You'll find out,' Adam told her, disappearing off down the hallway.

'Have we got news for you!' said Ben, heading over to the kitchen counter, where some cakes were cooling on a wire rack.

'Don't touch those!' said Molly quickly. 'They're for Amber and Josh to test for the wedding.'

'They're not going to want five different ones,' replied Ben, his hand hovering ever so close to the chocolate cake on the end.

'Here,' said Molly, thrusting a plate of cheddar and apple open top pies into his hand instead. 'Take these. They're still warm from the oven. Eat them all instead. But touch those bigger ones and you'll never eat any of my cakes ever again.'

'OK, OK,' said Ben, hugging the plate of pies to himself as he wandered to the other side of the kitchen. 'But you might want to be nice to me seeing as what we've got for you.'

'You've got a plate of pies and I don't seem to have anything in return as of this moment,' Molly told him with a grin.

'You have now,' said Adam, staggering into the kitchen carrying a large pile of heavy green plastic material. He dropped it onto the floor with an 'ooof' before taking a pie for himself.

'What's all this?' asked their mum.

'Do you remember Chris Stark?' said Ben, between mouthfuls. 'We were at school with him. Anyway, he runs an outdoor trekking company now over in Aldwych. Doing quite well from what he said.'

'So he told us over lunch that he was upgrading their camping equipment,' carried on Adam. 'You know, sheets of tarpaulin that they use for cover when they're going all Bear Grylls out in the wilderness. So we bought them for a knock-off price and there you go.'

'Am I going camping?' asked Molly, a little confused.

Ben laughed and nearly choked on his pie. 'No, sis! They're rectangular so you can tie them over the tables like those fancy sail covers that everyone uses in the summer. They're waterproof, but they'll keep off the sun as well.'

Molly looked at them in amazement before glancing down at the pile of plastic sheets on the floor. They were all different shades of green, but they would definitely work and would even be quite stylish in their own way.

'Oh, that's brilliant!' she told them, racing across the kitchen to give them both a hug.

'Yeah, yeah,' said Ben, giving her a wink. 'We truly are.'

'We've gotta get ready,' said Adam. 'We're going out for a pint tonight with a few mates.'

As they disappeared, Molly looked across at her mum who was smiling.

'Perhaps we did something right after all,' said her mum.

'Perhaps we did,' replied Molly, laughing. 'Oh, if only everything was that easily solved.'

'What do you mean?' asked her mum.

Molly's smile faded. 'Just worrying about all these changes I'm trying to make for the tea garden,' she said. She still had no idea as to whether the tea garden would be a success or another failure on reopening.

'It means this much to you?' asked her mum, sitting down at the table.

Molly nodded. 'It really does, although it's only for this month.'

'I never knew you dreamt about having your own place to run,' said her mum. 'You've never mentioned it before.'

'I don't think I realised it until now,' said Molly.

There was a short silence until her mum spoke. 'I found some tiny terracotta pots whilst I was tidying up the back garden. I've probably got enough to place one on each table if you want. I've got an idea for a tiny flower arrangement for each one that wouldn't need any upkeep. You know, for a bit of extra colour.'

Molly was thrilled. 'That would be great,' said Molly, reaching over to give her mum a hug. 'Thanks.'

It was certainly true that her mum was much more active since becoming involved with the community garden. Each day, the garden was filling up with more and more plants. In addition, to Molly's surprise, their own front garden at home was suddenly looking tidier as her mum had begun to clear that as well.

'I'll plant them up and take them to the tea garden tomorrow,' said her mum.

'Will Geoff be there?' asked Molly casually.

Rachel looked at her daughter. 'I'm not sure,' she said. 'Perhaps. Why?'

'Just asking,' said Molly, with a small smile.

But her mum didn't return the smile, merely shaking her head. 'It's not like that. He's just a friend.'

'Well, it's the first male friend I've ever known you have, so I think it's nice,' said Molly. 'That's all.'

'I don't want to muddle anything up,' carried on her mum. 'I mean, he's a very nice man. Kind and funny too, in his quiet way. It's just, I don't know, it's comfortable.'

'Comfortable?' asked Molly.

'Sometimes it's nice just being friends,' said her mum.

'And sometimes friends can turn into something more,' said Molly.

'Is that what's going to happen with you and Logan?'

Molly gave a start. 'We were talking about you,' she said quickly, feeling the blush spread across her cheeks. 'Logan's been amazing helping out with changing Del's awful chairs and then offering to make me some tables as well. I've told him that I can't possibly pay him.'

Rachel shook her head. 'I don't think he'll want paying,' she said. 'He probably just wants to help you.'

'Not sure why,' said Molly.

Rachel raised her eyebrows and smiled to herself as she got up from the table.

'Let me go check on those pots,' she said, heading into the garden.

Molly watched her go and was left wondering what her mum had been inferring. And whether her own imagination was reading too much into it.

Perhaps he just wanted to be friends. But Molly was starting to hope that maybe they could become something more.

32

Molly smiled to herself as she looked across the tea garden later that week.

Her brothers had certainly outdone themselves. With the help of Pete and Tom, they had fixed up the tarpaulin awnings and now a number of tables were protected, whatever the weather.

Of course, ever since the awnings had been put up, the sun had been shining but she didn't mind. The tea garden was now weather-proof which was one thing ticked off her to-do list.

However, they weren't the only new additions to the garden.

Geoff had fixed a tiered planter up against the far wall which had started to be covered with some hanging pink fuchsias which were cascading down the outside. Also, the Mothers and Toddlers group had finished their latest project. A rather large bug hotel had been placed in a far corner and apparently was already receiving visitors of the insect kind, much to the fascination of the children who checked on its progress daily. Molly was a little less fascinated and hoped that the bugs kept to their side of the garden and didn't venture near to her customers. Or her!

Best of all, whenever Molly arrived at the garden, another

couple of tables had appeared overnight from Logan. It was as if the garden fairies had magically conjured up a new piece of furniture.

Day by day, there were more places for any future customers to eat at. The only thing that was missing was actual customers until she reopened in two days' time, but Molly didn't have time to worry about that for now.

Logan was still refusing any kind of payment for the furniture, so Molly had begun to take him a piece of cake each day as well as lunch.

'You don't need to do this,' he told her as he lifted the lid on a freshly baked cheesy potato tart.

'But I want to,' she replied.

He sighed. 'I should really give this back to you, but my mouth is watering at the sight of that pastry.'

'All home-made,' she told him, in a proud tone.

Her years of experimenting meant that she remained confident in her abilities as a baker despite her serious doubts about her business capabilities.

'Besides,' she carried on. 'What's the harm in paying you back for all those lovely tables?'

He swallowed a piece of tart before giving her a stern look. 'Because life doesn't work that way,' he told her.

'You mean, kindness?' she said, smiling. 'Gratitude? That kind of thing?' She shook her head. Sometimes his inability to see the good in anyone amazed her.

'Everyone's out for something in this world,' he muttered, before finishing off the tart.

'Not me,' said Molly, determined to make him see the good in someone.

'No,' he said, staring at her. 'Not you.'

She shuffled awkwardly under his intense gaze.

'Or your grandad,' she told him. 'Surely we can agree on that?'

He scowled at her but his eyes were twinkling with humour. 'You've made your point.'

She grinned. 'Oh, I'm not nearly done trying to remove those cynical spectacles you insist on wearing.'

'Instead of the rose-tinted ones that you wear all the time,' he told her, balling up the paper napkin and throwing it into the bin.

'If you feel that everyone is awful, why are even bothering to help me?' she asked him, sticking up her chin, ready to take whatever blows would come her way.

But, instead, he surprised her by saying, 'Because you seem to spend your entire life helping everyone else.'

'Not my entire time,' she told him, thinking fast of an example to give him. The trouble was that she came up blank.

He smiled. 'You can't think of a single thing that you've done for yourself recently, can you?' he said.

'I'm still thinking,' she said quickly.

His smile grew wider and her train of thought stopped abruptly.

'You're so much better-looking when you smile,' she said before her brain could stop her.

He stared at her in disbelief whilst her blushes threatened to make her self-combust.

'I didn't mean that,' she said quickly.

He came to stand in front of her. 'Oh, you can't take it back now,' he murmured. 'I have an extremely good memory.'

She sighed heavily. 'Please let's forget this ever happened and let me die of shame.'

He suddenly reached out to take her chin gently in his fingers and lift her face up so she had no option but to look at him.

She was still mortified at blurting out what she had been thinking, for quite some time, actually. But still, that was private and should have remained hidden deep inside.

'If it makes you feel better, I think you're extremely pretty too when you stop worrying and smile instead,' he told her.

She blinked in surprise at his words before continuing to stare up at him. For a second, she couldn't breathe. Logan was staring down at her with something akin to fondness. And something else, deep inside his eyes.

He abruptly let go and she found herself feeling disappointed that they hadn't kissed. He headed over to a nearby worktop and bent down to continue planing a piece of wood.

'Thanks for the lunch,' he said. 'It was delicious, as always.'

Molly picked up her bag and said, 'You're welcome,' before quickly heading out of the shop.

She felt grateful to be able to leave and not make even more of a fool of herself than she felt.

She stood and looked at the river for a moment, watching a dragonfly hover on the surface before flying off downstream. Then she walked back along to her own shop.

But the fresh air did nothing to cool down her still warm cheeks. It was nothing to do with any kind of embarrassment and everything to do with the way that Logan had just looked at her.

Molly was left wondering whether her own longing had been mirrored in his eyes too.

33

There was still so much to do on the watermill. Logan really didn't need to waste any more time, especially as he was still so slow at manoeuvring himself around. His foot had yet to fully mend and he felt frustratingly slow. And yet he couldn't stop himself from pausing to peer out of the window every few moments on Saturday morning, looking out for when Molly arrived.

The reopening of the tea garden was that day and he found himself keen to see her reaction to what he had built for her the previous evening. He just hoped that she didn't mind that he had taken it upon himself to create something else.

Finally, just after 9 o'clock in the morning, he saw Molly go to open the gate into the garden before she gave a start. He waited for a moment, watching her reaction as she looked down at the gate in surprise. Then he heard her soft gasp of amazement.

Smiling to himself, Logan hobbled across the small bridge and along the garden wall. At least he could definitely cope without the wretched crutch now, he thought. He felt better without it. More healthy. Less reliant.

'Good morning,' he said.

Molly jumped and spun around, her eyes still wide. 'Good morning,' she replied, before looking down at the gate once more. 'Was this you?'

Logan followed her gaze. It really wasn't that much of a big deal, he told himself. The rotten gate had looked pretty awful and he had spotted both his grandad and the young children struggling to open and close it during the previous week so he had decided to replace it with a new one that he had spent the last couple of evenings working on.

'You made this new gate?' she asked once more.

Logan shrugged his shoulders. 'It's no big deal,' he told her, trying to sound nonchalant. 'I thought a fresh start deserved a new entrance.'

'I disagree,' she told him, her eyes shining bright. 'It's a very big deal.'

Logan was pleased by her reaction but it was just paying her back for taking care of him when he had hurt his foot. That was all, wasn't it?

'It's all wonderful,' she told him, turning her head to look up at him. 'The tables, the chairs and now the gate. It's just perfect.'

Then, before he even realised what was happening, she lifted her head and kissed him gently on the cheek. Logan felt something akin to shock with the feel of her soft lips on his skin.

'I can't thank you enough,' she murmured, giving him a warm smile.

Then she walked back towards the kitchen, leaving him alone in the garden.

Logan stood there for a moment before he realised that he was holding his breath. Finally he let it out with a long puff of air.

She was just being kind, he knew that. And he had helped her out of a tight spot. There was nothing more to it, was there?

* * *

In the safety of the kitchen, Molly groaned to herself. What had she done? She had kissed Logan! It had been an impulse thing, of course. The new gate was a wonderful surprise, but she didn't know why she had kissed him on the cheek. All she had needed to do was to say thank you, like a normal person.

Now he would think that she was some kind of idiot.

She sighed, and tried to concentrate on getting the food ready for the hopefully busy day ahead.

Meanwhile, Logan was still rooted to the spot. It could have been the warmth from the summer sun grazing his cheek, but he was pretty certain that it was Molly's soft lips that was causing the heat on his skin.

He was still stunned and yet found himself wishing he could return the favour and kiss her back in the very near future. Preferably on those sweet lips which had begun to fill his dreams each night.

34

Molly wrung her hands together and tried to look calm as opposed to reflecting the worry churning inside her.

Perhaps she should have left the tea garden closed and just suggested that they leave the whole area as a community garden. Perhaps she should have given up on the whole idea of a tea garden. Perhaps she shouldn't even have bothered getting out of bed that morning.

'Stop looking worried and smile,' said Belle, coming in through the front of the empty shop. 'It'll be fine.'

'Will it?' asked Molly, with a grimace. 'I'm not so sure.'

Belle put down the box she was carrying and took her friend by the shoulders. 'Breathe, nice and deep,' she told her. 'Of course it'll be fine. I just said so, didn't I?'

Molly sighed and nodded, her head agreeing with her friend even if the rest of her wasn't convinced. 'What's in the box?'

'Gifts from your girl squad, of course,' said Belle, with a grin. 'Lucy and Amber are on their way.'

Molly peered inside the box.

'The bunting is from me,' Belle told her. 'Don't ask me where I got the time, but I figured pretty fabric bunting was the way to go. Amber made the napkin rings and Lucy provided the fairy lights.'

Molly looked at the presents and was pleased. 'Oh, it's all perfect,' she said, with a teary smile before giving Belle a quick hug.

'Of course it is,' replied Belle. 'We've got your back. As always.'

The bunting was in the pastel colours that Molly had been dreaming about, all tiny triangles of pretty floral and striped fabric. The napkin rings were a small circle of silver wire with a different fake flower attached to each. And the fairy lights were a soft white.

'The bunting and the lights are going to look perfect along the garden walls and the edges of the new rain covers,' said Molly.

Belle nodded. 'You'd better show me,' she said.

So Molly took her outside and Belle whistled in appreciation.

'Wow, quite the transformation,' she said.

Molly was pleased that her friend agreed. The whole place looked far better. Each set of chairs now had a round or square table to sit at. There was no deep purple velvet or Playboy bunnies to be seen, thankfully. There was just classic rustic wooden furniture.

In addition, the flowers along the front wall were beginning to come out and provide some much-needed colour. Along one side, Geoff's raised vegetable beds were providing more greenery and interest and apparently the carrots and lettuce would soon be ready to be harvested. On the other, a rambling rose had been trained up the wall and was filling the air with its sweet perfume. On each table, her mum had placed a tiny terracotta pot filled with yet more brightly coloured flowers. It finished off the rustic and yet chic look to the place which, of course, was enhanced by all of Logan's hard work.

'It looks great,' said Amber, coming to stand next to them. She too was carrying a large box.

'Thank you so much for the napkin rings,' replied Molly, giving her arm a squeeze.

'They'll be perfect for each table with those white napkins you have,' said Amber, taking in the garden. 'Wow, I'd heard about the new tables but had no idea how much new furniture Logan had actually made.'

'Well, everyone's helped out,' replied Molly quickly.

'Hi, what did I miss?' asked Lucy, coming to stand with them with Keith the dog alongside her.

'Just Molly telling us how much everyone helped out with the garden, not just Logan,' said Belle, with a grin.

'Not sure about that.' Lucy laughed. 'I mean, I love Tom, but he's no handyman. Apparently he helped Logan fix the new gate last night. He was covered in splinters and cuts afterwards!'

'You need to get yourself a real man,' said Belle, her eyes gleaming. 'My Pete is very handy, especially in the bedroom.'

'And that's about as much as I need to know about my future brother-in-law,' Amber told her with a shudder. 'Come on, let's get all this set up before anyone comes.'

Molly was grateful for their support, but it wasn't just her friends who showed up that morning.

A while later, Geoff arrived with a large box of hanging baskets that were needing to be filled.

'I had some old hanging baskets in the shed,' he told Molly. 'I thought they could be today's project for my little team.'

The community garden had begun to build up quite a following in the community and soon about half a dozen helpers would arrive. Her mum had told Molly that a few of the newcomers were struggling with either bereavement or stress. Another was recovering from illness.

'But just focusing on planting up a few things and tending for them makes a huge difference,' her mum had said before adding, 'And to me too, I think.'

So Molly was smiling to herself as she walked back towards the kitchen.

'What's going on over there?' asked Belle.

'Geoff's found some old hanging baskets that he and the others are going to plant up today,' said Molly.

'Seems more like a man happier talking to his plants than to other people,' whispered Lucy.

'He's certainly a little quiet,' agreed Amber.

But Molly wasn't so sure. There was a quiet humour about Geoff and he certainly was more talkative whenever her mum appeared.

'Just like our new neighbour,' said Lucy, nodding at the watermill. 'He's still keeping himself to himself, from what I hear.'

Molly found herself shaking her head. 'Actually, Logan is very kind. Look how generous he's been with the furniture,' she said, waving her arm around the garden. 'And yes, he can be a little sharp sometimes, but he can be really funny as well.'

Her three friends looked at her with surprised smiles on their faces.

'It's not like that,' Molly told them all quickly before walking away.

And it really wasn't, she told herself. Although she could still feel the graze of his stubble on her lips when she had kissed him on the cheek.

She glanced over at the new furniture through the open doorway before shaking her head at herself and preparing the trays of drinks.

35

Molly was grateful that her friends remained to help out at the tea garden for the next couple of hours. Especially as Olivia turned up well after the agreed ten o'clock start time. It wasn't the best of beginnings for her new employee, thought Molly.

But she didn't say anything to Olivia when she arrived with an apology. As usual, Molly just smiled and said, 'It doesn't matter.'

Olivia nodded but didn't reply.

So Molly carried on to fill the silence. 'Why don't you dump your bag in the kitchen with mine and grab yourself a mug of coffee, if you'd like? Then I'll show you the ropes.'

'OK.'

As Olivia headed off, Amber and Grandma Tilly came up to Molly.

'Was she late? Not a great start to working for you, is it?' said Grandma Tilly frowning.

'She'd already warned me. It must have slipped my mind, with everything being so busy,' lied Molly.

'Like mother like daughter,' murmured Grandma Tilly, shaking her head.

'It's not like that, I'm sure,' Molly told her.

'What are you talking about?' asked Amber.

She and Lucy had only lived in the village for just over a year and so hadn't grown up and gone to the local school like Molly and Belle.

'Michelle Rivers,' said Grandma Tilly with a sigh. 'She's been trouble ever since high school. She never struck me as the parenting type.'

'She wasn't so bad.' Molly thought back to Olivia's bruised expression.

'Hopefully her daughter won't cause you any trouble then,' said Amber, frowning.

'She'll be fine,' replied Molly, ever optimistic. 'I think she was just grateful to get out of the house, to be honest.'

'I guess you'll find out sooner or later,' said Grandma Tilly, with a shake of her head.

'Well, it doesn't matter,' said Molly. 'It's not as if we're particularly overrun with customers so far, is it?'

She looked around and noting how few customers were there, gave a little sigh.

'They'll come,' said Amber, with a firm nod. 'You just wait and see. Besides, I hear Lucy's outdone herself putting the word out on every local social media account. I'm sure someone will have read about it.'

As it turned out, and to Molly's delight, Amber was right. Slowly but surely customers began to arrive throughout the morning including quite a few from the Mothers and Toddlers group who had heard all about the place whilst helping out in the community garden. Perhaps the change in weather helped, thought Molly as she relished the warm June sunshine on her skin.

There weren't hordes of people coming in, but luckily it was enough for her to teach Olivia how to serve people.

The cakes continued to be raved about from the customers, as well as the choice of quiches, savoury scones and biscuits.

'I was glad to see that you made my favourite,' said Stanley, when she settled the tray of tea and ginger snaps in front of him.

'I've dipped them in dark chocolate as well,' said Molly, placing the plate on the table. 'For extra antioxidants, of course.'

'Excellent,' beamed Stanley. 'What a splendid idea. I'm not sure my GP will agree though.'

'How's Logan getting on?' asked Molly, glancing over to where the door into the windmill was open.

'I think the help he has received so far from our friends has certainly helped in more ways than I had hoped for,' said Stanley.

'Good,' replied Molly. 'I'm glad for him.'

'I must say, the community garden is looking marvellous too,' said Stanley, nodding at the wall, where a few more flowers had begun to appear.

'Isn't it great?' said Molly. 'I've already seen a couple of butterflies this morning.'

She excused herself as she spotted her brothers walking across the tea garden.

'Hello,' she said to them. 'What are you doing here?'

'We heard there was free cake,' said Ben, with a grin.

Molly laughed. 'How do you expect me to make any profits if you eat all my food for free?'

'I've never figured you for a hard-nosed businesswoman, sis,' said Ben. 'There's hope for you yet.'

Both Molly and Ben looked over at their brother as Adam gave a start.

Molly followed his gaze across the tea garden. 'That's Olivia, my staff,' she told them.

'Very pretty,' said Ben, nodding his approval. 'Is she single?'

Adam rolled his eyes. 'I'm sure she doesn't want to be added to your ever-growing list of ex-girlfriends,' he told him.

'Probably not,' replied Ben with a grin.

'You should go over and introduce yourself,' said Molly, looking at Adam who couldn't seem to tear his gaze away from Olivia.

Her brother shrugged his shoulders. 'I'm sure she's busy,' he replied, shuffling from foot to foot.

'So maybe an offer to help would be a good start,' Molly told him softly.

Adam hesitated before walking across the garden away from them and towards the kitchen, picking up speed as he went.

Molly and Ben looked at each other with a knowing smile, with Molly thinking that Olivia could more than handle her younger brother.

She then found herself wondering whether anyone would ever want to cross the tea garden for her that quickly.

With a quick glance over to the watermill, she swiftly turned around and headed into the kitchen, hoping that her warm cheeks were only because of the hot weather.

36

From what his grandad had told Logan, the reopening of the tea garden had gone well.

'It perhaps wasn't as busy as it could have been,' said Stanley with a small frown. 'But I'm sure more customers will come in time.'

Logan had agreed with his grandad but wasn't quite sure where any new customers were going to come from.

He locked up the door to the watermill and headed towards his workshop. He looked in at the tea garden, but it too had been closed up. Molly was nowhere to be seen and he found that he was a bit sad about that as he would have liked to have heard her version of the day. He made a note to find time to visit her the following day.

He had had another long day working on the watermill and, with everyone busy, most of the work had fallen to him. Not that he minded, but his foot was aching somewhat.

So he carried on along Riverside Lane. He had to admit that he was feeling better these days. It felt good to give something back to others. He had lost count of the number of villagers who had stopped him to say how pleased and excited they were about the mill. But it was also having an effect on his own mental well-being. His grandad had been right. He suddenly felt valued again. They needed him and, in a way, he was beginning to need them as well.

He was slowly starting to feel as if he belonged. He had lost his sense of a community somewhere along the way. It was mainly his ex-wife's fault, but he had to admit that he had bought into that life-style as well. But here in Cranbridge, despite it being a simpler life, he felt a little less lonely than he had done previously.

Spending time by the river and in the gorgeous landscape helped as well. Being closer to nature was doing him the power of good. Sometimes he would spend his coffee break looking at the reflections in the water, the wildlife, the way the long branches of the willow trees trailed on the water surface. Now he had the time to pause and become aware of everything around him, from the nature to other people.

And Molly too was having an effect on him. Perhaps it was something in all that cake, but he felt it was more than that. Her charm and her smile were hard to ignore. Her enthusiasm too. She felt like a breath of fresh air to him. But just as a friend, that was all, he reminded himself.

The thought of an empty apartment wasn't tempting that evening so Logan found himself continuing to hobble along the road and then over the river to the Black Swan Inn.

He pushed the door and found a wall of conversation and laughter inside. As usual, the inn was busy, with customers all wanting the quality food. But Logan found that he was drawn to the stools at the bar, where Dodgy Del and Tom were chatting. Keith the dog was sprawled out on the floor between them.

'Hey,' he announced to the crowd. 'Everyone good for a pint?'

'Yes, thanks. You've just missed a round, luckily for you,' replied

Tom, with a smile. 'But take a seat. I can't stay too long as it's date night.'

'That makes you the lucky so-and-so then,' said Del, with a huff. 'Can't remember the last date I went out on.'

'I'm sure it's still crystal clear in the memory of the poor lady you took out though,' murmured Tom.

Logan greeted Pete and ordered his pint at the bar, as well as a plate of burger and chips to eat.

'I hear the tea garden reopening went well,' said Logan.

Tom nodded. 'A bit quiet, from the sounds of it. But it's a start.'

'What's that?' asked Del. 'Too quiet? You mean it needs some music?'

'Not your singing if that's what you mean,' said Tom, laughing, before looking more serious. 'No, unfortunately, more customers is what's required. Otherwise the business won't last the week, let alone the month.'

'Well, that's not on,' said Del, frowning. 'Not after I've spent so much time on that community garden.'

'Don't you mean your precious hops?' said Tom.

'It's the biggest of the bunch,' replied Del, looking proud of himself despite the others all rolling their eyes. 'So you're going to have to come up with a decent brewer for Del's Delicious Draft when those hops are ready later on in the summer.'

Pete nodded. 'Don't worry, I'm on it.'

'But Molly still needs customers.' Del frowned to himself in thought. 'We'll have to see what we can do about that.'

'I think Logan's done as much as he can with all that furniture,' said Tom, clapping him on the shoulder as he slid off his stool. 'Right, everyone, have a good evening.'

'The man's right,' said Del, nodding as Tom headed off, taking Keith the dog with him. 'You've made Molly's year with all that new stuff you've given her.'

'It was nothing,' replied Logan quickly.

At that moment, he caught Belle watching him and whilst Pete and Del were talking about the latest cricket scores, she leant forward over the bar.

'It's nice the way you and Molly are getting on,' she said softly so that only he could hear. 'But just so you know, you hurt her and I will make you pay ten times over.'

Logan looked at her in surprise. 'I would never hurt her.'

'Good.' Belle sighed, relaxing a bit. 'It's just that I don't think she'll ever realise just how beautiful she is on the inside as well as the outside. She doesn't rate herself and it's up to her friends to protect her.'

As she walked away, she was replaced by Pete.

'So your girlfriend can be a bit, er, fierce, can't she?' Logan said.

Pete laughed. 'Belle? Only a bit,' he replied. 'Put the frighteners on you, did she? Don't take it personally. She means well.' He suddenly looked thoughtful. 'Who was she protecting?'

'I guess she was protecting Molly, although there's really no need,' Logan added quickly.

'Don't worry about it,' said Pete with a shrug. 'I mean, Belle's like a mama bear protecting her young. But with me she's soft and...' His voice trailed off as his eyes held some secret between them.

'Anyway, I won't take advantage of her,' said Logan. 'Molly, I mean.'

'Glad to hear it,' said Pete, with a nod. 'Molly's like our little sister. Everyone in the whole village protects her. She's so sweet.'

But Logan thought she was stronger than they realised. And sexy too.

He gave a start. Where had that thought come from?

He shook his head to try to clear his racing thoughts. It was Molly. He respected her far too much to do anything about it. Of course, when she was concentrating and she bit her lip without realising, he couldn't help but stare. But that was just because she was so attractive, right?

Besides, that way lay only heartache and he would never fall for anyone ever again.

37

It had been a far better opening of the tea garden than Molly had hoped for, especially compared to the previous Saturday. Most of the villagers had come along and filled the garden with their conversation and laughter.

By Sunday, however, business had slowed considerably.

'The trouble is that not many people pass through our lovely village,' said Stanley, giving her a sympathetic smile as he cut the dead flower heads off the rambling rose that trailed up the wall behind them.

Molly nodded. 'I know. I was just hoping that it would be a tad busier than this, to be honest.'

She looked around the tables and chairs, of which not quite a quarter were filled with customers. Everyone was telling her how delicious the food was and that the setting was the prettiest they had ever seen. And yet, without any new customers discovering Cranbridge, she didn't have a hope of any passing trade.

She thought back to her visit to Willow Tree Hall and how busy it had been. But that was a stately home where many events were now staged. Cranbridge Stores and the Black Swan Inn had gained in popularity over the past few months, but any trade at the pub was unlikely to want tea and cake after their delicious Sunday roast.

'Morning all,' said Dodgy Del, coming into the garden. 'I'm here to check on my hops plant.'

'Have you tried talking to it?' suggested Stanley. 'I always find that helps with my tomatoes.'

'Good tip,' replied Del, with a grin. 'Especially if it makes a few more pints of Del's Delicious Draft.'

'Interesting name,' murmured Stanley.

Del looked around. 'Not many here yet, are there?' he said.

Molly shook her head. 'No,' she replied with a heavy sigh.

'Good morning,' said Glenda, the vicar, heading towards them with her Labrador, Noah. 'I do hope I'm not too early, but after my lengthy sermon this morning a coffee and a slice of poppy seed loaf would perk me right up.'

'And what about Noah?' asked Molly, reaching down to stroke the dog's furry head.

'Oh, he can share the cake with me, otherwise it'll go straight to my hips,' replied Glenda, with a wide smile. 'This is smashing,' she carried on, looking around. 'How much you've achieved, my dear.'

'Thank you,' said Molly. 'It's just a shame that we don't get much passing trade.'

Glenda frowned in thought. 'Well, I understand. We don't get a whole load through at St Barnabus's. Although there's always the ramblers walking past.'

Del brightened up. 'Oh yeah, the old lavender field at the back, I'd forgotten,' he said.

Glenda nodded sadly. 'It's pretty overgrown these days,' she said. 'But people seem to like the walk from Cranfield and the old railway station across the fields to see the river here. I must say, Cranbridge is looking a lot more prosperous than the other hamlets these days.'

'You could always put a sign up on the church noticeboard,' suggested Del. 'If the vicar don't mind, that is.'

'Splendid idea,' said Glenda. She looked enquiringly across at Olivia as she came out to serve another table. 'I see young Olivia is giving you a hand.'

'Do you know her?' asked Molly.

'Only her mother,' said Glenda, with a sad shake of her head.

'Didn't think my sister was the church-going type, to be honest, vicar,' said Del, rolling his eyes.

Glenda smiled sadly at him. 'She's not,' she replied. 'I tried to recruit her for the new mums' group but she didn't seem interested.'

'Michelle has never been interested in anyone but herself,' muttered Del.

Molly looked at him with raised eyebrows.

He shrugged. 'Can't choose your family,' he muttered.

'Talking of which,' added Stanley in a knowing tone.

Molly looked up to see Adam walking towards them.

'What are you doing here?' she asked.

'Thought I'd give you a hand if you needed it,' he said.

'Thanks, but I think we've got everything under control,' Molly told him.

But Adam was looking across at Olivia and not really listening. 'Uh-huh,' he replied before drifting away towards the kitchen.

'Ah, young love, ain't it grand?' said Del, grinning. 'Right, I'd best be off. There's a Sunday roast with my name on it in the pub.'

As Del wandered away, Molly looked across to where her brother had disappeared inside the kitchen. 'I'd better make sure he's not eating all the profit,' she said. 'I'll get your coffee and cake,' she told Glenda, before leaving the vicar with Stanley chatting.

But as she headed into the kitchen, Adam jumped guiltily.

'What are you doing?' asked Molly. After all, he was on his own as Olivia was serving another customer.

'Nothing, sis,' said Adam. 'You're always so suspicious,' he added with a cheeky grin.

But Molly didn't completely return it, thinking that something was possibly up with her brother. And hoping too that Adam didn't scare off her only decent member of staff as well.

38

Logan looked up at the inside of the watermill with a critical eye. But, for once, the feeling of doom didn't come over him. Everything was clean and, more importantly, connected once more. There was real hope that it might just work.

He was feeling hopeful. Thanks to the efforts of his new friends in the village, the wheel was clear of debris and the rusty pipes were now mended. It just needed testing.

But this was where Logan felt himself hesitate. The failure would be real if he couldn't get it to work. And yet, he knew he had to try for his grandfather. However if he failed to get it working, his grandad would never achieve his dream of hearing the water move over the wheel once more.

Logan headed out to look at the mill but was somewhat distracted by the sheer amount of noise outside. So unexpected was it in sleepy Cranbridge that he wandered around behind Riverside Lane to see what was occurring.

He hadn't expected to see a large somewhat dilapidated minibus in the lane, but there it was in front of him. As well as fifteen or so pensioners clambering down the steps and outside into the lane.

'Sorry about all this,' came a loud voice which sounded like Dodgy Del's from the other side of the vehicle.

'Hey, Del,' said Logan, heading towards where he was crouched in front of one of the wheels. 'What's up?'

'Puncture,' Del told him, almost shouting. 'It's gonna need changing.'

Logan peered down at the wheel which didn't look particularly deflated. 'Are you sure?' he asked, pressing against the rubber which felt firm under his fingers.

Del gave him a fierce look. 'Cool it,' he muttered under his breath. 'It needs fixing, OK?' He cleared his throat before standing up. 'Listen, ladies and gents. I'll have this fixed in a jiffy. There's a smashing tea room just opened around the corner. Why don't you take five in there? Logan here will show you the way.'

So Logan found himself leading a group of elderly ladies and gentlemen down the narrow passageway and around the side of the tea garden.

'Oh, how lovely,' said one of the ladies. 'I could just do with a cuppa.'

Molly looked up from the order she was taking at Logan in surprise. 'Hello,' she said, greeting the group. 'What's all this?'

'Del's minibus has a puncture,' Logan told her. 'It's parked up just around the corner in the lane. He suggested these ladies and gentlemen take respite here with you.'

'Of course,' said Molly, ever congenial and smiling at her new customers. 'Let's get you all seated.'

Whilst she settled the pensioners in their seats and took their orders, Logan headed back to where Del was now leaning against the engine, smoking a cigarette. He was taking a remarkably relaxed attitude to tyre changing, thought Logan.

'What's going on?' he asked.

Del looked around him. 'Are you on your own?' he asked.

Logan nodded. 'Yup. The whole party are enjoying Molly's delicious cakes.'

Del sagged in relief. 'That's good,' he said, nodding.

At that moment, Molly appeared around the corner. 'Everyone's settled in. What's happened with the minibus?' she asked.

'Absolutely nothing,' Del whispered and gave her a large wink.

Molly looked confused. 'What do you mean?'

Del gave her a sheepish smile. 'I figured that I owed you for the whole Playboy chairs thing last weekend,' he told her. 'Felt a bit bad for setting you up like that. And that woman shouting at you was awful. Anyway, thought if I got you a few new customers you might find it in your heart to forgive me.'

Molly looked at him in delighted surprise. 'Oh, Del,' she said, with a soft sigh. 'I knew that you meant well. It wasn't your fault.'

'Well,' began Logan. 'It was pretty much his fault.'

'Well, yes,' Molly said quickly, dismissing him with a wave of her hand. 'But his heart's in the right place.'

She leant forward and gave Del a soft kiss on the cheek before muttering her thanks once more and disappearing around the corner back into the tea garden.

Del looked delighted. 'I must say, this day's perking right up,' he said, with a grin. 'Figure I'll leave them ladies and gents for about half an hour or so and then we'll be on our way.' He looked at Logan for a moment. 'You don't mind, do you?'

Logan gave a start of surprise. 'About what?'

'About Molly giving me a kiss,' Del told him. 'We're just old friends, that's all. Think I'll go to the shop and grab an ice cream. Weather's turned that much warmer, thank goodness.'

And with that, Del wandered off up the lane, whistling tunelessly as he went.

Meanwhile, Logan was left standing on his own next to the minibus, still mulling over what Del had just said.

Mind? Why would he mind about Molly kissing Del on the cheek? After all, like Del had said, they were just friends. Friends like Molly and Logan, in fact.

The trouble was, as he walked slowly back to the watermill, he found that he minded about the kiss very much. And he had no idea what to do about it.

Because he had already decided not to fall for anyone ever again. And he wasn't about to break his own promise, was he? But for the first time in a long time, he found that he wasn't so sure any more.

39

'So how's the new staff working out?' asked Logan on Saturday morning as he leant against the door frame of the kitchen of the tea garden.

He popped by most mornings. Molly was now so busy that she didn't have time to visit his workshop each morning so was pleased that he would come and find her instead to chat.

She turned to look at him, surprised that he had noticed that Olivia was now working at the tea garden. She figured he mostly stayed within his own world.

'I need her now more than ever as we're getting busier and busier,' she told him, with a smile. 'All thanks to Dodgy Del, although don't tell him that. Turns out one of his minibus ladies is with some knitting circle to whom she raved about the tea garden and now the word is out.'

'That's good,' said Logan. 'Word of mouth is always important.'

Molly nodded. 'Everyone seems to be interested in the idea of a community garden as well. To be honest, I'm just grateful for the customers,' she told him.

Business had certainly picked up, she thought. There were

hardly any moments during the day where she could kick back and enjoy a leisurely cup of tea. Now it was snatched minutes between customers. But she knew it was only for another couple of weeks and the thought saddened her.

'So who is she?' asked Logan, looking out to where Olivia was tidying up the chairs ready for the first customers.

She had been late again that morning, much to Molly's dismay.

'Olivia,' Molly told him softly so they weren't overheard. 'She's Dodgy Del's niece. Had a few problems at home, so I think she's just grateful for the job.'

'Just keep an eye on the till,' said Logan, frowning.

Molly laughed. 'She's not like that,' she told him. 'I mean, Del's family have their problems, but none of them are thieves.'

'Nobody is like that until you realise one day that everyone is the same and out for what they can get.'

Molly was startled by the fierce tone in his voice. 'You don't trust anyone, do you?' she asked.

He shrugged his shoulders. 'I find it makes things easier these days.'

'Do you trust me?' she asked eventually, finding herself wanting to know the answer more than anything.

He looked at her. 'Actually,' he said, a smile playing on the corners of his mouth. 'You're one of the few people that I do trust.'

'Why?' she asked.

He laughed. 'You're an open book,' he told her. 'You hide nothing from anyone and therefore I know everything about you.'

Molly felt a little upset at this. 'I don't think I'm exactly like that,' she told him.

He shook his head. 'Don't be upset,' he replied. 'In actual fact, I'm almost a little jealous of you.'

Molly was amazed. 'Why on earth would you be jealous of me?' she said.

'Because your friendliness and openness with people comes so naturally to you,' he told her.

'Maybe if you were more friendly more often then it wouldn't be so hard for you either,' she replied.

'Maybe,' he said, his face softening.

He was a little softer these days, she realised. He smiled a little bit more.

'But I hear you're mixing more and more with the guys,' she told him. 'I'm pleased that you're fitting in.'

'Just for now,' he replied. 'They're good company whilst I'm here for the summer.'

She nodded, feeling a stab of disappointment inside. It looked as if everything was going to change after the summer and not necessarily for the better. She would miss him if he left. *When* he left, she reminded herself.

So, for now, she would enjoy their burgeoning friendship, despite his suspicious nature. What was wrong with trusting everyone anyway?

But later on, once the day was over and she was on her own, she realised that she wasn't so sure.

She looked down at her paperwork once more and added up the receipts for the fourth time. The credit card payments were correct as they were all via the machine anyway. But the cash in her little money box wasn't adding up properly.

Were her sums right? She went through the receipts and was certain. After all, if someone had written down the order wrong, then it would be roughly near enough. But the till was showing £20 less than the figures suggested.

Was it her? But Molly knew deep down in her heart that it wasn't. She had made sure every order was right and that every payment was double-checked.

She thought about Olivia. Perhaps she had just written down an order incorrectly. Or perhaps even forgotten one. But that would have meant more money than not enough.

Perhaps a customer hadn't paid?

Yes, Molly decided. That was perfectly understandable. People sometimes forgot to pay. That was it. That was the answer.

The trouble was, Molly didn't quite believe it.

She felt a cold chill. Somebody was stealing money from the till. Everyone from the community garden was invited into the kitchen at various times to make themselves a cup of tea. It was an open house. But mostly it was only her mum, Geoff, Stanley and Frank. And, of course, there was Olivia, but Molly dismissed that idea almost immediately as it didn't bear thinking about.

Whatever and whoever it was, Logan was right. You really couldn't trust people.

Molly gulped back the tears. Someone she knew was stealing from her and she felt absolutely wretched.

40

The light was fading but Logan wanted to get one more spoke fixed into the wheel of the watermill before he finished for the day so he stood in the cool water of the river trying to manoeuvre it into position.

He was tired but feeling satisfied with his work. Something would have to give regarding the furniture making, he was beginning to realise. He loved working with the wood, but somewhere along the way he had lost his love for the elaborate pieces that his high-end clientele demanded. In a way, he had enjoyed creating the rustic tables for the tea garden far more. There was a sense of satisfaction in helping others, he was finding. It wasn't just about making money any more. And when had it begun to be about money anyway? That wasn't how he had started out his business. He had become a victim of his own success, he felt. And he wasn't sure how it could change going forward but he knew that he wanted it to.

He focused back on the wheel and was just edging the new piece into position when he heard footsteps behind him.

He glanced over his shoulder at the riverbank and was surprised to see Molly stomping towards him, looking extremely angry.

'Hey,' he said, looking up at her, astonished. 'What on earth's the matter?'

'You were right,' she told him, crashing to a halt at the edge and crossing her arms in front of her chest.

'About what?' he asked, aghast at her obvious rage.

'About all of it!' she almost shouted in reply before beginning to pace up and down on the riverbank. 'What was I thinking? Trusting people! Strangers!'

Logan pulled out the plank of wood and waded over towards the riverbank. He had never heard Molly sound like this before. And it worried him.

'So, yes you were right,' she carried on. He tried not to stare at her long legs, bare and golden in the dusk as she strode back and forth along the grass in front of him. 'Of course people shouldn't be trusted. People are mean and horrid and I should just hold everyone at arm's length, like you.'

Logan felt saddened by what he was hearing. 'No,' he told her fiercely, standing in front of her, still waist-deep in water. 'That's my point of view. Not yours. You're trusting and good. Nothing like me.'

'Yes, and look where it's got me!' she told him, stopping at the end of the bank. 'You were right. People take advantage of me all the time. I don't say no and they all take, take, take. Well, I'm sick of it. I'm so angry, I could scream!'

Logan looked up and down and, seeing that nobody was nearby, said, 'Go on then. Go for it.'

Molly hesitated for a moment before coming to some kind of inner decision. 'Aaah!' she shouted. But it wasn't really a big hearty scream.

'That was pretty pathetic,' said Logan, trying not to smile. 'I don't think you even disturbed the ducks over there.'

She glared at him, even though there was now a hint of humour deep in her blue eyes.

'Go on,' he told her. 'Put a bit of oomph behind it.'

So she began to wave her arms around like windmills as if firing up her inner anger. However, before she could make any sound at all, the momentum of her arms made her trainers slip on the damp grass and Logan watched as Molly fell into the water.

He couldn't help but laugh in surprise.

Molly surfaced quickly and, spluttering, stood up in the waist-deep water next to him. 'What the...' she said, shaking her body free of the many droplets of water. 'Well, that's made my bad day a hundred times worse.'

He waded over to the riverbank where he hoisted himself out of the water. He then held out his hands for Molly to take and pulled her out as well, grateful that his foot had healed significantly well for him to do this.

'Thanks,' she muttered, flopping down onto the grass.

Logan sat down next to her. 'What's going on?' he asked gently. 'Why is everything suddenly so bad?'

'Someone's stealing from the cash till in the tea room,' she told him with a heavy sigh.

Logan was shocked. 'Are you sure?' he asked.

She nodded in reply.

'Who?' he asked.

She shrugged her shoulders. 'I have absolutely no idea,' she told him. 'The kitchen door is always open. It could be anyone.'

Logan dragged a hand through his hair. 'Well, maybe not anyone,' he said. 'I mean, I'm pretty certain Grandad wouldn't do that.'

'Yeah, I agree with you on that one,' said Molly. 'Which leaves absolutely everyone else.'

Logan felt she looked and sounded even worse than before. But it wasn't because she was wet. It was because she seemed thoroughly beaten and defeated.

'OK, so someone has been tempted by the ready availability of the money,' he said, thinking out loud. 'How much are we talking about?'

'Twenty pounds or so,' she replied.

'So it's someone in need,' he carried on. 'There's obviously a reason. Or, at least, I hope there is. My suggestion is to keep the money on you in some kind of belt so that it's safe and the temptation is thus removed.'

She nodded but stayed quiet, still downcast.

'You'll bounce back,' he told her. 'Because you're a good person. Deep down, I mean. Not like me.'

'That's rubbish,' she said quickly. 'You put yourself down, but you've helped me every step of the way.'

'Well, that's because I like you,' he replied and was thankful to see a small smile play on her lips. 'Be grateful,' he told her. 'It doesn't happen very often. Mostly I find people pretty annoying.'

Her smile grew wider. 'Are you saying you don't find me annoying? I thought I was too happy and cheerful all the time.'

'Yeah, but it turns out that when you're not, I kind of miss it.' A droplet of water hung to her thick eyelashes before it dripped down her cheek. He reached out to brush it away and felt his breath catch as he touched her soft skin. 'I really miss it.'

'You're always so tough-talking,' she told him, taking his hand and holding it in hers against her cheek.

Tough? Right at that moment, he felt as stable as jelly. He couldn't look away even if he had wanted to.

He wasn't sure if he had just made things ten times worse, but only for himself. He had wanted to protect Molly from herself as she was so sweet and trusting. But it turned out that the one he should have been protecting was himself. Because he was beginning to fall for Molly and was completely floored by the thought of it.

41

Molly felt herself shiver and it had nothing to do with the fact that she was soaked right through. It was the fact that Logan was holding her cheek with his hand. And that she had just covered his hand with hers.

She could hardly breathe. She had been so angry about the theft from the till. So cross about being taken advantage of. And then she had fallen in the river, for goodness' sakes! In front of Logan, of all people.

But somehow they had ended up on the riverbank and were now staring into each other's eyes. And she couldn't look away if she tried.

Logan suddenly cleared his throat and broke the spell, causing Molly to remove her hand. The heat of his skin still warmed hers even though his hand was no longer there.

'I don't suppose as you're already wet that you wouldn't mind helping me with the last spoke on the waterwheel, would you?' he asked after a short silence.

'Of course,' stammered Molly, still trying to make sense of what had happened.

She stood up and followed him back into the water. If anything, it seemed even colder now, despite the warmth of the evening. The sun was slowly sinking, hidden by the taller trees on the other side of the river, so she and Logan were in the shade as he showed her what he needed help with.

'If you can just hold it steady,' he said, reaching inside to the middle of the wheel. 'I should be able to fix it on.'

Molly stood as still as she could, which was saying something as the water was gently buffeting her as it slowly swept past on its way down the river. The goosebumps on her arms were growing larger in the cool shade, but she didn't mind.

Logan was standing very close as he fixed the spoke with his screwdriver. So close, in fact, that she could smell his citrus aftershave, which was making her senses reel. That and the fact that his T-shirt was also wet and clinging to every muscle.

This was ridiculous, she reminded herself. Logan was just a friend. A good friend, in fact, given the amount of listening to her woes that he had ended up doing. So it was good for her to be helping him out for a change, she decided. It was time to be giving something back.

The splosh of a fish leaping out of the river brought her to her senses as the ripples spread out across the water as it disappeared back under the surface.

Finally Logan stepped back to stand next to Molly as they both looked at the wheel.

'Well, I think it's done,' he said, sounding a little unsure.

'That's great,' said Molly. 'So what happens now?'

He gave her a hesitant smile. 'Only one way to find out, I suppose.'

She watched as he reached forward and seemed to remove some kind of heavy block from behind the wheel before swiftly stepping backwards and motioning for Molly to do the same.

'Can't be too careful,' he told her as they clambered back onto the bank.

But as they turned around to look at the wheel, she heard Logan take a deep intake of breath.

'It's turning,' he said, sounding incredulous.

Molly nodded, also somewhat dumbstruck. She had never seen the wheel turn before in her whole life of living in Cranbridge. The noise of the whooshing water as the wheel rotated was a whole new sound to her. It was relaxing and mesmerising as well.

'It's marvellous,' she told him, smiling.

But Logan was still looking somewhat dumbstruck. Finally, he turned to face her.

'It works!' he said, grinning.

She nodded at him. 'It does,' she replied, returning the smile.

'It actually works!' he said, even louder.

Then suddenly he was picking her up and twirling her around in his arms. Molly laughed as he whirled her around and around, repeating, 'It works! It works! At last!' Finally he stopped and put her down, saying, 'I don't believe it. After all this time.'

Molly was feeling slightly dazed as he was still holding her close in his arms.

She couldn't help but smile up at him. He was so excited, so pleased with himself. And she knew that it was for Stanley as well. He had never looked happier, in fact. Which, in turn, made her happier.

With a pang, she realised that she had to admit to herself that she cared for him. That she loved to see him so happy. And how much she had enjoyed being in his arms. She had a hopeless crush on Logan. But it would never be reciprocated, of course.

She automatically rubbed her arms, but it wasn't the cold that had given her goosebumps. It was being in his arms. She wanted anything to prolong spending time with him.

He seemed to blink back to life as he held her close before looking down at her.

'Let's celebrate,' he said suddenly, still smiling down at her.

'OK,' she replied, bemused. 'How?'

'Come on,' he said. 'I'll take you to dinner at the Black Swan.'

She hesitated and was surprised to see his face fall, as if he were upset that she might not want to go with him.

'Like this?' she said, glancing down at her sodden clothes.

'Ah. Perhaps not,' he replied.

She felt bitterly disappointed. What an idiot, she was. By not keeping quiet, she had ruined her chances of spending the evening with him.

But as she began to turn away she heard him say, 'I'll meet you outside the inn in half an hour, shall I?'

She spun back around and felt the thrill go through her as she nodded. 'OK,' she told him before rushing off to get showered and changed.

42

Molly found herself dithering over what to wear for her date with Logan at the pub. Except it wasn't a date, she reminded herself. She had to stop thinking like that. She was just meeting a friend. A handsome, tall, muscular friend whose arms she had very much enjoyed being swept up in only a short time ago.

She rolled her eyes at herself in the mirror as she applied some mascara. This was ridiculous. It was just Logan.

The trouble was, she wouldn't think of him as 'just' Logan ever again.

She checked her reflection one last time. A pretty skirt, T-shirt, denim jacket in case it got cold later and sparkly sandals. Not too over the top for dinner at the pub, she hoped, before grabbing her keys and rushing out of the front door.

She walked quickly alongside the river, where she found Logan standing outside the inn, waiting for her. He had changed into a pair of cargo shorts and short-sleeved shirt.

'Hi,' she said, coming up to greet him.

'You look nice,' he told her.

Molly blushed. 'So do you,' she said, before sighing silently at herself.

'Well, I'm dry in any case,' he replied, grinning at her, as he opened the door.

As usual on a Saturday night these days, the inn was packed with people. Most were sitting outside but many others were in the restaurant area, where everyone was enjoying the meals created by the new chef.

Logan and Molly managed to fight their way through the crowd of people to where Pete was standing behind the bar.

'Good evening,' said Pete, with the amiable smile of a happy landlord. After all, it hadn't been too long ago that the inn had been almost put out of business.

'Hi,' said Molly, aware of Pete very briefly looking from Logan and back to herself with an amused expression. 'We're celebrating.'

'Glad to hear it,' Pete told her. 'Are you celebrating life or something far more specific?'

'Logan got the wheel working on the watermill,' replied Molly.

'Seriously? That's fantastic news,' said Pete, delighted.

'And the tea garden is a success and has lived to survive another day,' added Logan.

Molly blushed but felt proud that he was speaking the truth.

'Brilliant,' said Pete, nodding.

'So bring on the drinks,' said Logan.

'And maybe something to eat too,' suggested Molly. 'I'm starving.' Although as she looked around, she realised that it might not be possible given the amount of customers being served on a busy Saturday night.

'Don't worry,' said Pete, noticing her worried expression and giving her a wink. 'Belle always has a spare table for friends.'

'Excellent,' said Logan, turning to Molly. 'What drink would you like? I presume anything but tea.'

She laughed. 'Definitely not tea,' she replied. 'A gin and tonic would be great, thanks.'

'And I'll have a pint of anything on tap,' said Logan.

'Coming right up,' replied Pete. 'And here's the boss so we can sort you out a table.'

'Hi,' said Belle, giving Molly an over-bright smile. 'I didn't know you were coming in tonight.'

'It was a last-minute decision,' Logan told her.

'They're celebrating,' added Pete, as he pulled out the pint.

'Indeed?' said Belle, raising an eyebrow in surprised question.

'Molly had a successful day at the tea garden and Logan got the waterwheel working,' Pete told her. 'After all this time, can you believe it?'

'I can't,' said Belle, looking surprised but thrilled. 'That's amazing. Both the watermill and the tea garden? That definitely deserves a drink.'

'And maybe something to eat too,' whispered Pete in her ear. 'Any ideas where we can seat them?'

'Leave it to me,' said Belle, smiling at them both before disappearing.

Only a few moments later, Belle was leading them to an outside corner of the pub garden.

'There was a cancellation,' she said airily, in answer to Molly's amazed question as to how there was an empty table on such a busy night. Although her eyes didn't quite meet Molly's as she sat down. 'Now, here's the menus,' said Belle briskly. 'I'll come back in a while to take your order.'

She gave Molly a knowing smile before walking off.

Did they all have to make it so obvious? thought Molly. She loved her friends, but sometimes subtlety was required.

Thankfully, Logan seemed oblivious to all the winks and nudges from everyone and was smiling at her as he too sat down.

'Cheers,' he said, holding up his pint glass. 'Here's to new beginnings.'

'To new beginnings,' said Molly, gently clinking her glass against his.

She took a welcome sip of the gin and tonic before looking around. It was a lovely evening, not a cloud in the sky as it turned to a deep raspberry-streaked pink.

Taking advantage of the comfortable silence, she glanced down at the menu whilst Logan did the same.

'I'm starving,' he said.

'Me too,' agreed Molly. 'We were so busy, I only managed to grab a slice of cake around 11 o'clock this morning.'

'Hiya,' said Del, coming to stand next to the table. 'What's this about the waterwheel turning? Is it true?'

Logan nodded. 'Yup,' he replied. 'Thanks to everyone's help recently, it's up and running.'

'That's amazing,' said Del, looking delighted as he sat down next to Molly on the bench. 'I've never renovated anything in my life.'

'Oh, I don't know, Del,' replied Logan. 'That minibus of yours was resurrected from the dead pretty quickly.'

'Yeah,' said Del, grinning.

Molly was pleased that Logan seemed to be enjoying chatting to more people these days. He was definitely opening up a little more day by day.

'Right,' said Belle, also joining them to place a bread basket on the table. 'What are you eating?'

Molly ordered a prosciutto and basil pasta which was from the new summer menu and Logan chose a chicken and asparagus risotto.

'Maybe I'll grab something as well,' said Del, reaching across for a menu.

But Belle was too quick for him and swiftly picked up the menus. 'Actually, I needed to talk to you about something, Del,' she told him. 'And I think Pete wants you to try out a new beer. Do you want to come and test it for us? On the house, of course.'

'Excellent,' replied Del, who was easily distracted and immediately stood up. 'Lead the way.'

'Let me just do this first,' said Belle, suddenly producing a small jam jar and lighting a tea light inside. 'It's a new thing we're trying out,' she added, with a ghost of a smile as she walked away with Del.

Molly looked down at the soft flickering light and then back up at Logan, giving him a sheepish smile. 'Well,' she said, clearing her throat. 'I wanted to thank you for listening to me earlier.'

'You know, I'm always happy to listen to you,' he told her, holding her gaze for a long time before Molly looked away first.

'So what's left to do on the mill?' she asked, steering the conversation onto safer matters. And far away from her heart which was hammering in her chest.

43

Molly enjoyed her evening meal at the inn. But she suspected it had nothing to do with the delicious food or the ambience of the twilight of the pub garden. And it had everything to do with Logan.

But she had been aware of a lot of local people glancing over at them throughout the evening.

'What's up?' asked Logan. 'You're looking uncomfortable.'

It was incredible how quickly he had got to know her, she thought. Or maybe what he had said before was true and that she was a complete open book.

'I think everyone's talking,' she said, glad the darkening light could mask her embarrassment. 'About us sitting here on our own, I mean.'

There was a slight pause before Logan said, 'So?'

She laughed. 'I guess you're right. So what?'

'See? Look at that.' She watched as he raised his eyes up to the darkening sky above. 'The sky isn't falling in.'

'Very funny,' she told him, relaxing once more.

Maybe it didn't matter. Maybe two friends could just enjoy each other's company and who cared what everyone else thought?

But as they walked along the river after finishing their meal, Molly knew that she could feel herself getting closer and closer to Logan with each passing day. She desperately wanted to be happy to just be friends with him, but something had shifted deep inside of her and she was reluctant to admit to herself how she really felt.

Dusk had fallen and the trees quietening down with one last birdsong. It was a beautiful night. Romantic, even, under the stars.

Molly looked briefly at Logan before looking away. Her crush was totally getting out of hand, but, that evening, she found she didn't mind. It was a precious moment, to be walking with him under a starlit sky, so she would take it and bury it away deep inside to cherish.

'When are you going to tell your grandad about getting the mill working?' asked Molly.

'First thing tomorrow,' said Logan, smiling to himself in anticipation.

'He'll be thrilled,' said Molly.

'Yes, he will,' replied Logan.

As they crossed the last of the narrow pedestrian bridges, Molly thought she spotted some movement in the darkness of the tea garden, but it was hard to tell with the shadow from the watermill at that time of the evening.

As they neared Logan's shop, he slowed up. He turned to her, just about to speak, when they both heard the sound of crying coming from the tea garden.

Molly and Logan exchanged a concerned look and immediately walked over to the wall.

'Hello?' she called out softly, stepping carefully through the open gate. 'Are you OK in there?'

Her eyes focused in the darkness and eventually found a small boy, of around eighteen or so months old, sitting in the darkness, giggling. Nearby, she realised that Olivia was scrabbling around on the damp grass, crying.

'Olivia?' said Molly, gently. 'What are you doing here?'

Olivia looked up startled and it was at that point that Molly realised she was clutching handfuls of petals.

'It's not his fault,' said Olivia, with a sob. 'He didn't mean to pick all the flowers. It's just he seems to like them.'

'It's fine,' replied Molly quickly, going to kneel on the grass next to Olivia. 'But what are you doing here at this time of night?'

'Sometimes he's awake during the night and won't settle. So we come here for some fresh air and to keep him from waking up Mum because that makes her angry. He seems to like it here,' Olivia carried on. 'Except he's destroying the flowers and everyone's worked so hard.'

'Flowers grow back,' said Molly. She couldn't be cross with either of them. Olivia seemed so downhearted and the little boy appeared so happy. 'Anyway he's just deadheading them for the gardeners, that's all.'

She glanced over to where Logan had crouched in front of the small boy. He was making silly faces behind his hands and then showing them to the toddler who was giggling with delight.

'He's your brother?' guessed Molly.

Olivia hesitated before nodding. 'Mum needs me to take care of him. You know, when she's out.'

Which Molly figured was probably most of the time, knowing Michelle. And the reason for Olivia's poor timekeeping was beginning to make sense.

She felt a connection with Olivia who had had to give up so much of her own life to take care of her brother. After all, that was exactly what Molly had done all those years ago with her own twin brothers.

'I know I should have told you before,' said Olivia, quickly. 'But when I've had to take time off before if he's sick, my other bosses didn't understand and I lost my job. So I figured it was better to keep quiet about him.'

'Well, that seems a shame when he's such a lovely little boy,' said Molly. 'What's his name?'

'Louis,' said Olivia. 'After my grandad.'

'Lovely name,' replied Molly. 'Look, please don't worry. I just need you to be honest with me, OK? So if you need to bring Louis to work with you or there's a reason why you're late, that's not a problem either. Just tell me the truth. That's all I ask.'

'OK,' said Olivia, with a teary smile. 'Thanks. Well, I'd better get him back to bed.'

They said goodnight and Molly and Logan watched as Olivia carried the small boy in her arms until they disappeared into the darkness.

Molly sighed. 'Poor kid.'

'Yeah,' agreed Logan.

'I think, perhaps, that nobody's given her any real attention or love so far in her life.' Molly came to a sudden decision. 'And I'm determined to make her feel better about herself.'

'Of course you are,' he murmured, looking down at her in the darkness.

She rolled her eyes at herself. 'I know, go on and tell me that I'm hopeless and daft and all that.'

'Actually, I'm beginning to think that you're incredibly special,' he said, staring down at her with such an intensity that she suddenly had trouble breathing.

He looked at her for a moment longer before softly saying goodnight and abruptly turning away. He left Molly standing under the wide starry sky, wondering what on earth had just passed between them again and how much she had been hoping for a goodnight kiss.

44

Molly was in the kitchen already when Olivia arrived the following morning, holding hands with Louis. She looked hesitant as she glanced down at her brother briefly.

'Hi,' said Molly, heading over to the large hot-water urn. 'And good morning, Louis! Coffee?'

'Thanks,' said Olivia, putting her handbag down onto a chair with a sigh.

'Well, it looks like it's going to be another lovely day,' carried on Molly, glancing out at the sunshine already filling the garden. 'So it could be a busy one.'

She caught Olivia biting her lip and looking concerned as she looked down at her younger brother.

'It'll be fine,' Molly told her, trying to reassure Olivia. 'Honestly. Just have something to eat and drink, if you like. There's no customers yet.'

As she headed out into the garden, Molly saw Grandma Tilly pushing open the gate. She had continued to show up to help out even though Molly had tried to dissuade her. But today, that wasn't

Molly's concern. She quickly went over and explained the situation to her about Olivia and young Louis.

'I told you about Michelle,' murmured Grandma Tilly in response, shaking her head. 'Poor little lamb. Right. Well then, let's see how our newest staff member gets on.'

Grandma Tilly took Louis under her wing and, to everyone's delight, he absolutely adored her.

Later on that morning, Molly overheard one customer say, 'Isn't he a bonny chap?'

'He certainly is,' said Grandma Tilly, who was holding hands with Louis. 'And he's been a dab hand at helping to hand out the napkins and lay the tables.'

They looked down as Louis handed over a napkin with a solemn face to the customer.

'Well, thank you very much,' said the lady to the young boy.

'Shall we go and see who's visiting the bug hotel today?' asked Grandma Tilly, leading the toddler towards the community garden.

Molly smiled to herself as she headed back into the kitchen, grateful that they had a resident childminder in Grandma Tilly and that peace was once more restored.

'We're running out of Victoria sponge,' said Olivia, taking the penultimate slice before placing the glass dome over the top.

Molly blew out a sigh. 'It does seem to be one of the most popular lines,' she said. 'Trouble is, I've got a meeting with someone from Aldwych online news about the tea garden in half an hour's time. It'll be really good for promotion and getting the word out but it leaves me no time to bake another cake.' She had a sudden thought and looked at Olivia. 'But you'd be able to whip one up in no time.'

Olivia looked startled. 'What do you mean?' she asked, frowning.

'I'm sure I bought some of your cupcakes at the Christmas fair last year,' said Molly.

Olivia shrugged her shoulders. 'The icing went all wrong,' she muttered, not making eye contact.

'I'm sure it didn't,' said Molly. 'All I remember is that they tasted amazing.'

Olivia blushed. 'Not as good as yours,' she muttered.

'I've had more time to practise,' said Molly. 'But here's your opportunity. All the ingredients and equipment are listed here.' She brought out her scribbled recipe notes. 'The mixer is quite simple. I can show you how it works. You just need to put them together.'

Olivia looked slightly panicked. 'But what about the customers?'

'We've got Grandma Tilly and Louis helping today,' said Molly, placing the recipe on the counter. 'It'll be fine. Right, I'd better clear those tables.'

Eager to leave Olivia before she could protest again, Molly headed towards the back door. She paused before walking outside, glancing over her shoulder to where Olivia was still hesitating and looking concerned.

'It's just cake,' said Molly softly. 'I honestly believe that you can do this. I trust you, but it doesn't really matter if it goes wrong, OK?'

Olivia finally met her eyes and gave her a small nod of her head.

Molly gave her a smile before heading outside, hoping that she hadn't pushed the girl too much. But she wanted to give her a chance and let Olivia know that someone believed in her.

She spent the next hour with the journalist from the blog chatting about the tea garden and how important it was to the village.

'It's certainly very busy here,' said the woman.

Molly looked around and realised how popular they had become so quickly. The weather was getting warmer by the day and the summer sunshine seemed to have brought everyone out. It wouldn't be too long before they might need extra staff, she thought to herself.

She was feeling pleased with the positive comments that she was beginning to receive from the customers. And there was also a sense of pride too as to what she had achieved. Of what they'd all achieved, because it wasn't just a tea garden any more, she explained to the journalist, it was a community garden as well.

She suggested that the journalist talk to her mum and Geoff as well. 'They're the real gardeners,' Molly told her. 'Not me.'

After the interview was over, she headed back into the kitchen.

'Sorry to leave you on your own for so long,' said Molly quickly.

But Olivia was looking more relaxed than before as she stood aside to reveal a beautiful-looking sponge cake on the counter, cooling down.

'Wow,' said Molly. 'That's perfect.' She gave Olivia a nudge with her elbow. 'Told you so.'

'Shurrup,' muttered Olivia, but she was blushing.

'I told you that you could do it,' said Molly, feeling something akin to pride.

'Yeah, but it's easy for you,' replied Olivia. 'You're the strongest person I know.'

Molly was shocked. 'Me?' she said, laughing. 'I'm the least confident person you'll ever meet!'

But Olivia didn't laugh. 'You're so nice and smiley and relaxed all the time. And look what you've done here. I could never open up a business like this, but you have. It's amazing.'

As Olivia headed back outside to serve some more customers, Molly stood in shock, mulling over what she had just been told. Maybe it really was amazing what she had achieved so far. Maybe what her friends had been telling her for a couple of years was true. That she was good enough. That customers were enjoying her cakes and were happy to pay for them.

Her phone bleeped just then and she glanced down at the text from Amber saying that she and Josh and chosen a three-layered wedding cake with flavours of lemon, chocolate and vanilla sponge.

Molly waited for the familiar nerves to kick in but, for once, they didn't appear.

Perhaps it was time to listen to her own advice for once, she realised. If Olivia could bake a Victoria sponge, then maybe, just maybe, Molly could bake a decent wedding cake for her friends.

And in that moment, Molly finally began to believe in herself and her abilities and felt stronger because of it.

45

Well, this was it, thought Logan. There were no more excuses. He couldn't hide any longer.

He stood near the entrance to the watermill and looked across at his grandad, who gave him a nod of approval.

Logan took a deep breath and pulled the lever to release the waterwheel.

There were a few nervy moments as the levers and pulleys ground together and clattered a bit, but they soon found their rhythm and the sound of gushing water filled the space.

Logan rushed outside to bend over the railing of the tiny bridge and saw that the wheel was turning and that the water was spilling over it in a smooth manner.

He straightened up to find Stanley standing next to him on the bridge with tears in his eyes. 'Well done, lad,' he murmured, his voice a little unsteady.

Logan felt quite overcome himself and placed a gentle hand on his grandad's shoulder and could only nod in reply.

He knew how much it meant to his grandad, but it turned out that in helping Stanley he had helped himself as well.

He would never have been able to do the heavy lifting by himself, of course, and when he'd hurt his foot, he had to ask for help for the first time in a very long time. However, in doing so, he had made friends. Good friends, in fact. Men that he trusted. People like Josh, Tom, Pete and even Dodgy Del.

'Well, just one more hurdle to jump,' murmured Logan.

They headed back inside, where Logan pulled the other lever and the two round querns began to gently bump together in the required motion.

Logan headed up the ladder and tipped the sack of grain that Josh had bought for him from a local farmer into one of the large vats just below the roof. As he headed back down, he waited nervously until, finally, he could see that the grain was being ground by the heavy quern stones.

He and Stanley watched as something akin to flour began to appear in the large tub nearby as it spilled out from between the two heavy stones.

'It's doing it,' said Logan, reaching out to touch the chalky white powder with his fingers, still not fully believing what he was seeing. 'It's actually flour.'

'I don't know why you sound so unsure,' said Stanley. 'I never doubted you for a second.'

Logan laughed and stepped forward to give his grandad a hug.

'Well, we've done it,' said Logan, stepping back to smile at his grandad.

'You mean, *you've* done it,' said Stanley. 'I'm so grateful, lad. I can't begin to tell you how thankful I am.'

But Logan, for once, found that he needed to disagree with his grandad.

'Just because I did the heavy lifting doesn't mean I get to take the credit,' said Logan, shaking his head. 'I had help from the others. But, to be honest, none of this would have been possible without your buying the mill in the first place.'

'It needed to be done,' said Stanley with a small shrug of his shoulders.

'And now we can share it with everyone else,' said Logan, hearing voices outside.

They headed back onto the bridge, where a small crowd had gathered.

'I may just have put the word out that the mill was finally going,' said Tom, grinning at them both as he came to stand at the front of the group.

'Then let us show you around,' said Logan, gesturing for everyone to come in.

He looked in the crowd for Molly's face but couldn't see her and felt a small pang of disappointment. She was obviously busy in the tea garden but even so, he wished she was there.

* * *

The rest of the day, Logan was busy showing everyone around the watermill. Stanley had many stories to tell about its history and Logan felt himself equally mesmerised as they all learnt about its past.

Finally, much later in the afternoon, the crowd began to subside and Logan and Stanley were left to admire the place on their own.

The clack and grinding of the gears was a gentle noise, almost as spellbinding as Stanley's storytelling. Outside, Logan could hear the water thundering over the wheel, a constant but pleasant sound.

'I'm so proud of you, Grandad,' he found himself blurting out.

Stanley looked surprised at his words but didn't reply.

'You've talked about the legacy of the mill today, but I think you need to appreciate what your legacy is as well,' Logan told him. 'All the villagers that came in today, so many of them were children that you taught and inspired, supported and encouraged. I think that's your true legacy. Maybe even more so than the mill.'

Stanley blinked his eyes rapidly. 'Thank you, my boy,' he said gruffly.

It was nice to make a difference, thought Logan. It wasn't about profit. It was about preserving some sort of heritage for the area. For Cranbridge. And for future generations too. It felt good.

He wandered outside with his grandad and listened to the water rushing through the wheel.

After a short but comfortable silence, Logan said, 'I know I haven't been around much, especially since you lost Granny and for that I'm truly sorry. But you can rely on me now. I promise.'

His grandad smiled. 'Does that mean that you're staying?' he said, sounding a little hopeful.

Logan sighed. 'I don't actually know, to be honest with you. But yes, perhaps.'

It was true. He was beginning to have doubts about leaving Cranbridge at the end of the summer. It felt right to be here. He felt at peace. Perhaps he could extend his stay for a while longer.

But all the time, his eyes were drawn across to the tea garden. Because he was beginning to wonder whether Molly would feature in his future plans as well.

46

Molly checked her emails for the third time that afternoon, but there was no reply from the council.

Such was the success of the twenty-eight-day trial of the pop-up business that she had emailed the council to request an extension of the tea garden business until the end of September. She was holding off contacting Barry, the landlord, until she had heard back.

She still couldn't believe it, but the figures that she entered into her spreadsheet each evening had begun to show a very healthy profit and so it must have been true. Not only was the tea garden financially successful, the feedback from all the customers was also extremely positive.

In fact, some customers told her how delighted they had been to find the tea garden, as if they had found some kind of secret place. But it didn't stay secret for very long. Suddenly almost overnight they were extremely busy.

Part of that was in thanks to the tremendous review that the journalist had posted on her blog. 'It's the perfect English country garden stop-off for a pot of tea and some extremely delicious home-made cake. Highly recommended!' the review had stated.

Everything was going well. In fact, Molly was considering taking on another member of staff to help with the customers as she and Olivia could barely keep up with the demand. That would then free up Olivia to help Molly with more of the baking.

Olivia had been a perfect person to employ, thought Molly. She was quiet but polite and quick to serve the customers. But almost better than that was to see her grow in confidence each day. Molly had begun to teach her how to make home-made cordials and lemonade, as well as some of the easiest bakes. She had achieved the required skills so quickly that Molly was eager to show her some more complex bakes.

'We need to add some more savoury food to the menu,' she had said only that morning. 'Not everyone wants cake.'

So Molly had planned to add a couple of savoury, summer tarts to the menu as well as cheese scones, which she was hoping that Olivia would learn to make and take responsibility for.

She had already picked some herbs from the community garden to add a bit of flavour to the tarts. The tomato and basil one tasted delicious.

She had almost forgotten about the missing money. She figured that she probably had just added up incorrectly. After all, it hadn't happened since.

Olivia still brought Louis along with her for about half the time, but there was always someone to help keep him occupied. Sometimes it was Grandma Tilly and sometimes it was Molly's mum, who was showing him how to plant seeds.

'He's a smashing little boy,' said her mum that afternoon.

'Isn't he?' said Molly.

'Reminds me of the boys when they were that little,' her mum remarked.

Molly laughed. 'They were never that well behaved,' she said. 'Or that sweet.'

Her mum smiled. 'Yes, they were.'

'I think all this sun must be making you a bit light-headed,' Molly told her, with a wink.

'Or the pollen,' she replied. 'Which reminds me. I treated myself to a couple of new dahlias at the garden centre. I thought they'd go well in our back garden as that's my next big project.'

Molly was overjoyed that her mum had got her mojo back and stepped forward to give her a hug.

'What's that for?' asked her mum, looking pleased but surprised.

'Because you're happy, Mum,' Molly told her.

Her mum nodded. 'You know what? I really am,' she said. 'And it's lovely to see your success as well.'

'Not just mine,' replied Molly, nodding at the watermill beyond the wall.

'This end of Riverside Lane is looking better and better with each passing day,' said her mum.

Everyone was talking about how exciting it was to see the mill finally working. There was quite a buzz about it in the village. It was the main topic of conversation in the tea garden as well.

'Isn't it marvellous to see?' said one rambler as she came through the gate. 'I've never seen a working watermill before.'

Molly offered her a spare table, where the woman gratefully sank down onto a chair.

'Such a hot day to be out walking,' she said, wiping her sweaty brow. 'I thought you were a mirage!'

'Not at all,' Molly told her. 'How about some home-made lemonade to cool you down?'

Later, the same lady told Molly, 'I wouldn't buy mass-manufactured cake any more. Not now I've tasted how good it can be.'

Molly relished the positive comments and was even starting to accept the compliments without the need to bat them away, embarrassed.

As she went to head back into the tea garden, her phone buzzed with an email. She held her breath as she read the contents.

The council had extended her licence! They were more than happy to give her until the end of September! Because the tables, chairs and awnings were all removable, there was no permanent structure involved. So that meant she could take the whole summer to keep the tea garden open.

Her excitement was only slightly dampened by the fear of what she would do when it was all over and she had to give it all up again.

But for now, she would enjoy being her very own boss and seeing what she could achieve. For once, the doubts didn't automatically spring to the surface and Molly found herself wondering just how much success all the hard work might bring her.

47

Logan looked up from the cabinet that he was working on and stared at Dodgy Del.

'Sorry, what were you talking about?' he said, with a shake of his head.

It had felt as if he were walking through fog for the past couple of days. He was having trouble sleeping and yet he wasn't really fully awake either.

'I said, have you got some length of wood that I could have,' said Del, sounding a little exasperated. 'My hops are getting too high for the canes we're using and I don't want to end up with only a half a pint of beer after all this hard work.'

Logan couldn't help but smile. 'Hard work?' he said, raising an eyebrow.

'It is, I tell you!' replied Del. 'It's all I'm thinking about. Everyone's saying how good this heatwave is and all that, but my hops need protecting otherwise they'll get scorched. I've read up on this. And then there's all the watering. It's exhausting.'

Logan took pity on him. 'Come on then,' he said, putting down his screwdriver. 'Show me what you're talking about.'

He locked up the shop and walked towards the tea garden. He could hear the buzz of the customers in there first before seeing the place. The whole garden was alive with conversation and the gentle clink of china from over the wall.

'Can't move for folks these days,' muttered Del, as Logan followed him through the open gate.

It was true that the tea garden was certainly successful these days, thought Logan. It was nearly always full whenever he went past and he was pleased for Molly and the village. The community garden also seemed to have at least one or two people in there each day as well. There was always something to be picked, weeded or potted, it appeared.

'So what happens to the watermill now you've got it working?' asked Del as they weaved their way past the packed tables and chairs.

'Not sure,' Logan told him. 'Grandad's talking about possibly employing a miller. You know, so we have local flour.'

'Well, it'll certainly be a good draw for tourists,' said Del. 'Which helps out the tea garden and all the other businesses.'

They arrived in front of the row of hop plants at the very back of the garden.

'Maybe your grandad could do a little tour of the place as well, once in a while,' suggested Del. 'He'd enjoy that.'

Logan nodded, thinking that was a great idea. 'Yes, he would. So what's up with your plant?'

'See?' Del pointed at his beloved hops, which was now towering over the top of the cane and flopping over. 'It needs to climb up something.'

Logan took a step back and studied all the plants. 'They're all going to need something eventually,' he said, nodding thoughtfully.

'This is what I found online.'

Logan looked down at the photo that Del was showing him on

his phone and laughed. 'You're joking!' he exclaimed. 'That's about twelve feet high. How am I supposed to build that?'

It was a row of vertical columns all upright like a parade of soldiers.

'Look, I can find you the wood,' said Del quickly. 'I just need your skills to fix 'em together. I know someone who's got some railway sleepers.'

Logan quickly shook his head. 'They're too big. Not to mention extremely heavy.'

'So?'

Logan rolled his eyes. 'So we don't want them to fall down and flatten any of Molly's customers, do we?'

'Oh.' Finally Del nodded in agreement. 'Yeah. Good point, I suppose.'

'Plus it's a question of aesthetics,' carried on Logan. 'You'd be better off making it into a pergola.'

'A what now?' asked Del.

'You know, a row of slim, vertical posts but joined at the top with either a trellis or something a little more sturdy,' Logan told him, whizzing through his own phone to show Del a photograph. 'Your vines will love it.'

'Sounds good,' said Del, nodding in agreement as he looked at the screen. 'How quickly can you whip one of them things up? My hops plant is desperate.'

'Yeah, yeah, I know,' said Logan. 'It's all about the beer.'

'Too right.'

Logan hesitated. 'I can't put it up by myself,' he found himself saying.

It was true that his foot was almost healed and that he was no longer hobbling. And yet, building a pergola was something that he couldn't possibly handle on his own.

But admitting he couldn't do anything by himself was a new experience for him.

'Of course you can't,' he heard Del say. 'No worries, you tell me what kind of wood we need and how much and I'll get the lads organised for one evening this week when the tea garden is shut.'

'OK,' said Logan, a little relieved.

And so, the following evening, he found himself with Del, Tom, Josh and Pete building a pergola in the back of the garden.

Occasionally, Molly would wander out of the kitchen where she was clearing up after another busy day and offer them all a cold drink.

'No beer?' said Del, with a grin.

'You've got beer on the brain,' said Tom, laughing.

'And the beer's in the pub waiting for us all after we're done,' added Pete, wiping his brow.

It certainly was a warm summer's evening, despite the sun beginning to sink below the rolling green hills on the horizon. Even Keith the dog was grateful for a bowl of cold water to slurp from noisily.

'That looks great,' said Molly, looking up at the pergola in amazement before handing Logan a glass of home-made lemonade.

'Thanks,' he replied, taking a grateful sip of the icy cold drink. 'You like it?'

She nodded. 'Absolutely.' Then she leaned forward to whisper, 'Do you think Del would mind if I wrap some fairy lights around it? Or do you think they'll affect the quality of the beer?'

He looked at her nose noticing that a few freckles had begun to appear as she spent so much time in the sunshine these days. Then he couldn't stop himself glancing at her lips briefly before forcing himself to stare back into her blue eyes.

'Go for it,' he said softly.

They locked eyes for a moment before she walked away.

Logan knew then the reason for the brain fog that he had been experiencing. It had nothing to do with being tired or the heat. It was all about Molly.

A few nights ago, when they had come back from the pub and found Olivia in the garden with young Louis, there had been a moment when they had been alone and he had found himself almost kissing her. Only some kind of self-preservation had stopped him.

But he couldn't stop running the moment through his mind over and over with Molly standing there in the darkness. And wondering what would have happened if the end of the evening had been any different.

48

Molly looked at her reflection in the full-length mirror and smiled. 'The dress is beautiful,' she said.

As promised, Belle had made them all stunning bridesmaid's dresses in purple silk for Amber's wedding. Molly hadn't worn anything so glamorous since her prom night.

'Hold still,' said Belle, kneeling down in front of her and pinning up the hem. 'It just needs to be slightly shorter, otherwise it won't drop to the floor properly.'

'I can't believe it's only six weeks until your wedding.' Lucy stirred up the large jug of Pimms she was making in the kitchen of her apartment.

'Nor can I,' said Amber, grinning as she sat on the sofa with her feet curled up under her.

'And I can't believe this is the first chance I've been able to arrange a final fitting with Molly,' muttered Belle. 'Good job I'm a speedy seamstress.'

'I know and I'm sorry,' said Molly, still standing still as Belle moved around her on the floor. 'You know I've been busy.'

This was an understatement, she thought. There had been no

drop in customer numbers at the tea garden since the extension to the council's licence had been approved two weeks ago. If anything, it was even busier.

The heatwave helped, of course. It was now the middle of July and the hot sticky air had brought everyone outside into the sunshine as the schools gradually closed for the summer holidays.

'Crikey, it's warm this evening,' said Amber, fanning herself with a magazine.

All the windows were open, but there wasn't much cool air wafting inside the apartment. The air was hot and still. Even Keith the dog was panting and hogging the cool air wafting from the fan that Lucy had switched on.

'It's going to be like this for at least another week or so,' said Lucy, bringing the jug and glasses over to the coffee table. 'Hurry up, ladies. I'm gasping for my drink.'

'All done,' said Belle, finally standing up.

Molly slid out of the dress and quickly changed into her shorts and T-shirt before joining them all in the lounge area.

'I now declare it Pimms o'clock,' said Lucy, pouring them all a drink and handing out the glasses. 'And the cucumber that I've used is from the community garden, would you believe!'

'Cheers!' they all chorused, clinking their glasses together.

'Mmm,' said Amber, after taking a sip of the cool drink. 'I needed that.'

'And it's long overdue,' added Belle. 'It's been weeks since we had a proper girly evening and not another snatched conversation somewhere down Riverside Lane.'

'It's Molly's fault for being such a successful businesswoman,' said Lucy, with a grin.

'I think we're all successful these days,' said Molly, blushing a little.

She still couldn't quite get used to the success of the tea garden.

Thankfully, Tom had been absolutely brilliant about her needing an extension to her month off work.

'I'll be back when it's closed for good in September,' she had told him.

But Tom had merely smiled at her and said, 'The job is always there for you, but hopefully you won't need it.'

Molly couldn't see how she could possibly extend the tea garden into the autumn months, so surely it would come to an end sooner or later. But, for now, she was enjoying her successful, albeit tiring days of work.

Of course, she had needed to ask Barry for an extension to her use of the kitchen and garden. But she had felt a little stronger in dealing with him this time around, although she had wimped out of calling him directly and had only sent him an email requesting the extension. Expecting a huff and a puff about it, she was surprised when she'd received an acceptance email the same afternoon. Perhaps Logan had scared him off a bit in those early days, she thought.

'Only a month until your hen night!' declared Lucy with a grin.

'Yeah, I just need confirmation from the strippergram,' said Belle with an evil smile.

'You wouldn't dare!' said Amber, looking horrified.

'Just try me,' replied Belle, as they all joined in the laughter.

'Is it really only six weeks until you're Mrs Kennedy?' asked Molly.

'Eeek!' squeaked Amber in excitement. But then her smile faded a little. 'I wish I'd been stronger with Mum about the venue.'

'It doesn't matter,' Lucy told her.

'As long as you and Josh get married, everything else like the wedding reception is just extra trimmings. Like the clotted cream on one of Molly's cream teas,' said Belle.

Molly smiled to herself. That had been Olivia's idea one day, to serve cream teas and it had proved a spectacular success.

'Actually I consider the cream an essential part of that,' said Lucy.

'Me too,' agreed Molly.

'And the wedding cake is going to look spectacular,' said Amber, with a nod of reassurance.

Molly nodded. She was still a little nervous about the cake being such an integral part of the wedding celebrations and yet, having now proved herself and her baking abilities day after day to satisfied customers, perhaps she was getting more confident in her abilities.

She could do this, she knew that now. And hopefully that inner strength and confidence would last long after the tea garden had closed.

49

As the heatwave continued, Logan found throwing open the front and back doors to the workshop at least helped some kind of cooling breeze waft through the shop. Although late in the afternoon, it was still pretty stifling, thanks to the full glass window at the front soaking up the sunshine.

'Here, hand me that drill, would you?' he said, as he stood on top of a stepladder.

Adam handed him the electric drill and watched as Logan drilled in the appropriate holes to fix up a blind.

Adam had taken to popping into the workshop most afternoons to hang around. He seemed to enjoy watching Logan work and chatting about various things.

He told Logan that Ben had gone with some friends to Ibiza for a fortnight.

'You didn't want to go?' asked Logan, as he climbed back down the ladder.

Adam shook his head. 'Can't afford it,' he said. 'I maxed out my credit card at uni this year.'

He helped Logan manoeuvre the blind into position and then

fix it against the wall. Logan twirled the handle and immediately the slats of the Venetian blind blocked out some of the sun's hot rays.

'That's better,' said Logan, turning to look at Adam, who was staring across the workshop in a kind of dream. 'Are you OK?' he found himself asking.

Adam blinked back to life and looked at him. 'What do you mean?' he asked.

'You just seem, I don't know, a little out of sorts,' said Logan. 'A bit listless, maybe.'

'Just a bit fearful, to be honest,' replied Adam with a sigh. 'I'm dreading going back to uni.'

He slid down the wall and onto the floor, his legs splayed out in the sunshine that shone through the open door.

Logan left the silence drag on for a minute until he prompted Adam with, 'Do you want to talk about it?'

Adam looked up at him nervously. 'You can't tell Mum or Molly, OK?' he said quickly.

'OK,' said Logan.

'No, I mean it. Otherwise I'm out of here.'

Adam's fierce tone surprised Logan, so he quickly said, 'All right.' Although secretly he was thinking that if it was something awful he would have to tell Molly.

'I hate university, my course, all of it.' Adam puffed out what appeared to be a relieved sigh. 'Wow. That feels better just saying it out loud.'

'OK,' said Logan slowly, wondering how to deal with this revelation.

'That's why you can't tell them,' Adam told him quickly. 'I mean, Mum and Molly have sacrificed everything so we can go to uni and it turns out that I don't really like it. Well, maybe the social scene, but I can do that anywhere.'

'You hate it? Do you mean the course?' asked Logan.

Adam nodded. 'Psychology,' he murmured. 'What was I thinking? I just thought it would set me up for something in the future, but I'm so bored. I get fidgety with all those words and lectures. I want to be doing something. Using my hands.'

'What about Ben?' said Logan.

'Oh, he loves his course,' replied Adam, with a wry smile. 'Trying to work out how to make his fortune in the coming years. He'll be all right. But there was something else...' His voice trailed off once more.

Logan waited patiently to let Adam speak in his own time.

'I went to see my dad.'

Logan was shocked. 'I didn't think he'd been in the picture for many years,' he said.

'He hasn't,' Adam told him, shaking his head. 'But I've always wondered, you know? Always been curious to see what he's like. Ben didn't want to know, so I drove myself over there one day. It was miles away. But money's so tight I had to borrow from Molly's till to pay for the petrol. Felt bad about that, to be honest.'

'I should think so!' Logan was trying not to shout. 'Do you realise that we thought it might be Olivia stealing from her?'

'No way!' said Adam, looking upset. 'Nah, it was me. Oh God! What have I done?'

'OK,' said Logan, thinking quickly. 'Well, you need to own up to your sister and repay her the money.'

'I will,' replied Adam, nodding. 'I didn't think about the consequences.'

'Well, maybe that's something you need to do from now on,' said Logan.

'Yeah.' Adam sat still for a moment, frowning as he stared down at the floor.

Logan realised that he wasn't a bad guy but perhaps just someone trying to figure out a few things in his life.

'So what happened with your dad?' asked Logan.

Adam finally looked up at him with pain in his eyes. 'Didn't want to know me, did he? Ben said it was no surprise when I told him about it later and didn't seem to care. But I care! I care that our own dad walked out. I thought that maybe he had had some kind of excuse, back then. You know, an illness or some kind of emergency.' His shoulders sank as he hugged his knees to his chest. 'Turns out he just didn't want anything to do with us.'

Logan watched Adam for a moment before speaking. 'Then I'm truly sorry. That must have been awful for you.'

Logan headed over to the small fridge he kept at the back of the workshop and grabbed a couple of bottles of beer and some left-over chocolate brownies that Molly had given him.

'Here,' he said, handing over the beer and brownies to Adam before sitting down on the floor next to him in the sunshine.

'Thanks,' muttered Adam before taking a bite. 'God, that's good.'

'Yes, it is,' said Logan. 'Your sister's got real talent.'

'Unlike me. I don't think I can do anything.'

Logan turned to look at Adam. 'Actually, that's not true. You showed promise when you helped me out with those chairs.'

'That was just a bit of sanding down,' said Adam.

Logan shook his head. 'No, you were responsible for removing the studs and filling the holes up as well. I was impressed at the time that they barely showed afterwards. It seemed quite a professional job for someone with no experience.'

'Maybe that's what I should do instead,' joked Adam.

'Well, I've done all right as a qualified furniture maker,' Logan told him.

'Yeah, but me?' said Adam, laughing.

But Logan was serious. 'Why not?' he replied. 'Listen, I'm

pushed for time with trying to get all these orders complete, as well as getting the watermill up and running. So would you like to give me a hand? You know, over the summer holidays.'

'Seriously?'

'Absolutely,' said Logan. 'It would give you something to do, as well as giving you a bit of experience. To see if it's something that you could take forward. You'll get paid, of course. Not a huge amount, I'm afraid.'

'Anything's better than nothing,' said Adam, his eyes gleaming. 'That would be so cool. I loved helping with those chairs.'

'I know,' replied Logan. 'That's what gave me the idea. So what do you say?'

He held out his hand for Adam to shake.

'Deal,' said Adam.

Logan thought later how nice it would be to have a bit of company around the place. And the hands-on help would certainly ease the workload.

But, he had to finally admit to himself, the main reason he had offered to help Adam was because he was Molly's younger brother. And everyone she cared for meant something to him too. Because he was beginning to care for her more deeply than he ever felt possible.

The hurt still ran deep from his failed marriage. Maybe it would never heal. But he found himself hoping that someday somehow his heart would mend. And with someone as special as Molly.

50

It had been another busy day at the tea garden and Molly was almost relieved by the time the day had ended.

She was tired, but at least she was making a profit. And she was sleeping well each night after all the hard work.

As she tidied up the last of the chairs, she glanced over to the watermill, but it was quiet that day. Logan must be in his workshop, she presumed.

But as she turned to lock up the kitchen, Adam suddenly appeared alongside her.

'Hey, sis,' said Adam, making her start. 'Sorry, didn't mean to make you jump. Or were you asleep standing up? Cos you look really tired.'

'Well, thanks very much,' said Molly in a sarcastic tone. 'Any other compliments you want to shower me with?'

Adam put his head to one side, appearing to think hard before saying, 'Your brownies are excellent.'

Molly rolled her eyes but still smiled at the praise. 'So what do you want? Olivia's left for the day.'

'Pity,' said Adam. 'I thought I might ask her out on a date and see if I could make her smile a bit. That's all. She always looks so sad.'

'Life is tough for some people,' Molly told him. 'Not everyone has an easy ride.'

'I know,' said Adam, nodding. 'That's why I thought if I wined and dined her, it might cheer her up a bit.'

'And how are you going to afford all this wining and dining?' said Molly, expecting the answer to be a request for another loan that she never saw the money returned for.

'I've got a summer job,' replied Adam, looking proud of himself.

'You have?' said Molly, astonished. 'Where?'

'I'm going to be Logan's apprentice,' said Adam.

Molly was stunned. 'His what?'

'Don't look so surprised,' he said. 'He suggested that I try my hand at furniture making this summer to see if I like it. So I'm going to help him with that. Isn't it cool?'

'Very cool,' murmured Molly, wondering why on earth Logan would offer Adam, of all people, a job.

'So it means that I can pay my own way,' said Adam, before looking serious all of a sudden. 'Which means I can repay you this.'

He drew out a £20 note and held it out for Molly to take.

'What's this for?' she asked.

Adam sighed and looked ashamed all of a sudden. 'I took it out of the till a few weeks back.'

Molly looked at him in amazement. 'I don't believe it!' she said. 'That was you? I was going crazy trying to work out who took the money from me.'

'I know, I know,' he said quickly. 'And I'm truly sorry, sis. It was a stupid thing to do and I should have asked you. I know that now.'

Molly stood and looked at Adam. He did actually look sincere in his apology.

'But I was desperate for the money,' he carried on.

'Then you should have asked me or Mum,' she told him, still angry. 'Not taken it for yourself.'

'I know,' he said again. 'But I couldn't ask you or Mum. You see, I wanted to go and see Dad.'

Molly took a deep intake of breath. 'What? Why?' she asked. 'Why on earth did you need to see him?' Suddenly she was terribly worried. 'Is everything OK? Are you in trouble?'

Adam shook his head. 'It's not that. I just thought that maybe he might want to see me now I'm grown up.' He dropped his face to the floor, but not before Molly saw the pain in his eyes. 'It was a mistake. He didn't want to know me, of course. Wasn't interested in seeing any of us.'

Molly sighed. 'I'm so sorry,' she said, stepping forward to give him a hug. 'That must have been upsetting for you.'

She felt him shrug his shoulders whilst she still held him close. Finally, she stepped back to look at him.

'You know, you can always talk to me or Mum,' she said.

'I know,' he said, with a heavy sigh. 'But sometimes it's nice to talk to a man, you know what I mean? Like Logan. He's a good listener.'

'Yes, he is.'

'But thanks, sis,' said Adam.

'For what?' asked Molly, trying to keep up with the conversation.

'For being a great sister,' he said, giving her another quick hug. 'You and Mum have given up so much for us growing up. We do appreciate it, you know.'

Molly blinked away the tears. 'You've never said that before.'

'Then maybe it was overdue,' replied Adam, with a smile.

'I think it was actually,' Molly told him before they both laughed. 'But you're right,' she carried on. 'Mum dedicated everything to us three. Which is why I've told her that she should definitely go out on a date now.'

'A date?'

'With Geoff,' she told him. 'He's invited her to a garden show, but I think she's too shy to say yes.'

Rachel and Geoff had continued to spend a lot of time together in the community garden so when her mum had told Molly about the invite to the garden show, Molly had encouraged her to say yes and go. However her mum had yet to decide.

Adam frowned. 'Not sure I like that idea.'

'Tough!' said Molly, laughing. 'She's allowed a life. Dad left when things got tough. Mum didn't. I think she's allowed out on a date once in nearly thirty years.'

'Yeah, I suppose so,' said Adam, nodding thoughtfully.

'And she's baking bread again which is a good sign,' Molly reminded him. 'I think working on the community garden has really helped her.'

'Yeah, I think it has too.'

Molly took the £20 note and put it in the till, ready to be included in the takings for that day.

'Well, thanks for repaying the money,' she told him.

Adam nodded. 'I'm truly sorry for taking it without asking,' he said. Suddenly he looked brighter. 'Hey, if Mum's going out on a date, then maybe you should as well!'

Molly shook her head. 'How am I supposed to make time for dating when I'm running a business twenty-four seven?' she asked, gesturing around the garden.

'I suppose so,' said Adam, suddenly breaking into a wide grin. 'I guess we'll have to find someone for you. I'm sure me and Ben can come up with a few suggestions.'

'The day I let the two of you run my love life is the day that I'll throw myself into the river,' said Molly, flinging a tea towel at his head as he disappeared out of the back door.

She was smiling to herself though as she closed up for the night. Because she had her own ideas as to who she really wanted to date.

51

After dinner that evening, Molly headed out to the shop to pick up some milk from Cranbridge Stores.

After a chat with Josh about his plans for the stag night, she headed back out onto Riverside Lane.

It was a beautiful summer's evening, still light at eight o'clock in the evening, although the sun was beginning to sink below the hills in the far distance. The sky was streaked with raspberry clouds, but there hadn't been any rain for a couple of weeks now. The river was getting very low. She realised that it was so low that the ducks were able to stand up in the shallow clear water to wash.

Seeing the river always made her think of the watermill and automatically Logan as well.

Molly wanted to thank him for taking on Adam as an apprentice, but when she looked, the workshop was already locked up for the evening.

She felt disappointed, not having had time to talk to him that afternoon. Which was ridiculous, because they were just friends and nothing more. Anyway, the conversation could wait until the following day.

She turned around and headed past the garden, checking over the scene once more. The chairs and tables were straight. Even in the light of the setting sun, it was gorgeous. Her mum's flowers were beginning to bloom and there were bursts of colour over the walls from the climbing roses as they scrambled up and over the top. Despite there being no breeze, she could smell their sweet perfume as she went past.

To Molly's surprise, there was a light on inside the watermill and she found that her feet automatically turned left and onto the narrow bridge across the stream.

'Hello,' she called out as she knocked on the open door.

'Hey,' said Logan, looking up from the large round stone which he had been checking. 'You only just heading home?'

'I finished a little while ago but I needed to pick up some milk,' she told him, placing her shopping bag on the floor next to her.

'I saw that you had another busy day of customers,' he told her, walking towards where she still stood in the doorway.

'It's been non-stop since we reopened,' she replied. 'How was your day?'

'Not bad, but I've had to stop the mill working for now because the water is getting too low,' he told her.

'Oh no,' said Molly. 'I've been enjoying the heatwave so much I didn't think the lack of rain would affect the mill.'

'Hopefully we'll get a break in the weather soon,' he said. 'But the forecast is for more sunshine over the coming days. On the plus side, I finished another piece of furniture today, so that was good.'

'And I hear you've taken on a new apprentice,' she added softly.

He smiled. 'Good news travels fast, eh?' he said, leaning against the door frame.

'Thank you for giving my brother that opportunity,' she told him. 'I'm not sure how much of a help he'll be to you.'

To her surprise, Logan shook his head. 'Actually, I think he's got a real talent for furniture making,' he told her.

Molly was nonplussed. 'But he's never expressed an interest or anything in that kind of thing before.'

'Maybe he never had the opportunity.'

'I guess not having an older male around the place, he probably never had the chance,' she said, frowning.

He reached out and took her chin with his fingers, lifting her eyes up to meet his.

'You've been a fantastic older sister,' he told her, his hazel eyes looking very solemn as he gazed at her.

'How do you know what I was thinking?' she said.

'I told you,' he replied, smiling. 'You're an open book.'

'Humph,' she mumbled, leaning away from his touch. 'That doesn't sound very attractive.'

'Trust me, when you've been surrounded by liars and people taking advantage of you these past few years, it's very attractive.'

The last two words that he spoke hung in the air as she looked up at him. Was he actually saying that she was very attractive? She wasn't sure.

But despite her muddled thoughts, only one thing was uppermost in her mind. So she leant forward and kissed him gently on the cheek.

The air inside the watermill stilled as she leant back. Logan looked at her for the longest time until she found that she was holding her breath.

Finally, she found her voice. 'Well, you're very kind to help out Adam,' she said, her voice a little croaky. 'I just wanted to say thank you.' She began to wonder if she had overstepped the mark. 'Sorry. I shouldn't have kissed you.'

Feeling embarrassed now, she turned to leave and would have

walked out if he hadn't had said, 'Well, you have already kissed me before.'

Molly spun around. Slowly a blush was creeping across her cheeks and she could feel the heat rise in her skin as he took a step towards her, his eyes never leaving hers. 'Oh well, yes, I suppose I have already,' she said. 'I'd forgotten about that.'

'I hadn't.'

The air was thick now and her breath was coming in short gasps as he stood in front of her, their bodies almost touching.

'Anyway, you probably forgot because they weren't proper kisses,' he said softly. 'A proper kiss is on the lips.' His eyes dropped to her mouth. 'It's intense. Romantic. It means something.'

As if in slow motion he leaned forward, but she didn't back away. In fact, she leaned forward a little as well so that their lips finally met.

He kissed her gently at first, but as they both got swept up in their emotion, the kiss grew deeper, more powerful, until she had no idea how many minutes, or even hours, had passed when they finally drew apart.

'That was a proper kiss,' he said, his voice sounding low and husky as he stared down at her.

She nodded, completely unable to speak as she stared up at him.

Then he reached out and stroked her cheek with his hand in a tender gesture before walking out of the watermill, leaving Molly still stunned as she stood there.

She was shocked. No kiss had ever got close to the intensity she had just felt. This was something else. Something special.

And then she knew. It was love. Hopeless, wonderful love.

But perhaps the fact that he had walked away meant that Logan didn't feel the same way?

52

Molly headed downstairs, having quickly got changed after another hectic day at the tea garden.

'Is that what you're wearing to Amber's hen night?' asked her mum, sounding a little surprised.

'Oh, didn't I tell you?' said Molly, glancing down at her simple pink top and denim shorts. 'Amber just wanted a girly night in, so we're heading to her apartment instead.'

'That's a shame,' replied her mum, making a face.

'I don't mind,' said Molly. 'To be honest, we're all so busy that a night in sounds like bliss right now.'

'Is the tea garden getting too much for you?' asked her mum, looking concerned.

Molly shook her head. 'No, it's great. I really love it. It's just...' Her voice trailed away. 'Well, it's only for another two months and then it's all over.'

Rachel came around the table to put her arm around her daughter and give her a squeeze. 'I'm sure something will turn up before then.'

Molly nodded, although she wasn't so sure. If she didn't go back to the community hub, what kind of catering jobs would be available in sleepy Cranbridge? And she was actually enjoying being the boss for once, making the decisions and taking responsibility. It was scary but good scary if she just about stayed within her comfort zone.

'So what are your plans this evening?' asked Molly, picking up a range of nail varnishes that she had brought downstairs.

'Well, I thought I might have a pamper evening as well,' said her mum, leaning over to choose a pale pink varnish. 'Could I borrow this one?'

'Of course,' said Molly, smiling to herself.

'What's so funny?' asked her mum.

'Just that you're doing your nails when you're going to a garden show tomorrow and will probably get your hands dirty with all those plants,' said Molly, laughing.

Rachel shook her head. 'You have obviously never been to a garden show,' she said. 'I won't be gardening tomorrow. It's about wandering around, seeing how the professionals have laid out their own gardens, getting ideas, all the plant stands...'

'A romantic lunch with a glass of something chilled too, I hope,' added Molly.

'I don't know about that,' said her mum quickly. 'Besides, I haven't definitely decided I'll go yet.'

'Why not?' asked Molly.

'Maybe the boys will need me for something.'

Before Molly could answer, the twins wandered into the kitchen.

'What's for dinner?' asked Ben, as usual.

'Whatever's in the fridge,' Molly told him before their mum could reply. 'You can both get yourself something because I'm going out and Mum's going to have a long soak in the bath and do her nails.'

'Why?' asked Adam, nonplussed. 'What are you doing yourself up for?'

'Because she's out tomorrow and she deserves a treat,' Molly told him. 'Not that it matters because you'll be at work with Logan, won't you?'

'Of course,' replied Adam, still frowning.

'I'm so pleased you've found yourself a job,' said her mum, sitting down at the table.

They all looked at Ben, who gave a nonchalant shrug of his shoulders. 'I don't need to work,' he told them. 'My Bitcoin investments have gone up tenfold this year.'

'I have no idea what that even means,' said Molly, shaking her head. 'Well, I'd better get going. I think Amber's ordering in pizza.'

'Not much of a hen night,' said Ben, making a face. 'What about Josh's stag night?'

'It's in the Black Swan,' Molly told him. 'But I think he's just having a drink as well.'

'FIFA first?' said Adam, looking at his brother.

'Deffo,' replied Ben, as they wandered away again.

'It's going to be a late one tonight and I might even crash at Amber's, so if I miss you in the morning, have a great time tomorrow,' said Molly, going around the table to give her mum a kiss on the cheek.

Rachel stayed quiet, so Molly looked down at her until her mum finally met her eyes.

'Just enjoy it, Mum,' she said.

'And you too,' said her mum. 'Shame it's a bit of a quiet send-off for Amber.'

Molly grinned as she picked up the large bag that she had placed on the kitchen counter earlier. The gin bottles inside clanked together as she lifted the handles. She peered in to make sure that the sashes and confetti that she had already bought were definitely in there. Then she reached in and pulled out a pair of pink fluffy handcuffs. 'Just because it's a night in, doesn't mean it'll be a quiet one!' she said, twirling them around on her finger.

She gave her mum a wink before saying goodbye and heading out of the house.

The evening was still warm as she walked along the river towards Riverside Lane. August had been ushered in, but still the heatwave held.

However, her good mood somewhat faltered as the watermill came into view. She glanced at it nervously, but thankfully it was all locked up.

It had been twenty-four hours since she had last seen Logan. Twenty-four hours since they had kissed.

Her heart immediately began to pound in memory of that kiss. It had been special, amazing, incredible. And yet he had walked away.

So she had deliberately managed to avoid seeing him all day. But she couldn't do that every day until he left Cranbridge at the end of the summer. And what on earth would she say to him when she finally saw him?

53

'Yeah, the boys are back in town!' said Del, spilling his beer all over the table as he put his glass down with the force of someone that was already on his fourth pint.

'Steady,' Logan told him, jumping up from the table quickly before he was covered in alcohol at the exact same time as Keith the dog sprang away as well.

'Del!' said Josh, in exasperation. 'Take it easy, mate. It's my stag night, not a scene from *The Hangover*.'

'Not yet anyway,' replied Del, with a grin. 'Where's your brother? I need to find out when the stripper's arriving.'

Josh sighed. 'I just wanted a few beers with my friends, that's all. No strippers. No wild party. Just a quiet celebration.'

'No strippers?' said Del, looking up at them aghast.

'Definitely not,' said Pete, coming to stand with the group. 'What kind of a place do you think I'm running here? There's families dining inside.'

The Black Swan was certainly doing roaring trade these days, thought Logan. But even so, Pete had cordoned off the pub garden for his brother's stag night celebrations. There were a few faces that he didn't recognise, but as it was a relatively small group, he knew most people.

It appeared that he had somehow got to know a few people in the short time that he had been living in Cranbridge, despite his first intention to keep himself to himself. He had also been handed a card from Josh a few days previously.

'What's this?' he had asked.

'A wedding invitation,' Josh had told him. 'You're our friend now so we'd like you to come and celebrate the big day with us.'

Logan had waited for the pang of regret that he had been included, but it never came. He belonged in Cranbridge. And it was a good feeling, he had found. To trust his new friends had been a revelation, but he was safe and secure that they wouldn't let him down.

Dodgy Del was still looking distinctly upset about the lack of strippers and was having a stern word with Pete, who was best man.

But Pete was just laughing. 'First of all, it's unpolitically correct these days, Del,' he said. 'Second, we don't need any women here. It's a stag night.'

Del scowled at him before downing his pint and getting up. 'I need another drink if I'm to deal with all this testosterone by myself,' he muttered, heading towards the back door.

Pete shook his head. 'I mean, honestly,' he said, rolling his eyes. 'We're all hooked up these days. What do we need strippers for?'

Logan stood quiet for a moment until Pete placed a hand on his shoulder.

'Well, I know you and Molly aren't exactly official or anything yet, but give it time.'

Logan opened his mouth to reply but wasn't given the chance as Tom wandered up to talk to them about the roles of the ushers at the wedding. Apparently the tiny church of St Barnabus would take some organising to squeeze all the guests inside to watch the ceremony.

Logan tuned out the conversation as the men discussed who was required at what time at the wedding and thought about what Pete had said. Was everyone really thinking of him and Molly as a couple?

Did anyone know about the kiss that had happened the previous evening? He didn't think so, but it was all he could think about. All he knew was that he had never known a kiss like it. But he made himself walk away from her because it just wasn't fair on Molly. He had made tentative plans to move on from Cranbridge at the end of the summer. However much he yearned for one more kiss. And another after that.

He tried to clear his mind. He felt as if he had been hit over the head every time he thought of Molly.

As he glanced across the garden in the twilight of the summer's evening, he spotted Adam and Ben sneaking through the back gate and past the notice that said 'Private Party'.

'Excuse me,' he said to Tom and Pete, and headed across the grass towards them.

'What are you both doing here?' he asked.

'It's Josh's stag night,' said Adam quickly. 'We've known him for years.'

'Yeah,' said Ben, nodding.

Logan couldn't help but smile as they both looked around him in expectation.

'There's no stripper,' he told them both. 'It's not that kind of stag party.'

'Exactly,' said Josh, coming to stand next to him. 'And are you two even over the legal limit these days?'

Adam looked hurt. 'We're twenty now,' he said.

'Wow, where did those years go?' said Josh, raising his

eyebrows in surprise. 'OK then. There's free drinks over there. Don't make me have to apologise to your mum tomorrow though, OK?'

'OK,' they chorused and headed over to the table to pour themselves a drink.

'I'll keep an eye on them,' said Logan.

'Good luck with that,' Josh told him with a grin. 'I've been trying to do the same for the past ten years, but it's never stopped them getting into many scrapes.' He narrowed his eyes as he spotted Del returning from inside the pub with someone that Logan recognised. It was Barry, the landlord of both Logan and Molly's shops and the tea garden. 'Invitation only,' said Josh in a pointed tone. 'No offence, Barry.'

'None taken,' replied Barry, with a shrug.

'He just wanted a quick word with Logan,' said Del.

Josh looked at Logan, who gave him a nod to say that it was OK.

Josh and Del wandered away and left them alone.

'What's up?' asked Logan, wondering what on earth Barry could say of interest to him.

'I seem to recall that you were only planning on staying here for the summer,' began Barry. 'So I was wondering what kind of end date you had in mind with regards to leasing my place.'

'Haven't decided yet,' replied Logan. For some reason, suddenly the thought of leaving Cranbridge brought him no joy or even peace. If anything, it almost pained him to think of it.

'Right,' said Barry quickly. 'Then I might have to hurry you along. Your contract ends at the end of September, right? And you need to give me two months' notice.'

Logan nodded. 'What's the rush?' he asked, beginning to feel nervous all of a sudden. 'Are you thinking about renting it out again?'

But Barry shook his head. 'Nah. I know a bloke who's interested in both of my shops on Riverside Lane, as it happens. He runs a chain of them private shops, shall we say?'

His lurid grin gave Logan no doubt that he was referring to the kind of places with blacked-out windows that sold various mail-order items.

'It's all sexy lingerie and whatnots,' carried on Barry, still grinning, spelling it out to him.

Logan nodded. 'Yeah, that much I understood.'

'It's good business, they say.' Barry leaned forward to whisper, 'Thinking of getting into it myself.'

He waggled his eyebrows in an alarming manner and Logan quickly stepped backwards.

'Yeah, I get the drift,' he said, trying not to shudder. 'Look, I'm not sure it's in keeping with Riverside Lane.'

He tried to imagine his grandad's reaction when he found out. Let alone the rest of the owners on the parade of shops when they saw the blacked-out windows in pretty Riverside Lane.

And then there was Molly...

'Doesn't he only need one shop?' asked Logan. 'Your mate, I mean? Surely two would just be too large for his requirements?'

'I told him what you'd done with the place, using it for storage as well,' said Barry. 'He said that's what made him consider both places.'

'Right.' Logan instantly felt guilty.

'So I'll be in touch about serving you notice on the end of your lease,' said Barry. 'And the girl with the cakes as well. Not that it really matters as she got the place so cheap off me. I suppose they could always use that garden next to it for parking. A nice bit of tarmac instead of all those messy flowers, eh?'

In a daze, Logan shook Barry's hand just to get rid of him. The village would lose the community garden as well? It was a terrible idea.

He stood there for a while, thinking about what on earth he could do to remedy the situation. He wasn't going to stay in Cranbridge, but it sounded as if both shops and the garden were going to be sold anyway.

He glanced over the river to the apartment above Cranbridge Stores where Molly was celebrating Amber's hen night and wondered how on earth he was going to tell her that her dream of the tea garden becoming more permanent was at an end already.

54

Amber's apartment was filled with much laugher and merriment as befitted a hen night celebration.

'Woohoo!' said Lucy, standing and swaying a little. 'Hey, how strong was that cocktail? My head's spinning.'

'So's mine,' said Amber, wincing a little.

Molly had to agree that she too was feeling pretty drunk. She had lost count of how many drinks she had had.

Belle had made up large batches of a cocktail in various jugs which were now empty. Nobody was quite sure what else other than gin had gone into the cocktail mix but it was certainly having the desired effect.

'Strong? It's my uncle's special recipe so of course it's strong,' said Belle, slurring her words ever so slightly.

Amber looked horrified. 'Your Uncle Mick's special punch recipe?' She giggled. 'No wonder my tongue's gone numb.'

'My legs too,' said Lucy, sliding down across the arm of the sofa to an almost lying position.

Belle's Uncle Mick had been the landlord of the Black Swan Inn at one time and his home-made punch had become notorious thanks to the effect that the strong mixture had on anyone who was unwise enough to drink it.

'What were we talking about again?' asked Amber, picking up her half-full glass and taking another sip. She was wearing a fake bridal veil which had twinkling fairy lights all over, giving her a festive halo.

'Your honeymoon,' said Molly, laughing.

But Amber shook her head. 'No, no, that wasn't it.' She looked at Belle. 'What were you saying before you filled up our glasses?'

Belle looked nonplussed for a moment before her eyes lit up as she turned to Molly. 'It wasn't me,' she said, shaking her head before saying 'ouch' and clutching her head. 'It was Molly. And Logan. Molly and Logan.'

'Ah!' said Lucy, struggling to get up from where she had been lying down. 'Lolly and Mogan!'

'Near enough,' replied Amber, giggling.

'We should be talking about Josh and Amber,' said Molly, not quite drunk enough yet to be relaxed about her friends talking about her love life, or rather lack of it. 'How romantic it is that they're getting married and all that stuff.'

'Nah!' said Belle, so loud that she almost shouted the word. 'Changing the subject!'

'She is!' slurred Amber. 'Stop, you know, changing the thingy. Tells us about, er, whatisname.'

'Logan,' said Belle, with a nod.

'Logan!' shouted Lucy.

'Logan!' said Amber, joining in.

'Sssshhhh!' Molly told them, glancing at the open window in the lounge. 'He'll hear you!'

'He's at the inn,' said Belle, pointing with her glass towards the window but managing to slosh some drink onto the floor in the process. 'My inn. Mine and Pete's. Lovely Pete.'

Molly clutched her head, which was beginning to feel a little woolly, and hoped that her friends were now getting too drunk to follow any kind of conversation. It wasn't that she kept secrets from them. She wasn't sure that she ever had kept anything from her friends. And she wasn't regretting kissing Logan because she would remember that incredible kiss for the rest of her life. For some reason, she just wanted to keep it close to her heart for a little while longer. It had been magical and the only way to keep it that way was to only whisper it to herself and not say the words out loud.

'Tom told me something about Logan.' Lucy then drained her own glass again and was holding it out for someone to replenish her drink. 'But I can't remember what he said.'

Molly focused on her friend. 'What did he say?' she asked, trying to keep her voice casual, but it was hard when she was feeling so drunk.

'Aha!' said Belle, laughing. 'I told you that she liked him!'

Molly went to wave her friend away with her hand but only succeeded in knocking a bowl of crisps to the floor.

'Of course she likes him,' said Amber. 'I like him. Just not like I like my Josh. I love him.'

'Yeah, we know.' Lucy gave her a soppy grin.

Amber giggled. 'I'm getting married. I still can't believe it.'

Belle reached over to the packet of sparkly confetti that Molly had brought and threw a bunch of it in the air. 'Da dum de dum,' she said, singing what was most likely to be the wedding chorus, although it was hard to tell as it was so out of tune.

'I know what it was!' said Lucy suddenly. 'Rain.'

'What are you talking about?' asked Belle, thankfully stopping her dreadful singing. 'Wayne who?'

Lucy laughed. 'Rain! You know, clouds and then rain! Rain!'

'I don't want rain on my wedding day,' said Amber, shaking her head. 'Don't let it rain!'

'No, not then,' said Lucy. 'Tom told me we need rain, otherwise the watermill won't work any more.'

'Well, yeah, duh!' Belle told them. 'It's a watermill, isn't it?'

'But if it doesn't work,' began Molly, before stopping.

Thankfully, nobody appeared to hear her and were having a complex and very drunken confused conversation about weather forecasts and how inaccurate they were. So it gave her a moment's peace to try and think through her muddled thoughts. If the watermill didn't work, then maybe Logan would leave. If he didn't have the watermill to take care of any more, then why would he stay? And she definitely, absolutely didn't want him to leave. Because she loved him.

Suddenly she knew what she had to do. The idea came through so clearly to her brain that she shot out of her seat to stand up.

'Are you off?' asked Belle, looking up at her with wide but somewhat hazy eyes.

'Off to see Logan.' Lucy laughed as she slipped off the sofa and onto the floor.

'We need a rain dance,' said Molly.

The others looked up at her. 'Dancing?' said Amber. 'Oh yes! Let's dance!'

The bride-to-be fiddled with her phone for a moment before Beyoncé suddenly began to sing out of the nearby speakers on almost full volume, the heavy bass making the oak floorboards shake.

But as her friends began to somewhat haphazardly stagger around the floor, Molly was still trying to link together a coherent thought.

It was Stanley who had been telling her recently when they had been chatting about the long hot summer. Something about native American tribes performing some kind of dance to invoke the rain.

And then, in her drunken state, Molly decided that was exactly what was needed to be done and headed towards the stairs.

'Wait!' screamed Belle, grabbing something off the table and throwing it at Molly, who by some miracle managed to catch it.

She looked down at the pink fluffy handcuffs that she had brought with her.

'So he can't get away,' said Belle, laughing before continuing her dance.

Molly slid them in her pocket and then headed downstairs, feeling determined that she could make it rain. Then everything would surely be all right and Logan would stay in Cranbridge. Preferably forever.

55

The stag do had gone well and Logan had certainly enjoyed himself, although he hadn't had as much to drink as the others.

Dodgy Del in particular was in a bit of a state, but thankfully Pete was going to let him sleep it off in one of the upstairs rooms of the inn.

Ben and Adam were sitting in a corner near the firepit, giggling away, and had also had a fun evening.

Logan left them to it. But he was in a good mood as he left the Black Swan and walked out into the dark night. In fact, it seemed even darker than recently. The sky had clouded over for the first time in weeks and so made the night seem blacker than it had done for ages.

He crossed the middle narrow pedestrian bridge deep in thought. August had arrived already. The summer was whizzing past at an alarming rate and he would have to decide what to do when September arrived. Leaving would be hard, that much he knew. Leaving his grandad even harder. But leaving Molly? That would be the hardest cut of all.

He sighed and slid his hands into the pockets of his cargo shorts as he wandered along Riverside Lane. What on earth was he going to do about his workshop? It sounded as if Barry was going to finish the lease, so he would have to move his business on. But the trouble was that he was actually enjoying working on the lane. It was a nice environment with good neighbours. Really good neighbours, he thought with a secret smile to himself.

He felt for his front door key in his pocket and was just about to draw it out when he heard singing. Drunken, out-of-tune singing.

At least they were happy, whoever it was, he thought, walking past his shop and on towards the tea garden. And that was when he saw her. Molly. She was dancing in the river just by the watermill. Thankfully the water was barely ankle-deep, as he well knew. But still, he was concerned enough about her to pick up speed a little as he walked towards her.

'Hey,' he said, coming to stand on the riverbank near to her. 'I thought you were at Amber's hen night.'

Molly stopped and spun around, staggering slightly as she did so. Logan immediately realised that she was not only very drunk but covered in many pieces of sparkly confetti. She appeared to shine like some kind of mesmerising apparition in the darkness.

'Hey!' she said, somewhat overenthusiastically, giving him a wide smile. 'It's you!'

'It's most definitely me,' he replied. 'What are you doing in the river?'

She rolled her eyes. 'Doing a rain dance, of course,' she told him, as if it were the most obvious thing in the world.

'I see,' he said, trying to humour her.

She really was very drunk. Her speech was a little too loud and a little bit slurred. On top of that, all her movements were completely exaggerated.

'Gotta keep going,' she muttered, beginning to spin around once more.

'Why?' he asked, suddenly keen to know what on earth had brought all this on.

'For the mill,' she said, somewhat exasperated. 'You know!'

'Er, right,' he replied.

Whilst it was true that the mill required the river to be more full than it was at present, he hadn't realised quite how much it had meant to Molly.

'You must dance as well!' she suddenly said, pointing at him.

Logan began to shake his head. 'I don't think that's necessary,' he began to say.

But it was no use. Molly had taken his hand and was trying to pull him into the river. He could stop her. He was certainly taller and stronger than she was. And yet, some small part of him wanted to be led into the river. Wanted to dance with Molly right there in the darkness. Because it was ridiculous and silly, something that he would never normally do.

So he held on to her hand and waded into the shallow water alongside her, despite the fact that his trainers were now soaking wet, and twirled her around, humming a tune as he did so.

And all the time he was smiling. Because it was Molly. And there was no one else he would rather be with in the world than her at that moment.

Because he was falling in love with her.

* * *

This was great, thought Molly. With Logan alongside her, it was bound to rain.

And rain was needed, oh-so desperately. She just couldn't quite remember why.

She held on to his hand as he spun her around gently once more. But the spinning wasn't helping her woozy head and she kept crashing into something hard, which she suspected was Logan's chest.

She held out her spare hand to steady herself, even though the world continued to sway long after she had stopped. It was only a short time later that she realised that she was clutching at Logan's shirt in an effort to stay upright.

'You OK?' he asked gently.

In the darkness, she could still see his soft hazel eyes looking down at her. Could still see that strong jaw and the outline of those lips that she could still remember touching hers.

'You kissed me,' she blurted out.

He nodded, still staring down at her. 'Yes, I did.'

She so wanted him to stay in Cranbridge. And then she suddenly thought of a brilliant idea! She slipped her hand inside her shorts pocket and drew out the pink fluffy handcuffs. Then she swiftly snapped one end onto her wrist and quickly snapped the other onto Logan's wrist.

'I've got you!' she told him, triumphantly.

He opened his mouth to speak again, but something weird happened instead. He made a strange rumbling noise.

'How did you do that?' she said, looking up at him in wonder.

He shook his head. 'That wasn't me,' he replied. 'I think we're about to get a thunderstorm.'

'We are?' She looked up at the sky and heard the rumble of thunder again. 'I'm not dreaming this?'

'Only if I'm having the same dream,' he told her, reaching out to stroke something from her cheek.

Then she felt something else land on her forehead.

'What is it?' she asked, rubbing her skin.

'It's rain,' he told her, smiling.

'It is?' She looked around and then down on the water surface, where she could see the droplets of rain as they landed on the river. 'Yippee! It's raining!' she shouted. 'I did it!'

'Yes, you did,' he said.

She went to move her hands up to behind his neck but remembered that she had locked their wrists together with the handcuffs.

'And you've most definitely got me,' he reminded her softly with a smile.

She reached up with her free hand and brought his head down towards hers so that their lips could meet again.

But this time the kiss didn't deepen. It was just as sweet as before and gave her as many tingles as she had felt the previous day, but he stepped away almost immediately, or so it felt to her.

'We'd better get out of the water in case we get struck by lightning,' he said softly.

'I don't care!' she said.

'Then it's a good job that I do,' he told her, taking her hand and leading her towards the riverbank.

* * *

Logan already felt as if he had been struck by lightning. Molly reaching up to kiss him had been one of the sweeter moments in his life.

He led her onto the riverbank and realised that the rain was coming down a lot heavier now.

'It really worked!' whispered Molly, standing next to him and still holding his hand in hers.

'I'm glad the mill is so important to you,' said Logan, turning to face her.

But Molly shook her head. 'Not the mill. You,' she told him, smiling.

Logan gulped. This was his worst fear. She was beginning to have feelings for him and that was bad. So very bad.

It was his fault. He had kissed her when he had known it was a terrible idea. The trouble was that he so wanted to do it again and he had needed to summon every ounce of willpower not to kiss her back when she had just kissed him. Because she was drunk and there were rules about these things, of course.

But also because he wasn't sure once he started that he would ever stop wanting to kiss Molly.

'We need to get you home,' said Logan, as the rain continued to pour down.

She seemed unwilling to let go of his hand and, truth be told, he liked the feeling of her smaller hand in his. So they walked hand in hand all the way back to her cottage, where he waited until she eventually found her front door key and opened up the front door.

As she turned around to face him, he looked down at the pink fluffy handcuffs and realised that they were only pretend ones and he quite easily managed to free his wrist.

She suddenly leaned forward, as if to kiss him once more.

But this time, he forced himself to turn his head so that her gentle lips landed on his cheek instead. She frowned up at him as if his rejection registered somewhere deep inside.

'Goodnight,' he said, walking back down the garden path.

It was only then that he realised how empty his hand felt without hers to hold.

56

The rain was still hammering down against the bedroom window when Molly woke up with a raging hangover the following day.

Perhaps she had been a little too zealous with her rain dance, she thought.

She sat bolt upright in bed, eyes clicked wide open before groaning at her aching head and slumped back against the pillow. But she could feel her cheeks burning red hot as she squirmed under the covers with embarrassment. Had she really danced in front of Logan in the middle of the river? Had she truly performed a rain dance?

She groaned as she glanced down at the fluffy pink handcuff still on her wrist. Of course she had. What on earth must he think of her?

She grabbed her phone and realised that she must have slept through her alarm. It was gone nine o'clock and the tea garden was due to open in an hour's time! She threw off the covers and staggered around, quickly getting dressed, as well as extricating herself from the handcuffs.

Once she had splashed her face, she felt a little more human, although really not that much better.

All was quiet upstairs apart, from her brothers snoring away their own hangovers, from the sounds of it. Downstairs was quiet too as she remembered that her mum had intended to leave early for her day out with Geoff at the garden show.

As she left the house, she quickly sent a text wishing her mum a lovely day before trying to get her fuzzy brain in gear for the busy day ahead.

She kept her head down, in deference to the rain that was still hammering down, as well as eager not to make eye contact with anyone. A quick glance at the watermill made her feel even worse and she picked up speed as she headed across the garden towards the back door of the kitchen.

To her surprise, it was already open as Olivia must have turned up before her.

'Good morning,' Molly said, as she headed into the kitchen, trying to sound as if she weren't dying inside of a hangover.

'Morning,' replied Olivia with a small smile. 'I let myself in. I hope that was OK.'

'I wouldn't have given you the key if I didn't trust you,' said Molly, reaching out to sink gratefully onto a nearby stool.

'Are you OK?' asked Olivia. 'You look a little pale.'

'It was Amber's hen night last night,' Molly told her with a groan.

Olivia smiled. 'Ooof, no wonder you're suffering.'

'At least we won't be getting many walk-in customers this morning,' said Molly, glancing out at the pouring rain.

'Actually we still have a few cream teas booked in the diary,' said Olivia. 'If they're sitting under the awnings, then they'll probably still come as it's still warm. Such a change in the weather though,' she added, shaking her head. 'I don't know where all this rain has come from.'

Molly gave a soft groan. Had she broken the heatwave with her dance? She sighed. 'I don't know about you, but I need a strong coffee.' She glanced at the large coffee machine but couldn't face setting it up yet. 'Actually, I'm going to try one of Amber's drinks from the new coffee machine in the shop for a change. Do you want one?'

'Yes, please,' said Olivia. 'In the meantime, do you want me to start on another couple of cakes? We're running low on carrot cake, scones and those white chocolate and rose petal cookies as well.'

'That would be great,' said Molly, thinking how much more confident Olivia was these days.

She left her assistant to her baking and put up the hood on her jacket once more to scurry down Riverside Lane to Cranbridge Stores.

She found Amber sitting on one of the benches on the veranda outside, looking equally pale.

'Good morning,' said Molly, sinking down gratefully next to her friend.

'Morning,' said Amber, with a grimace. 'But it's in no way good.'

'Hangover?' asked Molly.

'The worst. You?'

'God, yes,' replied Molly, leaning back against the bench so that her head rested against the wall of the shop. 'What on earth was in that cocktail?'

'If it was Belle's Uncle Mick's recipe then probably everything,' said Amber, rubbing her head. 'I may never eat anything again.'

'What happened after I left?' asked Molly.

'I have no idea,' said Amber. 'I can only vaguely remember you leaving, to be honest. I passed out on my bed with Belle next to me and Lucy on the sofa. Josh had to go back to the inn and grab a room there.'

Molly laughed and then immediately regretted it as she winced at her sore head. 'Thank God it's raining. I'm not sure I'm in any fit state to serve too many customers today.'

'Well, that doesn't sound like much of a business plan,' said Josh, who had just come out of the shop.

'How come you look so normal and healthy?' asked Molly, scowling at his almost sunny disposition.

Josh grinned. 'I stuck to beer, so I'm not too bad. Del may never recover from the embarrassment.'

'Why?' asked Molly, agog. 'What did he do?'

'Fell flat on his face, only narrowly avoiding the firepit,' Josh told her.

Molly gave a grunt. 'He's not the only one who's embarrassed.'

Amber looked at her, somewhat startled. 'Why? What happened to you?'

'Nothing. I'm fine,' muttered Molly.

Thanks to Logan, thought Molly, nodding ruefully. She always seemed to be owing him a favour in one way or another.

'If this rain keeps up, at least it sounds as if we might be able to get the watermill up and running again,' said Josh. 'Who wants a coffee?'

Molly and Amber both nodded, content to sit outside and hope the fresh air made them feel better.

But Molly wasn't sure anything would make her feel better. Logan had been a proper gentleman, of course. He had made sure she was safe and had even walked her home. But he hadn't wanted to kiss her again. Maybe once was enough as far as he was concerned.

Molly stared at the rain which was still pouring down. At least the river was beginning to look a little more healthy already, she thought. But she realised that in her haste to help Logan out with the watermill, she was likely to take a hit with the tea garden business instead. She truly was an idiot. A lovestruck idiot who cared more about him than she did about herself.

Because she did really care for him. She loved him.

But she had no idea how he felt about her, apart from that one scorching kiss. And the fact that he had rejected her kiss last night.

Now she wasn't sure what felt worse, her aching head or her breaking heart.

57

Logan looked out at the pouring rain from the open door of his workshop and smiled to himself.

The sight of Molly dancing in the river the previous evening would stay with him for a long time. Perhaps even forever.

He turned away, still smiling, to look over at Adam, who was struggling with his own hangover.

'You really didn't need to come in today,' he told him.

'Better than feeling rubbish at home,' said Adam, concentrating on a chair that he was helping to make. 'And it's only my second day so I didn't want to skive off already!'

'That's good work,' said Logan, wandering over to check on the join that he had just connected.

'Thanks,' said Adam, beaming with pride. 'I was quite pleased with this bit.'

Logan nodded his approval before walking over to his desk to check his to-do list. He was enjoying being part of a team and having a bit of company throughout the working day. It had always just been him and the business. But it was nice having a sort of apprentice for the summer. Someone with whom to hopefully pass on the skills that he had managed to teach himself. He could see now why his grandad had always enjoyed his teaching career. He would be sad when it came to an end and Adam headed back to university, he realised.

Of course, the chances were, the workshop would be closed by autumn as well, with Barry not renewing the lease. But he was finding that decision harder and harder to come to terms with. He had thought that life in Cranbridge would be dull and that everyone would be secretly pointing fingers at him after his wife's notorious affair. However, that couldn't be further from the truth. People had welcomed him but left him to his privacy. He was also enjoying seeing his grandad most days and felt better that he could contribute and help him out when needed.

Most of all, it was the thought of Molly that was stopping him from being so sure about leaving. Quiet Molly who had been so lacking in confidence but had hidden talents and secret rain dance skills as well.

Logan found he couldn't stop himself smiling once more and wondered how hungover she was feeling that morning.

However, his good mood quickly faded when he looked up to see who had just entered the workshop. It was Barry.

'What can I do for you?' asked Logan, going up to him.

'Thought we could have a further discussion about business matters,' said Barry. He was obviously desperate to sell the shop and needed an answer from Logan as to when he would be vacating the premises.

Logan looked over at Adam and decided that he wanted to have the conversation on his own and so asked Adam to give them five minutes and to take a break.

Adam nodded and headed out the front door past Barry. Logan noted that he headed in the direction of the tea garden, although it was still raining and likely to be closed. He knew that Adam had a rather large crush on Olivia.

Barry cleared his throat. 'About what we were talking about last night...'

'You mean the private shop?' said Logan, still somewhat aghast that such a thing would ever fit in somewhere like Cranbridge.

'Shops plural.' Barry gave him a smile that was a borderline sneer. 'And if the weather has broken, then that tea garden will be closing up pretty darn quickly and I can get that land included in the sale as well.'

'I'm sure it's just a rainy day to clear the summer air,' said Logan quickly. It would surely break Molly's heart to have to give up the tea garden any earlier than September. But that left the question of what she would do when the weather turned and autumn finally began.

His mind was racing as he tried to tune into what Barry was saying about the end of his lease.

'So you'll vacate by the end of September,' said Barry. 'Sounds fair to me as that was the original agreement.'

Logan realised that he had no choice. After all, the place wasn't his.

'Sounds good,' said Logan in a dull tone.

But suddenly he wasn't so sure that leaving Cranbridge was the right thing for him at all. How on earth could he turn this nightmare around for everyone?

He headed over to the window and looked out at the river. Then, slowly, Logan began to see the light.

He turned around and smiled at Barry. 'Tell you what,' he began. 'Let me give you a counter-offer and see what we can agree on.'

An idea was beginning to form in his mind. It was crazy and yet nothing had ever felt so right in the whole of his life. And, if he got everything right, it might just be a brand-new beginning and not just for him.

* * *

Molly stood still outside Logan's workshop, holding the coffee for Olivia that she was taking to the tea garden.

She certainly hadn't meant to eavesdrop, but she had recognised Barry's voice when she had neared the open door and hadn't wanted to see him in case he decided to increase the rent of the shop or something.

So as she stood nearby out of sight, she heard Barry and Logan agree that he would vacate the shop at the end of September.

Shocked to her core, Molly quickly walked off in the other direction without being seen. It was just as she had feared. Logan was definitely leaving. There hadn't been anything between them this summer. Or even if there had, it hadn't been enough to keep him in Cranbridge.

It sounded as if Logan would head off soon after Josh and Amber's wedding and everything would revert back to how it was. The tea garden would close and she could forget about her summer with Logan altogether.

If only that were true. Because the thought of forgetting him might just break her heart forever even though he was obviously ready to move on without her.

The rain quickly mingled with the tears running down her cheeks as she walked in a daze alongside the river and away from Logan.

58

Everything looked and felt fresh and green again when the rain finally stopped after a few days of heavy downpours, thought Molly. It was now late into August and the heavy morning dew had kept the grass green along the riverbanks and in the tea garden.

Tidying away the last of the menus after another busy day at work, Molly could hear the mill working over the other side of the stream. The gentle clacking and crunching of the turning wheels was a soothing sound. She liked it. It reminded her of Logan.

She missed him terribly. It had been two weeks since she had overheard his conversation with Barry. Two weeks since she had performed her rain dance. Two weeks since she had tried to kiss him and he had literally turned the other cheek.

It was hardly surprising, she thought. He was a kind enough man that he didn't want to hurt her. He was planning to leave and so he had kept her at arm's length that evening in the thunderstorm.

So she had reciprocated in kind ever since. Therefore it had been two weeks of polite, brief conversations about the weather and how busy the tea garden was. Two weeks of her heart aching for him and missing him. But it wasn't meant to be. That much she had to accept now.

But she could feel her heart breaking at the thought of him leaving for good.

Thankfully for now there were other things to concentrate on.

Like, Amber and Josh's wedding the following day.

Molly stood back and looked at the cake that she had made them. It probably didn't suit the fancy reception hotel at all, but Amber had left the choice of decoration up to her. She felt her choice was the best reflection on their personalities. They weren't bling and glamour kind of people. They liked home-made and eco-friendly ideas. So she had iced the cake with a soft buttercream and covered it in edible flowers, all picked from both the tea garden and her mum's garden which were placed like confetti falling down and around the three tiers.

Molly thought that the design suited Amber and Josh and just hoped that they would like it. Which, thankfully, they did.

'Oh, I love it!' said Amber, when they popped in on the way to their wedding rehearsal. She had tears in her eyes. 'Thank you so much.'

'You're welcome,' replied Molly, giving her a hug.

'It's great,' Josh told her. 'It's the perfect cake for us.'

She smiled at him as he too embraced her. 'I hoped you'd like it. I'll take it over to the hotel in the morning.'

'It's brilliant,' said Amber.

'Isn't it,' said Dodgy Del, appearing at the doorway where the back door was open.

They all looked at him.

'When did you care about our wedding cake so much?' asked Josh, laughing.

'The cake?' said Del, looking confused. 'No, I meant the hops! They're in flower, aren't they?'

Somewhat bemused, they followed Del outside into the early-evening air.

'Look!' he said, walking over to the pergola, where the hops were now almost ten feet high and had scrambled eagerly up the oak towards the skies.

Molly peered at the flowers that had been in bud for a week or so and were now bursting into life. She could even smell their sweet, spicy aroma in the air.

'Lovely,' she said. 'They're very pretty.'

'I don't care what they look like,' said Del. 'It means that my beer's finally on the way! I tell you, I've never waited this long for a pint in my life!'

They all laughed and left Del to talk sweet nothings to his hops whilst they walked towards the tiny village church of St Barnabus to rehearse the following day's wedding ceremony.

Thankfully a warm, sunny day was predicted for the wedding.

The other bridesmaids and ushers all joined them for the rehearsal, along with Josh's best man, Pete and Keith the dog who was an unofficial usher. Molly found herself tearing up a little as Josh and Amber practised their vows and made a mental note to make sure she had a tissue tucked somewhere in the beautiful bridesmaid dress that Belle had made for her.

They wandered back along the river afterwards, with everyone chatting excitedly.

'Oooh, let's go and see Logan,' said Lucy, heading towards the narrow bridge. 'The door's open, so he must still be in there.'

Molly hesitated and held back from following the others. She could hear the gentle clacking and crunching of the turning wheels and wood as the wheat was ground into flour. It was a soothing sound but did nothing to quiet her distress that he was leaving.

Belle and Amber waited with her as everyone else headed into the mill before leading her over to the wall by the tea garden.

'What gives?' asked Belle in a hushed tone.

'What are you talking about?' asked Molly.

'You and Logan,' said Belle, raising her eyebrows in question. 'I thought you two were getting along OK. Better than OK, in fact.'

'We were,' said Molly quickly. 'We are, I guess.'

'You guess?' Amber looked at her with concern in her eyes. 'What's happened? You've been so sad these past two weeks.'

Molly hadn't said anything about the conversation she had overheard between Barry and Logan. Maybe after the wedding, but not now. For now it was all about Amber and Josh.

'Nothing,' she told Amber. 'Look, don't worry about it. Let's just concentrate on the wedding tomorrow.'

'Oh that's all in hand,' said Amber, with a wave of her hand. 'To be honest, as long as Josh is waiting for me at the church, everything else will fall into place.'

At that moment, Amber's mobile rang and so she stepped away to take the call.

'You want to tell me what's really going on?' asked Belle gently. 'Because I thought you liked him. *Really* liked hm.'

'I do,' Molly told her, with a heavy sigh. 'I even think that I've fallen in love with him.'

'That's great,' said Belle, looking delighted for a moment before realising that Molly was still looking miserable. 'Well, maybe you should be having this conversation with him instead of me.'

'I can't,' said Molly, shaking her head. 'He's leaving soon anyway, so what's the point.'

Belle looked confused and went to say something more when Amber came up to them, still holding her phone in her hand. She looked dazed and shocked.

'What's the matter?' asked Molly. 'What's happened?'

'It's the hotel,' said Amber, bursting into tears. 'Apparently there was a fire earlier today. A big one. There's no way we can hold our wedding reception there. What on earth are we going to do?'

59

Logan was chatting with his friends and showing them the workings of the watermill when there was a shout of distress from outside.

There was a scramble as everyone headed outside to see what was going on.

Amber was crying and looking very upset as Josh raced across to reach her.

'What's going on?' asked Del.

'I don't know,' said Tom, as Lucy ran over to Amber as well. 'I've never seen her so upset.'

Everyone followed Josh to find out what had happened.

'It was the wedding organiser at the hotel,' Amber was saying by the time Logan reached the small crowd. 'There was a fire in the kitchen which is next to the main ballroom. The whole place is filled with smoke and debris from the fire. We can't possibly use it tomorrow for our reception.'

There was a pause as everyone took in the terrible news. Logan looked at Molly for a moment, but she appeared to be deep in thought, staring across the river.

'Can you postpone the wedding?' asked Lucy gently.

Amber shook her head. 'The banns have been read in the church already and we've got relatives coming from all over the country who are already on their way.'

Keith the dog, sensing unhappiness, came over to sit on Amber's feet and lean against her legs which at least made everyone's mood lighten slightly.

Amber stroked the dog's soft fur whilst everyone else scratched their heads and tried to think of an alternative.

Josh began to pace up and down. 'What about the Black Swan?' he asked, looking pleadingly at his brother.

Pete and Belle looked at each other before speaking.

'It's possible,' said Pete, sounding a little unsure. 'Just a bit complicated, that's all.'

'It'll be fine,' said Belle quickly. 'We'll just cancel all the lunch and dinner reservations for tomorrow. Everyone will understand, I'm sure.'

Knowing how full the Black Swan Inn was every weekend, Logan could understand their hesitancy in making sure no customers were upset with the sudden cancellations.

'Or what about that place in Aldwych?' said Tom. 'The Red Lion or whatever it's called.'

'Nah, mate,' said Del, with a grimace. 'Got shut down last month after it failed a food hygiene test.'

'There's no need to reorganise or cancel anything,' said Molly suddenly into the short silence.

Everyone turned their heads to look at her as she broke into a wide smile.

'We'll hold it right here in the tea garden,' she said.

* * *

Molly was aware that everyone was looking at her in complete amazement, but for once, she didn't mind the attention. In fact, she had never been so sure or so confident in herself at any time before that moment.

Amber said, 'Here? In the tea garden?'

They all looked in the direction that Molly was facing, trying to imagine how it would look. But Molly could see it all perfectly in her mind's eye. It was all she'd been thinking about for the past few minutes since Amber had told them about the cancellation of the wedding reception. It would absolutely work, she felt.

'Well, it's pretty enough,' said Amber slowly.

Josh nodded, also looking around. 'And right here in Cranbridge, so everyone can just walk from the church and not worry about getting back in their cars.'

'We've already got all the tables and chairs,' said Molly.

'Thanks to me,' added Del, with a grin.

'Thanks to Logan, they're now Playboy bunny free,' said Pete, rolling his eyes.

As well as the extra tables and chairs that Logan had made for her, thought Molly, looking across at him. He met her eyes with his hazel eyes and for a second she almost lost her train of thought before concentrating back on the bride and groom.

'It's big enough for everyone who's invited,' Molly told them. 'Everyone can sit down to eat and there's room for the little ones to play as well. The weather forecast is for fine and sunny weather, so it will be warm too.'

'What about decorations?' asked Lucy.

'Amber's always got spare bunting,' said Belle, nodding and smiling her approval.

'We'll make sure there's extra flowers on the tables and fairy lights everywhere,' Molly told them.

'But what about the band that the hotel were providing?' asked Amber.

'We'll try to organise someone else, but if not, Pete can play something,' said Belle, looking across at her boyfriend, who nodded.

'It would be my pleasure,' he said, looking directly at his brother with an emotional look on his face.

Josh smiled. 'Brilliant,' he murmured. 'Not sure why we didn't think of that before.'

'But what about the wedding breakfast?' said Amber, still looking concerned. 'The whole thing was going to be catered by the hotel.'

'People will be happy to help themselves to a really fancy buffet,' Molly told her.

'But who's going to provide the buffet?' asked Amber frowning in thought.

'Me of course,' said Molly, smiling at her friend. 'Who else?'

Molly was full of confidence and self-belief. She knew deep down that she could and absolutely would be able to organise everything for her best friend. After all, she could do anything now, couldn't she?

Amber gave a little cry of joy before rushing forward to give Molly a huge hug. Then she turned around to look at Josh.

'So?' he said, smiling at them both. 'What do you think?'

Amber gave her fiancé a teary smile. 'I think it sounds perfect,' she told him. 'Maybe even more so than the fussy hotel reception that we didn't really want. But I'm worried about all the work for Molly.'

Molly shook her head. 'I think I'll have plenty of volunteers to help me,' she said, looking around the group, who were all nodding and agreeing.

She looked at Logan last, who was also nodding and saying that he was happy to help.

Perhaps she would have some time with him at the wedding. She might even let herself have a dance with him. But it would be their last dance before he left.

In the meantime, she had twenty-four hours to organise a wedding reception in the tea garden. In the past, the thought of such a huge undertaking would have horrified and stressed her but now she only felt excitement. She had finally realised that she could meet any business challenge head on and succeed, whatever the odds.

If only she felt as confident about her love for Logan having a happy ending.

60

It was late in the evening and the sun was already sinking behind the horizon. However, Molly had no time to enjoy the glorious summer sunset that evening. She had a wedding reception to organise.

She looked up as she heard the gate to the tea garden click open and was pleased and somewhat relieved to see Olivia walking towards her.

'Hi,' Molly said. 'You got my text? Thanks so much for coming in. I'm sorry to ruin your Friday night plans.'

'No worries,' said Olivia, with a shrug. 'I wasn't doing anything anyway.'

'Look, Josh and Amber's wedding venue has had to cancel,' Molly told her. 'So we're going to hold it here instead.'

Olivia's eyes widened in alarm, but she didn't say anything.

'We're going to put on a buffet for everyone to help themselves,' carried on Molly. 'Here's what I was thinking,' she added, as they walked into the kitchen. 'We'll need some large quiches. Just what we normally make here, OK? Some vegetarian, the others with salmon or ham, OK?'

Olivia nodded. 'What about those savoury tarts?'

'Great idea,' said Molly. 'We'll need some of those pea, feta and mint ones that you learnt to make this week, OK?'

'That's fine,' said Olivia.

'It's going to be a late one, I'm afraid,' Molly told her.

'I don't mind,' said Olivia.

'And I can help,' added Adam, who had been standing in the doorway. He had arrived a short time earlier after the calls and texts for help had gone out to as many people as possible.

Molly looked at her younger brother. 'You are strictly on washing-up duties only, you hear me? No dawdling, flirting or distracting.'

'You're not half as much fun when you're so bossy,' replied Adam, but he smiled at her and gave her a wink.

'There should be enough ingredients in the fridge to get going with the pastry,' said Molly. 'I'll get someone else to pick up whatever else we need. OK?'

'OK,' said Olivia, looking a little unsure. 'I'm not sure how perfect my pastry is going to look.'

'It'll be fine,' Molly told her gently. 'You can do this and nothing has to be perfect. Just delicious! Listen, just treat it like a really crazily busy day, all right?'

Olivia gave her a little nod and so Molly left her and Adam to the kitchen whilst she headed outside.

'Right, where's the list?' asked Molly, taking the paper that Amber and Josh had scribbled down lots of notes on. She ran her eyes down the many things that needed to be done before the reception could be held. She felt a faint twinge of alarm at the many items on the list before pushing the feeling to one side. There was simply no need to panic. And no time either.

'OK,' she said. 'Let's designate. Pete and Josh!'

Pete came over to stand in front of her.

'We need to organise drinks,' she said. 'Alcohol and non-alcoholic as well. You know how much we'll need. Oh, and glasses too, if you have some spare at the inn.'

'No worries,' said Pete. 'Hey, do you want me to see if Brad is around to give you a hand in the morning for a while?'

Brad was the chef at the Black Swan Inn.

'That would be great,' said Molly.

As they headed off, Molly looked at Amber and Belle, who were still seated at a nearby table.

'You two are on decorations duty,' she told them.

Between Amber's designer skills and Belle's talent for sewing, she was sure that the additional bunting would soon be whipped up.

'This will be fun,' said Amber with a grin. 'Why didn't I think that I could decorate my own wedding reception in the first place?'

'Tom and Lucy!' called out Molly.

They came to stand in front of her; Lucy in particular was wearing a wide grin at the new and improved Molly.

'We're going to need quite a few ingredients for the food,' she told them. 'The supermarket in Aldwych is open until 10 p.m. I'll text you the list in a couple of minutes so you'd better get going and I'll send it to you before you get there.'

'Yes, ma'am,' said Tom with a smile.

Molly grinned with the absolute belief that she could do this. She knew it. And now everyone else did as well.

Next up was Dodgy Del and Logan.

'We're going to need more fairy lights,' she said to Del. 'As many as you can find.'

'Yes, ma'am,' said Del, grabbing his phone. 'Let me call my mate...'

As he wandered away, for the first time Molly realised that she was in front of Logan. Everyone else was a little way away from them.

She hesitated and tried to focus on the job in hand.

'Any spare chairs or tables that you have would be really welcome,' she told him. 'Anything will do.'

'Yes, ma'am,' he replied.

He gave her a wide crooked smile and her heart leapt in her chest. It was no use. She was completely and utterly in love with him, but she couldn't think about that now.

She gave him a nod and was turning to head back to the kitchen when he touched her arm.

'We'll talk tomorrow,' he told her softly, and then he was gone.

And she shivered despite the warmth of the summer's evening, but for now she had to concentrate on the wedding.

* * *

Everyone worked until almost midnight to get the tea garden ready for the wedding reception.

Eventually Amber and Josh had been ordered home to rest before their big day, with everyone else following suit in the early hours.

Logan had watched Molly and felt so proud of her. She had come so far and he was in awe of how strong she actually was. But he was still sad that something had broken between them. Ever since the night of the hen and stag parties, everything had been different. She had been polite and smiled at him, but the connection felt lost. Something had happened and he wasn't sure what it was. Had he overstepped some kind of boundary between them? Offended her somehow?

He was determined to make it up to her, whatever it was that he had done. He just hoped that she wanted to listen to what he had to say.

61

The following morning, Molly looked around the tea garden for one last inspection.

She couldn't quite believe it, but it was ready to host Amber and Josh's wedding reception in a couple of hours' time.

It had been a crazy twelve hours and she sincerely hoped that the scant few hours of sleep she had managed to get wouldn't show up in the wedding photographs.

But for now, she was happy with how well everything had turned out. She and Olivia had baked into the early hours, but there was lots of food to be served, that was the main thing. The fridges and countertops were groaning with delicious food for all the guests. Alongside, the wedding cake was covered, ready to be brought out with all the desserts that they had made in addition to all the savoury fare.

If possible, the tea garden looked even prettier than normal in the summer sunshine. Amber and Belle had enjoyed a few glasses of champagne, apparently, but the bunting was still finished and now hung all along the walls, the low wall at the front and around the pergola. Although Dodgy Del had made sure that both the bunting and the fairy lights didn't touch his precious hops.

Belle had even found some spare purple material from the bridesmaids' dresses with which to tie a couple of bows around the chairs designated for the bride and groom.

Each table now had an additional white candle placed in each of her mum's terracotta pots along with a white bow wrapped around the outside. Later on, when night fell, there would be lots of tea lights in jam jars and fairy lights waiting to give a soft glow to the evening celebrations. They had even cleared an area to act as a dance floor.

Molly gave a satisfied sigh. It really had come together even better than she had hoped for. She had done it. Now she could relax and enjoy the wedding.

She checked her watch and realised that time was marching on, so she closed the gate to the tea garden, which now held a sign proclaiming it closed for the day for a private party.

Molly dashed up the stairs to Amber's apartment to get changed and join in with the preparations. Amber's parents were due to arrive in a short while, but Amber had wanted to have a private celebration first with her friends. So when Molly arrived, they were ready to toast the bride with a glass of champagne.

'To Amber and Josh,' said Lucy, as they clinked their glasses together.

'To the happy couple,' replied Molly.

'To the honeymoon,' added Belle, with a wink.

They all laughed.

Blushing, Amber finally said, 'And to my bridesmaids for making my day so special.'

There were a few tears and then Molly dashed off for a quick shower and to get changed into her bridesmaid dress.

'Belle, you're a whizz,' she said once changed, as she looked at her reflection in the mirror. 'It fits perfectly.'

'Of course it fits,' said Belle, pretending to be affronted.

Molly showed off the dress to the others. 'Isn't she clever?'

'You look great,' Lucy told her. 'Hopefully Logan won't be able to keep his hands off you.'

Molly's good mood immediately faded. 'Let's just leave it for today,' she said, with a heavy sigh. 'I don't want to think about it.'

'But you do love him, don't you?' asked Amber, looking concerned.

Molly looked at Belle, who shrugged her shoulders as she pinned a flower to her hair. 'I'm surprised you even considered the notion that I wouldn't tell them,' said Belle with a sheepish smile of guilt.

'Why don't you tell him how you feel?' asked Lucy gently.

'Yeah, what happened to scary, bossy Molly from last night?' said Belle, laughing. 'Just show up like that, and say, hey Logan, come here! And then kiss him.'

Molly rolled her eyes and began to pin her own hair up.

It was true that she had finally found some self-confidence, but she could never be as forward as Belle. It was just wasn't in her nature.

Thankfully, she was saved from having to reply as Amber came out of her bedroom wearing her wedding dress.

'You look beautiful,' they all said.

And she really did. It was a gorgeous, floor-length dress of white silk with a white lace overlay which glittered with tiny diamanté jewels. It was simple but elegant.

Molly was equally thrilled with the bridesmaid dresses that Belle had made for them all. They all differed slightly but were all made from the same purple silk. Belle's was a halter neck. Lucy's had a scoop neck which showed off her curves. Molly's dress had tiny spaghetti straps which hung over the tops of her arms, leaving the dress almost strapless in design. She had never worn anything so elegant and pretty and couldn't believe what it looked like as she twirled this way and that in front of the mirror.

'You look amazing,' Lucy murmured, coming to stand alongside her.

'Thanks. So do you,' said Molly.

Time went past quickly after that. There were a huge amount of tears when Amber's parents arrived and saw how beautiful their daughter was looking on her wedding day.

Suddenly it was time to get going. So they all picked up the bouquets of flowers that they were each going to carry and headed down the stairs to walk to the church.

62

A little past four o'clock on Saturday afternoon, Logan sat at the back of the church of St Barnabus in Cranbridge. It was a small but very pretty church, with the sun gleaming through the stained-glass window which was placed above the tiny altar.

Logan looked at his grandad, who was sitting on the bench next to him, and smiled. Stanley had his best suit on for the occasion. At the front, Josh was looking fairly relaxed as he stood waiting for his bride, with Pete as his best man alongside him.

All their friends and family were on the first couple of pews, including Keith the dog, who appeared to be wearing a purple bow tie in honour of the occasion.

As the bridal march music rang out, the bridesmaids began their entrance ahead of the bride. Both Belle and Lucy looked very pretty in their mauve silk dresses, but it was the sight of Molly that took Logan's breath away.

Her blonde hair had been swept up into an elegant bun at the back of her head, pinned with tiny twinkly flowers. Her dress was the same colour as the other two bridesmaids, but it was her bare shoulders and back that Logan couldn't help but stare at. The soft skin at the back of her neck where her hair was swept up. He gulped as she walked down the short aisle and then turned around to wait for the bride.

Amber came in on her father's arm, but Logan barely noticed her. He was sure that she looked beautiful because of the look in Josh's eyes as she reached him. But Logan had eyes for no one but Molly throughout the ceremony.

Amber and Josh exchanged vows and rings whilst a few people, including Molly, dabbed their eyes.

Logan thought back to his own wedding, which had been a cold, sterile ordeal. It hadn't had the relaxed, happy atmosphere of St Barnabus's church that day. This was how a wedding should be, he thought. Surrounded by family and friends to love and support you.

And with the one that you love next to you at the altar.

His eyes were once more drawn to Molly.

He realised that in the failure of his own marriage, he had allowed himself to be cut off. From friends and family and, yes, from love as well.

What was the point in getting the great gift of life if he didn't want to take it and kiss it, like he had with that first kiss with Molly. Life was for living. And loving too, he now knew. Especially with the right person by your side.

* * *

It was a lovely ceremony, thought Molly. She didn't think she had ever seen a happier bride and groom than Amber and Josh.

Glenda the vicar announced, 'And I am delighted to now declare you husband and wife!'

A huge cheer went up as Josh took a step forward and swept his new wife into a kiss, whilst everyone stood up, applauded and shed a few more tears as well.

Afterwards, once many photographs had been taken outside the church and confetti had been copiously thrown, the congregation wandered back alongside the river past the watermill.

Molly thought it a comforting sound, hearing the water rushing over the wheel. It had been so quiet for so long, much like herself, and it too had finally found its voice.

She pushed open the gate to the tea garden and let everyone in before rushing off to the kitchen to organise the food. Olivia had been busy for the past couple of hours making sure that all the last minute preparations were complete.

Her brothers, mum and Geoff had left the church soon after the ceremony and were all ready and waiting with drinks to hand out to everyone as they arrived. Molly blew her mum a kiss as she headed past, picking up two glasses of Buck's Fizz as she went.

Molly was so proud of her mum. Not only was she wearing a brand new dress, she had even had her hair highlighted. There was pride in her appearance these days and in her work at the community garden as well.

Olivia was already in the kitchen, cutting up the many pies, tarts and cakes into generous slices.

'By the way,' said Molly, coming to stand next to her and handing her a drink. 'If I forget to say later on, thank you. And well done. You've done amazingly good work considering how last minute this was.'

Olivia looked up at her surprised but pleased. 'Thanks,' she said.

'Your pastry is incredible,' Molly told her. 'If the place was going to be open for longer than one more month, I'd train you up in puff pastry as well.'

Olivia blushed. 'Really?'

'Of course,' said Molly. 'You could totally handle it.' She hesitated before speaking again. 'I hope you know how good a baker you are. I'm sure you'll be able to get a job anywhere using the skills that you've mastered these past couple of months. And I'll happily give you a glowing reference.'

Olivia smiled but looked a little sad. 'It's such a shame that the tea garden has to close.'

'I know,' replied Molly, with a sigh before placing a wide smile on her face. 'But for now, let's celebrate.'

'Oh, I don't think I'm invited,' said Olivia, frowning.

'You are totally invited,' Molly told her. 'Amber reminded me to tell you. So let's go and toast the happy couple.'

So she persuaded Olivia to take her glass outside for a while and join in with the celebrations.

'Ladies and gentlemen!' called out Tom, bringing a temporary halt to the flow of conversation. 'I would like you all to welcome Mr and Mrs Kennedy!'

A huge cheer went up as Amber and Josh walked into the garden hand in hand, smiling and looking every inch as happy as all the friends and family smiling back at them.

Molly cheered along with everyone else but couldn't help but wonder whether she would have her own happy ever after one day.

63

It was one of the best wedding receptions Molly had ever been to, although she knew that perhaps she was ever so slightly biased on that point.

But all the planets had aligned and the whole celebration was wonderful. The weather was glorious and the sun shone down on the group of family and friends that gathered in the tea garden after the ceremony.

The garden itself looked beautiful. The bunting and flowers gave off just the right ambience to the whole party.

Of course, the best decorations were the smiles that everyone was wearing, especially the bride and groom. Josh and Amber held hands tightly as they went around chatting to all their families and friends who wanted to offer their congratulations.

Amber's mum had finally stopped crying about the fire at the glamorous hotel she had so desired for her daughter's wedding and was embracing the new venue with gusto.

She hugged her daughter and Molly could hear her say to Amber, 'I'm sorry for being a pain in the bottom. I just wanted it to be perfect for you, my darling.' She gave a little laugh. 'And, you know what? It truly is.'

The champagne and other drinks that Pete and Belle had brought over from the inn flowed freely and the sound of laughter and joy filled the sweet summer air.

Even Del was in good spirits, showing off his prized hops plant to a somewhat bemused but interested audience.

Occasionally, Molly caught sight of Logan, who looked incredible in his dark suit. So used to seeing him in his casual clothes, there was no denying that the man could out Bond James Bond looking that good in his smart clothes.

Thankfully, Molly was still keeping an eye on the buffet and was able to just about keep her wandering eyes from Logan's handsome face.

The choice of buffet meant that everyone was able to mingle and leave their seats and conversation and filled the air as the guests chatted about the food and wedding.

One of the longer tables was being substituted as an open bar, where everyone could help themselves.

'This food is tremendous,' one very well-spoken lady told her, helping herself to another slice of tomato and basil tart. 'Do you happen to know who the caterers are?'

'Actually, it's my daughter,' said a voice behind them.

Molly turned around to see her mum wearing a very proud look on her face.

The woman looked from mother to daughter, comprehension dawning as she burst into laughter.

'Well, you've done marvellously and I'm all for supporting our local businesses,' carried on the woman, reaching out to give Molly's arm a squeeze. 'I'm holding a small soiree next month and it would be simply wonderful if you could cater for me.'

'I'd love to,' stammered Molly.

'Magnificent!' said the woman, with a wink. 'I shall be in touch, my dear.'

As the stranger walked away, Rachel looked at her daughter with a huge smile on her face. 'You do know who that was, don't you?' she said.

Molly shook her head. 'One of Amber's distant family?'

Her mum laughed. 'That was Rose Harris, sister to the Earl of Cranley himself!'

Molly was amazed. 'But doesn't she live at Willow Tree Hall?' she said. 'And so the little soiree she wants me to cater for...?'

'Will probably be at a very elegant stately home,' said Rachel, laughing once more. 'Oh, my dearest, loveliest daughter. You are going up in the world.'

Molly's mind was racing. Next month was September and the tea garden would be closing up. How was she supposed to cater for a member of the aristocracy from her small kitchen at home?

Molly was still standing there in astonishment when her mum stepped forward to give her a hug.

'I'm so proud of you,' she said, stepping back and smoothing back a lock of hair that had come free. 'By the way, I'm out tomorrow night.'

'With Geoff?' said Molly, with a sly smile.

Rachel sighed but she too was smiling. 'Yes, actually. So you'd better get used to it.'

'Are you?' asked Molly softly.

Her mum looked more serious. 'I am,' she said. 'It's taken time, but you told me to be brave and look where it's got me. And you too,' she added, looking around the garden.

Molly nodded. She was proud of herself, she realised. It had been an amazing summer, despite her heartbreak over Logan.

'Maybe it's time for you to be brave all over again,' said her mum, giving her arm a squeeze.

'What do you mean?' asked Molly.

'I mean that life is about more than work.' Her mum gave her a knowing look.

'It's nice that you're dating again,' Molly told her, trying to change the subject. 'You like him.'

'I do.' Rachel thought hard for a moment. 'But it's more than that. I trust him.' She looked at her daughter. 'Do you trust Logan like that?'

Molly took a deep intake of breath. 'I do. Or at least I did. But I'm not sure he's ready for a relationship, especially with me.'

Her mum gave her a soft smile. 'There's only one way to find out,' she said before walking away.

Molly stood still. It was true, she had trusted Logan, but all this business about leaving Cranbridge and not telling anyone was making her rethink everything she had ever felt about him.

With a heavy sigh, she headed into the kitchen and picked up the wedding cake. Then she very carefully began to carry it outside ready for the cutting ceremony.

64

The wedding cake was oohed and aahed over by everyone who saw it, such was the level of expertise of the decorations that Molly had done. It was then cut by the happy couple before Molly handed out slices to all the guests.

As Logan had expected, the cake was absolutely delicious. Almost as delicious as Molly looked that day, in fact. He watched as she handed out the cake to everyone who had lined up so eagerly for a piece, finally joining the queue and taking his own slice of cake from her.

They locked eyes briefly, almost the first time she had looked at him all day, and then quickly looked away.

Logan sighed and carried his cake back to the corner of the tea garden where he had been previously sitting.

The sun was lower in the sky now, causing a golden glow over the proceedings as it began to set on the horizon.

He couldn't help but worry that something had caused Molly to think badly of him and to back off so much. He missed her warm smile, her positive way of thinking. He missed kissing her most of all.

After everyone had enjoyed their cake, it was time for the speeches.

Pete gave a memorable take-down of his big brother but finished his best man speech by telling of the love and respect he had for Josh, which had their mum, Cathy, Grandma Tilly and everyone else in tears.

When it came to Josh's turn, he thanked his beautiful new wife for making him 'the luckiest man on the planet' and then thanked everyone for their help.

'I need to finish with an extra special thank you,' said Josh, coming to the final part of his speech. 'All of our bridesmaids are special, but we have to give extra thanks to Molly for giving us the most memorable and perfect wedding reception we could have hoped for. Or even dreamed of. So here's to Molly.'

Everyone raised their champagne glasses at Molly, who blushed furiously at the attention. But Logan hoped she was proud of what she had achieved in such a short space of time by giving her friends their dream wedding reception.

He continued to watch her long after the speeches had ended, chatting with various people, and yearned to take her in his arms.

Pete brought out his guitar and began to play a gentle tune for the bride and groom to have their first dance.

It was a beautiful setting, thought Logan, as dusk arrived by the river. The fairy lights had just been switched on and someone had begun to light the tea lights on the tables. Everywhere was covered with a magical, soft light. Although no one and nothing looked more magical and beautiful than Molly.

Pete was soon replaced by a local band, whom he had organised to play some classic tunes throughout the evening.

Logan watched as more and more people began to dance, as the music tempo picked up. Molly was being twirled around the dance floor by Stanley and he smiled as he watched them both.

'What's the word for being jealous of your own grandad?' murmured Pete, who had come to stand next to Logan without him even realising.

'Not sure,' said Tom, on the other side. 'But at least you can guarantee that Stanley won't have wandering hands.'

'Excuse me, that's my grandad you're talking about,' said Logan, looking at his friends.

'Yes, but what we really want to know is why he's dancing with your girl and you're not,' said Pete in a pointed tone.

Logan had no reply to this and just stayed quiet as Belle also came up to join them.

'What do you think of Molly's dress?' she asked, looking directly at Logan.

He remained silent, keeping his sizzling thoughts about Molly's body to himself.

Belle broke into a winning smile. 'I'd say that making you speechless was a pretty good reaction,' she said, taking Pete's hand and dragging him onto the makeshift dance floor.

In their place, Josh wandered up to Logan and Tom.

'How's everyone doing?' he asked, beaming with happiness. 'Enjoying yourselves?'

'I am,' said Tom. 'Can't say the same for Logan, standing here brooding over Miss Hopkins over there.'

Josh placed a hand on Logan's shoulder. 'Listen, mate,' he told him. 'You obviously care for each other. So why not go for it? Look at how happy Amber and I are.'

Tom nodded alongside him. 'He's right,' he said. 'What's the worst that could happen?'

'That she could pulverise my heart into tiny pieces and shatter it so badly that it will never love again,' replied Logan in a dull tone.

'Crikey,' said Josh, looking stunned.

'Are you sure we're talking about the same Molly Hopkins?' said Tom, looking equally amazed.

'You mean, gorgeous, warm, kind, generous, beautiful, sexy Molly?' murmured Logan.

'Oh, you have got it bad, friend,' said Tom, with a sad nod.

'I miss her,' confessed Logan. 'I really miss her.'

'Then don't you think you should be telling her that and not us,' said Josh, looking directly at him.

Logan nodded slowly. 'Yeah. You're right.'

He realised it was true. Time was short and life needed to be grabbed by both hands.

'Thanks,' he said, looking at his friends.

'For what?' asked Tom, looking confused. 'Nothing's happened, has it?'

'Not yet,' said Logan, with a grin. 'Excuse me.'

Then he headed through the crowds to find the woman who had mended his shattered heart.

65

Molly was enjoying a lovely dance with Stanley when they were interrupted.

'Excuse me, Grandad,' said Logan, coming to stand next to them. 'Do you mind if I cut in?'

'Of course not, dear boy,' said Stanley, giving them both a warm smile. 'I shall go and find some more of that delicious cake.'

'Do you want some help?' asked Molly, suddenly nervous about being so close to Logan.

But Stanley waved away her concern with his hand. 'No need, my dear,' he said, disappearing off into the crowd.

She felt Logan take her hand in his as the music slowed down in tempo to a love song. Keeping her eyes on anywhere but him, she felt him place his other hand on her back and draw her closer until they were almost touching.

This was fine, she told herself. She could totally act nonchalant about having him so close to her, despite her hammering pulse and the fact that she was having trouble drawing breath.

She tried to look around to catch someone's eye, but she couldn't see past his large chest in front of her.

'You look very beautiful,' she heard him murmur.

'Thank you,' she replied. But she still couldn't look at him.

So for a while, they danced slowly in a circle as the setting sun cast a golden glow over them both. They both stayed silent, neither seemingly knowing what to say. But it was comfortable.

She sighed. And that was the problem. She had always somehow felt comfortable with him. From falling in the water to showing her nervousness about starting a business, he had listened patiently and been totally supportive of her each and every time.

'Please look at me,' she heard him say.

She finally looked up into his face, which was staring down at hers. She tried not to lose herself in his hazel eyes as he spoke again.

'That's better,' he said, giving her a soft smile. 'You know, you're the hero of the hour. Or rather the heroine, I should say. Look at what you've achieved here. It's amazing.'

She gave a shrug. 'I had help,' she told him.

He shook his head. 'Could you just accept the compliment for once and be proud of yourself.'

'I am proud,' she found herself saying. 'Whatever happens in the future, I know that I've achieved something memorable here. And for that I'm truly glad.'

'Then why do you look so sad?' he asked.

She gulped back the tears that came into her eyes. 'It's just all coming to an end, that's all,' she told him, figuring that she should just speak the truth.

'Or maybe it's just beginning,' he said.

'You're right,' she told him, her voice becoming a little harder as she tried to cope with her aching heart. 'You've got a new start, wherever it may be. I know, you see, that you're leaving and that's fine. Thank you for all your support this summer. It's meant a great deal to me.' She had thought she was doing so well until her voice broke on the final couple of words.

She went to draw away from Logan and the dance floor but he didn't let go of her hand.

'Come with me,' he told her in a low voice before leading her away from the music and out of the tea garden, all the time holding her hand in his.

He led her around the corner to stand in front of his workshop. In the soft twilight, it was just them with the river flowing past in the background. She could still hear the laughter and music of the celebrations and yet felt far away from everyone.

'Now,' he said, turning to face her but still holding her hand. 'Let's start again, shall we? Why don't you tell me what's up?'

She looked down at the pavement. 'I heard you talking to Barry the other day. I know everything.'

Logan frowned at her. 'Like what?' he said.

'That when your lease is up at the end of September you're moving on. From Cranbridge.' A tear rolled down her cheek before she could stop it. 'From me. And that's fine.' She paused and took a deep breath. 'Except it's not. Because it's like I'll be missing a part of myself if you go.'

He reached out with his free hand and brushed the tear away from her cheek with his thumb. 'You don't need anyone to make you whole,' he told her. 'You're already there.'

But she was shaking her head. 'But, you see, I'm not whole without you. I love you.'

She heard him take a sharp intake of breath.

'I know it's not what you want to hear and that you're leaving anyway,' she carried on quickly. 'But you'll always be welcome back here. Just as friends, if that's what you want.'

But Logan shook his head slowly and Molly felt her heart burst into pieces. He didn't even want to be friends?

'I can't be just friends with you,' he told her, drawing her close. 'Not when I want to kiss you over and over and over.'

He ducked his head down and she was powerless to stop him kissing her. Powerless to stop herself from kissing him back as she wrapped her hands around his shoulders and pulled him even closer.

Finally, they both drew back at the same time.

'Maybe it's better if you did leave,' she told him, still staring up at him in wonder. 'We'll never get any work done otherwise.'

She tried and failed to smile at him. It was just all too sad for her to make light of it. To have this chemistry and intensity between them and not be able to do anything about it was heartbreaking.

'I'm not going anywhere,' he murmured, pulling her close to him once more. 'Yes, it's true that the lease is going to end, but that's because I'm buying the shop from Barry.'

'You are?' she said, amazed. 'I don't understand.'

He nodded. 'You see, it turns out that when you find the love of your life, you want to stay as close as possible to that person. So you'll move heaven and earth to make sure that happens.'

She stared up at him, trying to make sense of what he had just said.

'The love of your life?' she repeated.

He nodded. 'Yes,' he told her, kissing her gently on the lips. 'You are. Thanks to you, I believe in love again. Can feel love again. And it's true love. Forever love.'

'For me too,' she told him, the words slowly sinking in. 'I can't believe it!'

He laughed. 'Well, this is going to be a fine relationship if you can't believe a thing I tell you.' He held her close to him. 'How can I persuade you that I'm telling the truth? I need to impress you and make you believe me.'

'You never need to impress me,' she told him, reaching up to touch his face in wonder. 'You've done that ever since I first met you.'

'When I ran over the rabbit head?' he said, laughing.

She joined in with his laughter. 'Well, maybe not at that exact moment. But I knew you were someone special.'

'Well, you're my someone special,' he told her. 'And you always will be.'

They both gave a start as suddenly fireworks began to appear overhead.

'That's my present to you both!' they heard Dodgy Del shout.

So there, under the dark night sky full of fireworks, Molly and Logan kissed each other once more.

And it was a kiss of promise and love. And a kiss for the future too. For their own future together.

66

Two weeks later and it had been the happiest, most wonderful fortnight that Molly could ever remember. She had spent nearly every free moment with Logan when she wasn't working. Each night, they would talk and kiss endlessly. Each morning, she would wake up wrapped in his arms. They were happy, blissfully so.

And yet, she was almost certain that he was hiding something from her.

He had told her that he loved her and she believed him. Almost. She was ninety-nine per cent positive about her relationship with Logan, but there was a tiny niggle of doubt that she just couldn't shake.

He would take secretive phone calls and wouldn't tell her who he had been speaking to.

'I'm allowed some secrets, aren't I?' he would say, smiling at her before stealing another kiss.

And she wanted to believe that he wouldn't hurt her and would treat her well. But she had been hurt so many times in the past that she almost couldn't bring herself to believe that their love story would end happily.

She looked at him as he sat on the bench next to her in the tea garden, his arm casually wrapped around her shoulders. She sighed and closed her eyes briefly in the late afternoon sun. It was September now and the sun was a lot lower in the sky. She shivered, realising that she had forgotten her sweatshirt.

'Are you cold?' murmured Logan, drawing her closer to him so that she could feel the heat from his own body.

'Not too bad,' she replied. 'And I want to see this.'

She looked over to where a small crowd of people were hovering near the back of the tea garden. The flowers on the hops plants had finally been deemed ready to be harvested and Dodgy Del had insisted on a ceremony to celebrate the occasion.

Watching everyone carefully pick their own flowers, she felt sad suddenly. The summer was at an end and thereby the tea garden too was at an end. Maybe next summer she could reopen, but who knew where her life might be by then. Maybe it wouldn't be possible. Maybe the circumstances wouldn't be right.

She had tried to remain cheerful and optimistic as always, but the tea garden was precious to her. It had been all of her own doing – admittedly with a lot of help along the way. But it had been hers in name and now Molly's Tea Garden was at an end.

Logan gave her a nudge with his shoulder.

'What?' she asked, looking into his eyes.

'You just gave the heaviest sigh,' he told her.

She smiled at him. 'I'm just sad it has to end,' she replied, resting her head on his shoulder.

He leaned forward to kiss her gently on the lips. 'Maybe it doesn't have to,' he said softly. 'Come with me.'

He stood up and took her hand, leading her out of the garden.

'What about the others?' she asked, looking over the wall at the crowd of people who were still chatting excitedly about their harvest.

'This won't take long,' he told her, still holding her hand as he led her over to stand in front of her shop.

He looked at her for a moment and she realised that he was nervous.

'Is everything OK?' she asked, suddenly worried.

He gave her a tight smile. 'I hope so,' he said. 'I took a risk, to be honest. But I just hope that you'll be happy with it.'

'OK,' she said slowly, wondering what on earth this was all about.

'I've started renegotiating with Barry,' he told her.

Molly gulped. It was worse than she had feared. He had changed his mind about buying the place after all.

But as she glanced up at him, she realised that he was shaking his head. 'I've been negotiating on your behalf,' he said. 'You see, I thought we could buy the end shop and garden as well. For you. I just needed to wait long enough for him to agree the sale before I told you. It's taken much longer than I wanted it to but I had to be certain before I told you.'

'Buying the shop and the garden?' she said, spinning her head around to look briefly at the empty shopfront and then back at Logan.

'Well, I figured that if we apply to the council for a change of use of business, then maybe you would be able to move inside for the winter months.' He gave a her a small smile. 'A tea room as well as a tea garden. And it means we don't lose the community garden either.'

Molly was stunned. Every once in a while she had daydreamed about changing the front of the shop into a tea room but had never believed it to be even remotely possible.

'I don't believe it,' said Molly. 'Seriously?'

He nodded. 'I know how much it means for you to be your own boss,' he told her. 'And this way, we both have a business on Riverside Lane.'

She couldn't stop herself from flinging her arms around him. 'Oh, you're so lovely,' she said, as he spun her around.

He placed her gently back on the ground. 'You're pretty special yourself,' he murmured, bending his head to kiss her on the lips. 'My sweet, adorable neighbour.'

It was only after a few minutes that Molly realised that somebody, somewhere was clapping and cheering.

She drew her head back and glanced back to the tea garden, where all her friends stood on the other side of the low wall whooping and grinning at them both.

'They all know?' she asked.

Logan nodded. 'I needed some help with the legal side of things, so I went to see Tom.'

'Who told Lucy, who told Belle and Amber,' carried on Molly, with a giggle, looking over at her best friends. She could see Amber's honeymoon suntan even from this far away. Amber, Lucy and Belle were all smiling at them and nodding their approval.

'Can you forgive me?' Logan said, holding her close. 'For all the secrecy? I wanted to be certain about the sale but I don't like having secrets from you. It didn't feel right.'

'Forgive you for giving me all my dreams at once?' she said, looking up at him. 'Absolutely.'

'And it's not just for you,' he told her. 'It's for both of us.'

She nodded. 'It will be.'

She knew that he needed her as much as she needed him. It was to be a partnership on equal terms.

'So I thought if I've got the workshop next door and you use the end shop for your tea room,' he carried on. 'Then maybe we could knock the two apartments upstairs into one at some point.' His eyes gleamed wickedly. 'I've got big plans for those bedrooms.'

'Me too,' she said, laughing softly.

And as they both leant forward to kiss at the same time, Molly knew what true love was. And how special it could truly be.

67

Logan dug his cold hands into the pocket of his jeans as he stood on the bridge next to the watermill. The nights were certainly drawing in now that October had almost arrived.

The trees along the river were a kaleidoscope of fiery yellows, ambers and reds as autumn rushed in and the river had certainly swollen to a much higher level since the summer weather had broken a few weeks previously.

He smiled to himself at the memory of Molly's rain dance and wondered whether he might need her to do the same again next year if there was another drought. But for now, the watermill was working just fine. He glanced at the new wheel turning slowly and steadily.

To his amazement, the flour produced by the mill had quickly become much in demand. He had never gotten around to employing a miller, preferring to keep it in the family, which pleased his grandad immensely.

He had never thought he would be a part-time miller but it turned out that there was a huge appetite for local flour from many of the residents as well as businesses in the area, including Molly's new tea room.

The corner shop was selling many bags of flour as well and the Black Swan used it too for all of their catering needs. The community hub had even begun a breadmaking course in the past week to serve the uptake in demand.

To keep up with the progress, he had begun to work a couple of days a week in the watermill, which meant he needed help with the furniture making side of business.

But thankfully his apprentice had become a more permanent member of staff than he could have dreamed of. Adam had finally confessed to his mum and sister that he hated his university course. So, with some gentle negotiations by Logan, Adam had been allowed to leave and begin working for Logan full-time, along with one day a week at college studying carpentry. His first project had been to build a bird table for the community garden which was a huge hit with the Mothers and Toddlers group who were eagerly filling up the bird feeders every day for the new winged visitors.

So the furniture making could continue alongside the flour producing side as well. It was an odd mix but Logan found that he enjoyed working with both materials.

Most importantly of all, he was happy. Really happy for perhaps the first time ever in his life. He had a partner in Molly who was his equal and she was both loving and supportive of him.

The purchase of the shops had finally gone through and at last they owned both premises at the end of Riverside Lane. New shop signs had gone up only the previous week and, to him, it made it feel permanent. As if he had finally made his mark on something, as well as the watermill of course.

But there was also a sense of belonging and being part of the community. He was home at last.

He looked beyond the village to the distant hills and could see the fields were full of bales after the wheat harvest. In the nearby rose bushes, ruby rose hips were appearing, signalling the changing of the seasons. And the changes in his life too.

He still needed a hand occasionally, such as helping to clear the old shop to make way for Molly's new tea room. But these days he wasn't afraid to ask for help from other people. Molly had taught him that life was better full of friends, rather than trying to face every trial alone.

His own shop on the King's Road in Chelsea had finally closed. It was the end of a chapter in his life. But he had no desire to rush back to London any time soon. His life was here in Cranbridge, with Molly and his grandad.

He turned around and locked up the door to the mill. There was always lots more work to do, but for now, it was time to celebrate an important harvest.

* * *

'Cheers, everyone!' said Dodgy Del holding up his pint glass full of frothy beer to his friends after taking a sip. 'Cor, this stuff really does taste better when you've grown it yourself.'

Molly laughed alongside everyone else. It seemed only fitting that the drinking of the home-grown beer should be done in the tea garden. After all, that was where it had all begun several months ago.

When ready, the flowers that the hops had produced had been snipped off and carefully collected. Pete knew of a local beer brewer who had made them each a keg from their harvest. Each small barrel was labelled accordingly, so everyone got to drink the beer made from their very own hops plant.

'Next year, I'm going to get a good dozen pints worth,' said Del, his eyes gleaming at the thought. 'I'm thinking of adding loads more hops plants to go alongside my other one.'

'In *my* tea garden?' asked Molly in a fake prim tone. But she was smiling as she spoke. After all, it was still the community garden as well.

'Oh, er, yeah,' said Del, giving her a sheepish grin. 'If it's OK with you, boss.'

As she nodded in reply, Molly realised that she really was the boss these days. She still couldn't believe the changes that had happened over the summer but she was slowly getting used to them all.

Being in charge of her own business was immensely satisfying, if not a little nerve-wracking at times. But she believed in herself these days and was hopeful of what the future would bring. After all, it said Molly's Tea Room on the new sign above the shop.

The new tea room had only been open for a couple of days and was already doing a roaring trade, with people wanting to shelter from the autumnal weather. New customers appeared from every direction, including ramblers who had used the ancient lavender field walk to head into Cranbridge from the next village.

She had a whole new menu full of autumnal flavours debuting the following week but was so full of confidence in her baking that she knew they would be just as popular.

In addition, a healthy side business in catering had begun to open up. After the success of Josh and Amber's wedding reception, she had been inundated with requests to cater for birthday and other parties even up to Christmas. That included a very special dinner at Willow Tree Hall, catering for Rose, the sister of the Earl of Cranley.

Thankfully, she had Olivia to help her. The young woman had pride and confidence in herself and her abilities these days. Her romance with Adam was in its early days, but they seemed to suit each other with their quiet personalities. And now that Adam had found his passion in furniture making alongside Logan, he had a future in the village as well.

Ben would take a little more encouraging to stand on his own two feet, but he had his final year at university to complete and then the world would be his oyster, wherever it took him.

Their mum was proud of them all and it was wonderful to see her so happy with Geoff. Even now they were laughing softly in the soft light of dusk as they watched the harvest celebrations.

The boys teased their mum about her romance but they approved of her choice of partner. She had found her happy place both with Geoff and taking responsibility for the community garden. She was even teaching gardening classes in the community hub which were proving especially popular to people who were trying to manage their stress and anxiety levels.

The community garden was hugely popular in the village now that the word had got out with the hops tasting. In addition, more and more people were now contributing to helping sowing new flowers and vegetables, as well as collecting the produce and distributing it amongst the villagers. In fact, a fine crop of pumpkins would be ready in time to be distributed around the village for Halloween and there was already a big campaign planned for spring bulbs to be planted out across the garden.

Molly looked up as Logan came through the garden gate and walked towards her. She couldn't help but break into a smile whenever she saw him. He had made her life utterly and blissfully happy and she couldn't stop herself from kissing him when he sat down on the bench next to her.

'Mmm,' he murmured against her lips. 'Whatever have I done to deserve that? Not that I'm complaining, of course.'

'Absolutely nothing,' she told him, leaning forward once more. 'Just because.'

'My favourite reason,' he replied.

She leant her head against his shoulder and looked across at her friends who were all laughing and enjoying the evening. It was quite remarkable the changes that had occurred over the past couple of years both for her friends and for Riverside Lane. But it was all for the better. Riverside Lane looked so much prettier these days. Each shop was painted, decorated and had a proper sign above the window. Most importantly, the village was a community, somewhere everyone could gather together and help each other out with whatever problems life threw at them.

'I've got a great idea,' announced Del with a large grin. 'Forget Oktoberfest. Next year it's going to be CranbridgeFest!'

Everyone laughed.

Molly took Logan's hand and squeezed it. As she looked across the tea garden and all that she had achieved so far that summer, she had no doubt regarding her own talents and potential. She was going to live a life that excited and fulfilled her, both at work and in love.

Because, just like Riverside Lane, she and Logan deserved their happy ever after.

ACKNOWLEDGMENTS

A huge thank you to my wonderful editor Caroline Ridding for always knowing exactly what each of my stories needs to make it better and for her endless enthusiasm in my work.

Thank you to everyone at Boldwood Books for all their hard work on this book, especially Nia Beynon and Claire Fenby for all their marketing skills behind the scenes. Also I would like to thank Jade Craddock and Shirley Khan for their great work yet again on the edits.

I would also like to thank my lovely fellow Team Boldwood authors for their good cheer and support which make working alongside them all such a joy.

Thank you to all my friends, especially Jo Botelle who has been tireless in her support of my research needs to visit a garden centre as frequently as possible!

Special thanks to Christiane and Robin Bonham for providing me with so much information about their wonderful and inspiring work on the Mumbles Community Orchard near Swansea.

Thanks to my wonderful family, especially Gill, Simon, Louise, Ross, Lee, Cara and Sian.

A huge thank you once more to my husband, Dave, for letting me drag him to various tea gardens and suffering with having to taste all those wonderful cakes! As always, this book could never have been written without your love and support.

Finally, a heartfelt thank you to all the readers out there who have been so wonderful in their enthusiasm for the Riverside Lane series. I began writing the first book in the series *The Village Shop for Lonely Hearts* in January 2020 and, much like everyone else in the world, I had no idea what was about to happen to us all. It hasn't always been easy writing about an idyllic place such as Cranbridge when real life has been so very hard for us all. However, I have taken huge comfort in the feedback from readers who have found it somewhere to escape to during difficult times.

So, dear reader, this book is for you.

Alison x

MORE FROM ALISON SHERLOCK

We hope you enjoyed reading *The Village of Happy Ever Afters*. If you did, please leave a review.

If you'd like to gift a copy, this book is also available as an ebook, digital audio download and audiobook CD.

Sign up to Alison Sherlock's mailing list for news, competitions and updates on future books.

https://bit.ly/AlisonSherlockNewsletter

Explore more feel-good novels from Alison Sherlock.

ABOUT THE AUTHOR

Alison Sherlock is the author of the bestselling *Willow Tree Hall* books. Alison enjoyed reading and writing stories from an early age and gave up office life to follow her dream.

Follow Alison on social media:

facebook.com/alison.sherlock.73
twitter.com/AlisonSherlock
bookbub.com/authors/alison-sherlock

ABOUT BOLDWOOD BOOKS

Boldwood Books is a fiction publishing company seeking out the best stories from around the world.

Find out more at www.boldwoodbooks.com

Sign up to the Book and Tonic newsletter for news, offers and competitions from Boldwood Books!

http://www.bit.ly/bookandtonic

We'd love to hear from you, follow us on social media:

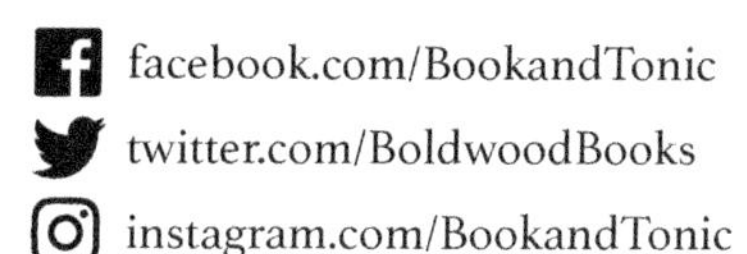

Printed in Great Britain
by Amazon